MW01118820

# THINGS UNSEEN

# Also by C. J. Brightley

# THINGS UNSEEN

## A LONG-FORGOTTEN SONG
## BOOK 1

C. J. BRIGHTLEY

Egia, LLC

ISBN 9781497389755

Published in the United Sates of America by Egia, LLC.

www.cjbrightley.com

Cover art by Vuk Kostic

*For Stephen*

# ACKNOWLEDGEMENTS

Thank you for being my hero, Stephen. I am immensely grateful to my parents for their encouragement and advice. I also owe a debt of gratitude to my wonderful beta readers, Sarah, Megan, Laura, Pat, and Doug.

# CHAPTER 1

*RESEARCHING THIS THESIS is an exercise in dedication, frustration, making up stuff, pretending I know what I'm doing, and wondering why nothing adds up.* Aria swirled her coffee and stared at the blank page in her notebook.

*Why did I decide to study history?* She flipped back to look at her notes and sighed. She couldn't find enough information to even form a coherent thesis. The records were either gone, or had never existed in the first place. *Something* had happened when the Revolution came to power, but she didn't know what, and she couldn't even pinpoint exactly when.

The nebulous idea she'd had for her research seemed even more useless now. She'd been trying to find records of how things had changed since the Revolution, how the city had grown and developed. There were official statistics on the greater prosperity, the academic success of the city schools, and the vast reduction in crime. The statistics didn't mention the abandoned buildings, the missing persons, or any grumbling against the curfew. At least it was later now; for a year, curfew had been at dusk.

She glanced around the bookstore at the other patrons. A man wearing a business suit was browsing in the self-help section, probably trying to improve his public speaking. A girl, probably another student judging by her worn jeans and backpack, was sitting on the floor in the literary fiction section, completely engrossed in a book.

Aria flipped to the front of the book again. It was a memoir of someone she'd never heard of. She'd picked it up almost at random, and flipped to the middle, hoping to find something more interesting than dead ends. The words told of a walk in the forest, and for a moment Aria was there, her nose filled with the scents of pine and loam, her eyes dazzled by the sunlight streaming through the leaves swaying above her. She blinked, and the words were there but the feeling was gone. Rereading the passage, she couldn't figure out why she'd been caught up with such breathless realism.

It wasn't that the words were so profound; she was confident they were not. Something had caught her though, and she closed her eyes to imagine the forest again, as if it were a memory. Distant, faded, perhaps not even her memory. A memory of something she'd seen in a movie, perhaps, or a memory of a dream she'd had as a child.

Something about it troubled her, and she

meant to come back to it. Tonight, though, she had other homework, and she pushed the book aside.

Dandra's Books was an unassuming name for the best bookstore in all of the North Quadrant. Dandra was a petite, grey-haired lady with a warm smile. She also had the best map collection, everything from ancient history, both originals and reproductions, to modern maps of cities both near and far, topographical maps, water currents, and everything else. She carried the new releases and electronic holdings that were most in demand, but what made the store unique was the extensive and ever-changing selection of used and antique books. If it could be found, Dandra could find it. Aria suspected she maintained an unassuming storefront because she didn't want demand to increase; business was sufficient to pay the bills and she refused to hire help.

Dandra also made tolerable coffee, an important consideration for a graduate student. Aria had spent hours studying there as an undergraduate; it had the same air of productive intellectualism as the university library, but without the distraction of other groups of students having more fun than she was. She'd found it on a long, meandering walk avoiding some homework. Something about the place made concentrating easier.

Except when it came to her thesis. Aria told herself that she was investigating what resources were available before she narrowed her focus. But sometimes, when she stared at the blank pages, she almost admitted to herself the truth, that she was frustrated with her professors, her thesis, and the Empire itself. She didn't have a good explanation, and she hadn't told anyone.

Something about this image of the forest felt true in a way that nothing had felt for a very long time. It was evidence. Evidence of *what*, she wasn't sure. But definitely evidence.

She finished her homework and packed her bag. She put a bookmark in the memoir and re-shelved it, resolving that she would come back later and read it a bit more. It was already late, and she had an early class the next day.

After class there were errands, and homework, and more class, and lunch with a boy who'd seemed almost likable until he talked too much about his dysfunctional family and his abiding love for his ex-girlfriend, who lived down the hall in his apartment building. It was a week before she made it back to Dandra's.

The book was gone.

Dandra shook her head when Aria asked about it. "I don't know what book you mean. I've never had a book like that."

Aria stared at her in disbelief. "You saw me read it last week. It was called *Memories Kept* or something like that. *Memory Keeper*, maybe. Don't you remember? I was sitting there." She pointed.

Dandra gave her a sympathetic look. "You've been studying too much, Aria. I'm sorry. I don't have that book. I don't think I ever did."

Aria huffed in frustration and bought a cup of coffee. She put too much sugar and cream in it and sat by the window at the front. She stared at the people as they came in, wondering if her anger would burn a hole in the back of someone's coat. It didn't, but the mental picture amused her.

Not much else did. The thesis was going no-where, and the only thing that kept her interest was a line of questions that had no answers and a book that didn't exist.

Was the degree worth anything anyway? She'd studied history because she enjoyed stories, wanted to learn about the past. But the classes had consisted almost entirely of monologues by the professors about the strength of the Empire and how much better things were now after the Revolution. Her papers had alternated between parroting the professors' words, and uneasy forays into the old times. The research was hard, and getting harder.

The paper she'd written on the Revolution, on how John Sanderhill had united the bickering political factions, had earned an F. Dr. Corten had written, "Your implication that Sanderhill ordered the assassination of Gerard Neeson is patently false and betrays an utter lack of understanding of the morality of the Revolution. I am unable to grade this paper higher than an F, in light of such suspect scholarship and patriotism." Yet Aria had cited her source clearly and had been careful not to take a side on the issue, choosing merely to note that it was one possible explanation for Neeson's disappearance at the height of the conflict. Not even the most likely.

For a history department, her professors were remarkably uninterested in exploring the past. She scowled at her coffee as it got colder. What was the point of history, if you couldn't learn from it? The people in history weren't perfect, any more than people now were. But surely, as scholars, they should be able to admit that imperfect people and imperfect decisions could yield lessons and wisdom.

It wasn't as if it was ancient history either. The Revolution had begun less than fifteen years ago. One would think information would be available. Memories should be clear.

But they weren't.

The man entered Dandra's near dusk. He wore no jacket against the winter cold, only a threadbare short-sleeved black shirt. His trousers were dark and equally worn, the cuffs skimming bare ankles. His feet were bare too, and that caught her attention.

He spoke in a low voice, but she was curious, so she listened hard and heard most of what he said. "I need the maps, Dandra."

"You know I don't have those."

"I'll pay."

"I don't have them." Dandra took a step back as he leaned forward with his hands resting on the desk. "I told you before, I can't get them. I still can't."

"I was told you could on good authority." His voice stayed very quiet, but even Aria could hear the cold anger. "Should I tell Petro he was wrong about you?"

"Are you threatening me?" Dandra's eyes widened, but Aria couldn't tell if it was in fear or in anger.

"I'm asking if Petro was wrong."

"Whatever you were promised was wrong. I couldn't get them." Dandra clasped her hands together and drew back, her shoulders against the wall, and Aria realized she was terrified. Of the man in the black shirt, or of Petro, or possibly both.

Aria glanced around as she rose and stepped to the counter. Everyone else seemed to be pretending that absolutely nothing was going on. It was up to her to help. "Excuse me? Can I help you find something?" She smiled brightly at him.

He glanced back and she had the momentary impression he was startled at the interruption. He stared at her for a split second with cold blue eyes, then looked back at Dandra. Without another word, he brushed past Aria and out the door, and disappeared into the darkness.

Dandra looked at her with wide eyes. "That wasn't wise, but thank you."

"Who is he?"

Dandra shook her head. "Don't ask questions you don't want to know the answer to. Go home, child. It's late."

"Are you in trouble?"

Dandra shook her head wordlessly and glanced at a note she held crumpled in her hand. *Was she holding that earlier? I don't think so.* The contents seemed to disturb her even more and she announced in a slightly unsteady voice that the store would be closing early for the evening.

Aria pulled on her gloves and shoved her notebook back in her pack. Dandra shooed out the few remaining customers and locked the door with a sigh of relief.

Aria looked around, but the man in the black shirt was long gone.

"You want a ride home?" Dandra asked.

"No, thanks. I'll walk. It's not far." She hesitated. "Are you okay, Dandra?"

Dandra's smile and nod were so forced it was obvious even in the reflected lamplight. "Goodnight."

Aria wandered down the block and around the

corner, holding her now-cold cup of coffee. If she went home, she'd have to work on her thesis. If she stayed out, she could tell herself she was planning. She followed the sidewalk and the lighted windows toward the river. She'd walk to the bridge and turn around; she couldn't justify more procrastination.

The cozy shops didn't hold her attention, though the light and bustle kept the walk from feeling too morose. She took a last swig of coffee and tossed the cup in a trashcan, then stuffed her hands in her pockets. The wind whipped around the corners of the concrete buildings, and she pulled her hat tighter over her brown curls. The lighted shops behind her, she headed into the edge of the shipping district. Her friend Amara would tell her to be more cautious, but Aria had never been afraid of lonely walks. *Just stay alert*, she told herself.

One of the ubiquitous posters flapped in the wind, then detached from the light pole and fluttered down the street, finally stopping when it hit a puddle of icy water. She didn't need to read it to know what it said. *See it, say it! Report suspicious activity to the Imperial Police Force.* And underneath that admonition: *Enemies hide in plain sight.*

She'd never seen any enemies of the state. The warnings were everywhere, but even the Revolution itself had been seamless, with barely a whimper of protest from the old government. Everyone knew things were better now.

She approached the bridge at an angle, almost ready to turn around. The water was a black void between the lights behind her and the distant streetlights of the bustling harbor on the other side, which caught the tops of small waves whipped up by the wind. Now and again a faint reflection would wink at her, a bright spot in the sea of darkness.

A movement caught her eye.

Later, when she thought about it, she was surprised she'd seen him at all. He sat on one of the steel girders underneath the bridge, some forty feet above the water. He was doing something with his hands, perhaps writing, but she couldn't see clearly. One leg swung beneath him, relaxed. He was still in shirtsleeves and barefoot.

It was cold enough for snow, and she stared at him, wondering if he was crazy. Contemplating suicide? Trying to catch pneumonia? She shivered in her sweater, with a thick coat over it against the icy wind.

Perhaps he needed to see a mental therapist. As she finished the thought, he swung his leg back onto the girder. He rose with easy grace and ran along the slick metal to leap fifteen feet to the ground. He jogged up the slope toward her but turned while he was still some distance away, and jogged another two blocks before entering into a dark building, perhaps an abandoned apartment or condominium tower.

She slipped into the building a few moments after he did, her heart pounding. The doors were well-oiled and silent. The hall seemed black as coal after the streetlights outside, and she blinked, hoping her eyes would adjust. After a moment, she could make out the faint rectangles of light from windows in adjacent rooms, but the spaces between remained dark and empty. She crept another step forward, wondering where the man had

17

gone. No light from a distant doorway hinted at a destination, and she hesitated again.

He twisted her arm up behind her back and clamped a hand over her mouth, so her shriek of fear and surprise was caught in her throat. "Why are you following me? *How* are you following me?"

His face was close to hers, his breath nearly in her hair. He lifted his icy hand from her mouth just a little, so she managed to gasp, "I was just curious. No reason."

"You are not welcome here." He opened the door and shoved her outside into the cold.

And that was that.

Or it should have been, anyway. She was too curious for her own good, and she knew it.

Something about him drew her, though she could not say why. The next day, while eating lunch at the campus cafe with Amara, she almost mentioned him, but stifled the impulse. He was a baffling secret, not meant to be discussed over toasted hummus sandwiches.

Aria went back to his apartment three days later, after she'd gathered up her courage again. She circled the building and found an outer door unlocked. Perhaps he never locked it. She closed her eyes for several minutes outside to let her eyes adjust to the darkness before she slipped inside. While she waited, she listened for him, but heard only the traffic of electric cars on the road to her left, the whoosh of wind through the buildings, and the rustle of a bit of paper caught in the grating over a drain near her feet. Her heartbeat thudded in her ears.

The building felt deserted, long disused. *Why*

*didn't I bring a flashlight?* Faint streetlight made it through the windows in the rooms along one side to light the hallway. Long rectangles of light crossed the floor. A stairwell at the end made her pause again, and she crept downward, heart in her throat. The darkness grew deeper, and she remembered her phone. She pulled it out and let the screen shed pale light down the stairs. Another hallway, with a closed door a short distance ahead on her left.

She put her ear to the door and listened. Silence. She waited, her heart in her throat, for some sound that would tell her he was there. *Why am I doing this?* Absolute silence, both in the room and in the hallway.

She glanced around and tried the door tentatively. If he was there, it was dangerous. Even if he wasn't, it was still dangerous.

There was no sound from inside, and she took a deep breath before pulling a plastic card from her pocket. The building was old, and the lock looked simple and loose. Perhaps this would work.

She needed both hands, so she put the phone back in her pocket, wishing she still had its faint light. It seemed to take too long, her heart in her throat while she jiggled the card, twisting and pushing and hoping.

There was a barely audible click, and she breathed a quick sigh of relief as she turned the doorknob.

Too soon.

He spun her about and slammed her against the wall, one hand on her throat and the other pulling the card from her hand.

"Why are you here?" His voice growled into

her ear, cold breath brushing against her cheek.

She thrashed, trying to kick him, but he evaded her efforts easily, barely acknowledging her effort. He loosened his hand, just a bit, and she gasped before he tightened it again. Sparkles swam before her eyes, dazzling in the darkness of the hallway. This had been a very bad idea indeed. *How did he sneak up on me? I didn't hear him at all.*

"Why are you here?" He repeated his question, and she shook her head obstinately. She wouldn't answer his question, not while he was choking her. She opened her mouth, trying to curse him, beg him, something, and no sound came out. The sparkles began to fade.

She could see nothing, but his breath moved gently against her face. He was staring at her, as if the darkness meant nothing to him. *I'm going to die. He's going to kill me, and no one will even know.* Suddenly he let go and pushed past her through the open door.

She fell to one knee and rubbed her neck, blinking back angry tears at the pain. It was her own fault. His hand had been as cold and hard as steel, and her breath burned in her throat.

She pulled the phone from her pocket and pointed the light at him through the doorway.

She hadn't had a good look before, and even now, in her fear, the curiosity rose up. *It's going to get me killed someday.* He wore well-worn dark trousers and a threadbare short-sleeved black shirt, perhaps the same one, so thin his pale skin showed through across the shoulders. His hair was black, or close to it; she couldn't tell in the dim light. He moved with taut grace, an athlete or a soldier, perhaps. Of average height, with a slim, muscular build. Thirty? Perhaps younger? There was the slightest touch of grey in the hair near his temples but his face was unlined. Sharp features, because he had no fat to soften them, but they were attractive, she had to admit that. An ancient oil lantern sat unlit on a wooden desk. He tossed a rucksack beside it and packed with swift economy. Three more shirts. A pair of pants. She craned her neck to see more.

"Leave me alone," he said without looking up.

She hesitated. "I only meant to see if anyone lived here."

He grunted. It was an unfriendly sound. And why should he be friendly? She'd been trying to break into his apartment. But he could have killed her, and he didn't.

She pressed her luck. "Well, I thought you might need something. Since the power is off." She rubbed her throat again.

He didn't answer. He picked up all six books from the desk and stacked them in the rucksack, then jerked the worn blanket off the cot, folded it, and tucked it in on top. He turned away for a moment and buckled something around his waist, and she frowned.

"What are you doing?"

"Leaving." His voice was cold.

"Because of me?"

He grunted again. He turned back to the cot and threw the rucksack over his shoulder. Her eyes widened. He was wearing a sword, a long straight blade with a worn, leather-wrapped scabbard. Another, shorter sword hung from his right hip. *What kind of lunatic carries swords, as if we lived back in ye olden days? If he wanted to defend himself, a gun would be better, but if he wants to look intimidating, I guess this works.*

He finally met her eyes, and she flinched at the icy blue stare. She took a step backward, and he walked past her into the hallway.

He dropped the key at her feet without looking back. "It's yours now."

Aria stared at his back. He disappeared at the end of the hallway, and she hesitated. She was almost crazy enough to go after him.

No, she would look in the room. She picked up the key and stepped inside his apartment.

He'd left the lamp, and she lit it with a match from the box sitting beside it. It was impossible to tell how long he'd been there. He'd packed little yet left nothing behind. The ancient wooden bureau was empty, the drawers loud as she tried them. There was a desk with a single drawer, also empty. Nothing in the trashcan. Nothing in the old wardrobe. There was a tiny refrigerator, but it was off. She opened the door, half-expecting some horrible rot to assault her nose, but there was nothing inside. It had been empty and cleaned before the power was turned off. He'd probably never used it then. She tried the light switch. Nothing. No hum of electric power or devices charging. It might have been a bank vault for how silent the room was.

She turned in a circle in the middle of the room. The cot was pushed against the wall, and she eyed it. A cheap camping cot, well-used, devoid of padding and comfort. *He didn't have a pillow. Odd.* The room was a concrete box with nothing to see and nothing to recommend it.

Aria took the lantern with her when she left.

She walked slowly down the hallway, thinking so hard she forgot the pain in her throat as she climbed the stairs toward the exit. The adventure had yielded little, and she felt the whole thing had been foolish. *More than foolish. Idiotic. Some men would have done worse, you know. You're not exactly imposing, and he* did *have reason to be angry with you. What did you expect?*

She sniffed. There was an odd smell, musky and rank, and she caught her breath suddenly. It smelled dangerous. *Big* and dangerous. She pressed herself against the wall, her heart racing.

It was inside the building. She heard it, a rumbling growl, perhaps from the next hall. She swallowed hard. It was coming closer. Another growl, low and echoing in the concrete hallways.

*Why did I decide this was a good idea?* Aria tried to figure out where the sound was coming from. Was it between her and the exterior door? Could she make it outside without being seen? What good would that do, if it caught her scent? She found an open doorway and slid inside the darkened room, trembling, her back pressed against the concrete block wall. She turned the lantern down as far as it would go without going out completely. She pushed the door closed, wincing at a soft squeak. She turned the doorknob, her fingers trembling, trying to get the latch to catch without another sound.

*Maybe it won't hear me.*

*Maybe it can smell me. It sounds big enough to break down the door.*

It growled again, closer. A roar brought her heart to her throat. Terrible snarls echoed in the hallway. An inhuman shriek. Thumps and crashes, with deafening snarling over it all. She sank down against the wall and tried to breathe silently. *Be brave, Aria! Don't lose it, girl.*

Sudden silence. She caught her breath. Was it coming closer? Had it killed someone? What *was* it?

There was a faint thump, very different than the sounds before. Perhaps someone was alive and needed help. There were no cries of pain or shouts for help, but perhaps they couldn't cry out. She waited.

*Is it dead? Is it gone yet? What if someone needs help?* She took a deep breath and rose from her hiding place. She unlatched the door and pulled it open to peek around the doorframe.

The flickering lamplight showed nothing, and she turned it up. She crept carefully down the hall, grateful for her soft, quiet shoes. The hall was short, and at the corner she caught her breath. The walls and floor were covered in blood, great streaks and smears of gore. There was no body. The blood led to the left, and she held her breath as she followed the trail.

The lamp flooded a room with yellow light and her mouth dropped open in horror. It might have been a classroom at some point; there was a blackboard on one wall and a large desk to one side, though there were no small desks for children. A great hulk lay in the middle, the face turned away from her. Blood smeared the floor, the ceiling, and three of the four walls. Paw prints showed how the beast had fought, how it had leaped from the floor to a wall and back into the center of the room.

Her eyes rested on the creature, and she stayed

well away from it, holding the lamp higher as she edged around to examine its head. A wolf of sorts, though not exactly. It was easily three hundred pounds, perhaps more, lean and muscular. Long-legged. Its muzzle was shorter than a wolf's should be, and the teeth were larger and more uneven. Its mouth gaped open, a slime of blood and saliva pooling beneath the tongue. *Is it dead? It's not moving.*

"I told you to leave me alone." The growl came from the other side of the beast's body.

Aria started so badly she almost dropped the lamp.

"Are you hurt?" she managed. She could barely hear her voice over her own thudding heartbeat.

He must have been holding his breath, for he let it out in a rush. "It is none of your concern."

She stepped closer anyway, giving the creature a wide berth. Her eyes were transfixed on its face for another long moment. It looked *wrong*.

Then she looked at him.

He was on his knees, sitting on his heels, the longer sword on the floor in front of him in easy reach. The hilt and blade were smeared with blood, and so was his face. She brought the lamp closer. He sighed in weary frustration, turning his face away from the light.

"Let me help you."

He was covered in blood, the thin shirt sticking to him wetly. His shoulders dropped and he grunted again. "You should leave." It wasn't so unfriendly this time.

She didn't answer. She reached forward to push his hands away from the wound. One of the wounds.

It looked like the creature had tried to gut him, his stomach ravaged. She brought the lamp closer to see the damage, but it was hard to make out in the flickering light. Everything was red blood, soaked dark into the ripped fabric. He'd been trying to tie his extra pair of pants about his waist, but the fabric was difficult to knot tightly. Especially since one of his hands was badly mangled. A broken bone glistened white against the red flesh and blood.

She tried not to look at it, feeling bile rise in her throat.

"What is that thing?" she asked. She had to keep him talking. He would go into shock and die.

"A *vertril*."

"Are there many of them in the city? I've never seen one before." She felt panicky at the thought. Blood smeared her hands, and she stared at them, appalled. *I have to stop the bleeding.*

He snorted, and she looked up at his face. "You wouldn't have," he said.

"I'll take you to the hospital. You need better care than I can give. And you need it soon." *He shouldn't still be talking. He should be dead. How much of that blood on the floor is his?* She pulled the knot tight, the fabric slick in her fingers.

"I'll be fine." He leaned forward and rested a moment on his right hand, holding his left close to his body, then stood. He blinked, and swayed a moment, then focused on her. "You need to leave. It isn't safe here."

She reached out for his mangled left hand. "Let me bandage that."

He ignored her, knelt to pick up his sword and

wiped it on his pants.

"I don't think that helped much," she ventured. "You're pretty gory."

He slanted a look at her sideways. His mouth twitched, as if he was going to say something, but then he only frowned and said nothing.

"I need to take you to the hospital," she repeated. "If it doesn't hurt too much now, it's because you're in shock. You need medical attention."

He bent to pull his rucksack over one shoulder and straightened again, more steadily this time, and looked at her. "Thank you for your help. I hope I never see you again." One corner of his mouth twitched upward in a ghost of a smile, and he turned away.

She let him go.

She stayed on her knees, too queasy to rise just yet. She stared at the great beast in horrified fascination. It was covered in grey-brown fur, layered as if it were a cold-weather creature. The teeth were white and sharp, and she peered at them in the lamplight. The largest was nearly as long as her hand. Bloody smears across the floor highlighted long gouges in the linoleum. *Claw marks.*

He should have been dead. It had bitten him, savaged him. The beast too, should have been dead two or three times over. It was cut and stabbed in twelve or thirteen places. Two sword strokes went deep into its gut, but she guessed the throat wound had killed it.

She startled at the sounds in the hallway. The Imperial Police Force was here. The IPF was reassuringly competent, and they would handle this.

"What happened here, ma'am?" the corporal at

the front asked. "Are you injured?"

"No." She gestured helplessly toward the beast.

"Yes, I see it. What do you know about it?" He didn't seem as surprised as she'd expected. *Has he seen one of these before?*

Aria licked her lips. "I think he said it was a 'vertril'? Is that a word?"

He looked at her sharply. "Who said that?"

"The man who killed it. You didn't think I did, did you?"

He blinked at her. "Wait a moment." He pulled an electronic tablet from his pocket and tapped the screen a few times. A light pulsed softly on the end pointed toward her. "Start at the beginning."

She hesitated. She wasn't supposed to be here. Not exactly. "I was here because, well, I heard a sound, and I thought it was suspicious. It wasn't loud. It might have been only a cat or something. But I was just trying to do my duty, and check to see if anything was wrong, so I came in. And I was walking through the hall there when I heard a growl."

The man stared at her. "Wait a moment." He tapped on the screen a few times, then frowned. "Continue."

"Well, it sounded big. And I was frightened. So I waited in that room and when it sounded like everything was over, I came out to see if everything was okay. It sounded like it might have killed someone." She felt panic rising up again at the thought. The smell. The sound of the fight. What if it had found her first?

"Breathe, miss. Take a deep breath. Continue." The man was looking at her with a combination of compassion, disbelief, and suspicion.

"This man had killed it. With a sword." She heard her own choppy language and thought distantly, *I think I'm in shock.* "He was hurt, and I tried to take him to a hospital, but he refused. He left."

"Did you see where he went?" The man's eyes were sharp on her face.

"Down the hall." She waved vaguely.

He called out over his shoulder, eyes not leaving her face. "Teams one and two, ready for retrieval ops. Direction unknown. One target, armed and dangerous. Standby." Then, to Aria, "What did he look like?"

She blinked. "He's not a criminal. He killed it. That's a heroic thing, I'd think."

"What did he look like?" He barked the question at her.

"Medium height. Dark hair. Blue eyes." She felt obstinately unwilling to help them. What did they want with him anyway? He hadn't done anything wrong. If anything, they needed to find him to save his life. He'd be bleeding out now, if she guessed right. Probably no more than a block away.

"Anything else? Distinguishing marks?"

"He's hurt." She stared at him sullenly, wishing she'd lied.

"Medium height, dark hair, blue eyes, wounded. Go!"

All but three of the IPF squad sprinted away.

"Is that all you know?"

"I... think so?"

He studied her for a moment and said carefully, "I'm not questioning your truthfulness, but in cases like this, there is often some... confusion...

in the witnesses. I'm going to prompt you a little where things don't seem to make sense. Just tell me what you actually remember, not what you think I want to hear. If you can't remember, you can't remember. But don't be afraid to add things or change your story if you think of something you didn't say before. If you realize you were confused and said something that wasn't true, now is the time to tell me."

She licked her lips.

"So, you hadn't seen the man before? You just came in here because of a strange noise?"

Aria swallowed. It wasn't really believable, was it? If they thought she was lying, or even just not telling everything she knew, she could be arrested. Kicked out of school. Who knew what else?

"Um. Well, actually I saw the man earlier, in a bookstore. I thought he was... odd, somehow. He didn't do anything wrong. He just caught my interest, I guess. Maybe he reminded me of someone?"

The man's gaze sharpened at this.

"So I guess I followed him here without really thinking much about it. I was out walking, and this was as good a way as any. It's not that far out of my way. I didn't think much of it before..." she gestured at the vertril corpse on the floor.

"He reminded you of someone? Who?"

She shrugged. "I don't know. Maybe he didn't at all. Maybe it was something else about him. He just seemed a little strange somehow, and we're supposed to pay attention and report strange things, aren't we?"

He relaxed a little and glanced at the screen before him. "Where did you first see him? Did you speak with him?"

Oh. They thought she might be associated with him somehow. That was not good at all.

"No, not really. I saw him, just for a minute, in a bookstore where I do homework. It's called Dandra's. He was looking for something and I asked if I could help him, but he turned and left without answering me. I hadn't seen him before that. I left the store a few minutes later and happened to see him again on the street while I was walking around, and I guess I just followed him here without meaning to. Then I heard the noises." That was a better story. They could verify with Dandra that she'd been at the shop, and hadn't seemed to know the man. And she hadn't really said anything that would help them catch him.

"Is any of this blood his?"

She nodded uncertainly. "Take samples," he said over his shoulder to the other men. "Your name? Age? Address?"

"Aria Forsyth. Twenty-four. 19 McKenna Walk."

"That's North Quadrant. Why are you here?"

She blinked at him innocently. "What do you mean?"

"This is East Quadrant. Why are you here?"

"Like I said, I was just on a walk. This isn't where I'd normally go, but it's not any farther."

"Three miles from home." He frowned at her skeptically.

She blinked back at him innocently. "I'm a student. I walk everywhere."

"Hm." He noted something on the tablet. "We're done here. Gert, call cleanup." Then to Aria, "Go home. Have a good evening. I'd recommend staying in North Quadrant for your walks from now on." He smiled at her coolly and pointed her toward the door.

As she left, she heard another IPF officer say quietly, "It's number 235, sir."

She hurried down the hall, away from the blood streaks and terror. She'd gotten more than she bargained for. What had she expected if she broke into his apartment, anyway?

Any man would be annoyed, at best, at finding someone breaking and entering. Dandra was frightened, either of him or of those he worked with. *Worked with*, as if she knew what his connection was with Petro. Or who Petro was. Not to mention the danger of other things. Some men couldn't be trusted alone with a girl at all. She'd thought she could take care of herself, but he'd taken her by surprise. Twice.

Now, in the aftermath of the... what would she call it? Her attempt at breaking into his apartment? The incident with the great wolf beast? The second time he could have killed her but didn't? In the aftermath, as she walked into the light winter sleet, she thought about him.

He meant to be frightening, but she wasn't frightened. Not of him, anyway. The thought of another vertril in the streets was enough to make her look over her shoulder and hurry a little faster. She was curious, still. Worried, too. Guilty.

*What if they caught him?* The IPF hadn't seemed concerned about his wounds at all. She tried to put into words what she'd seen in the corporal's face. Bloodthirsty? It sounded harsh but yet terrifyingly accurate.

She heard IPF teams as she hurried through

the darkness. They were quiet, but she was alone in the street and she could tell that many people moved through the darkness around her. Their boots squished softly on the damp asphalt.

"That way." She heard them running swiftly past her. She stopped, her heart in her throat, at the quick flash of a laser sight. It disappeared, and she heard them moving again. No shot sounded.

She stood frozen in the street. *They're trying to kill him!*

She tried to follow the sounds, but they were fast and she was already tired. She lost them some blocks away. Not that she had any idea what she would do if she caught up with them.

Maybe she was wrong.

Maybe they weren't going to kill him. But what were "retrieval ops" and why did they merit weapons with laser sights? The whole team had been armed, once she thought about it. Heavily armed. Their guns had silencers. She'd assumed it was to deal with the vertril, but now she wasn't sure. How had they known to come in the first place? Number 235? What did that mean?

She walked home briskly, huddled in her coat. It was a long walk with the sleet picking up, and she wondered why she'd thought it was a good idea to walk in the first place. She stayed under the lights on the busier streets. Even at this hour, there were plenty of people out in the commercial district.

*How many of them know about the vertril?* Would they hunt here, among the crowds? How had she lived in this city for twenty-four years and not known of such monsters? She slipped into her little apartment with a sigh of relief. She locked the door behind herself and pulled off her coat and sweater, her boots, and finally her pants. She ran her hands over her face and through her hair.

*A shower. I'll feel better after a shower.* She shivered.

As the hot water ran over her, she felt some of her tension and fear melt away. No vertril would get her here. But it didn't soothe her guilt. Somewhere, a man was dying, and she had barely tried to save him.

# CHAPTER 2

ARIA SPENT the next day inside. She had plenty of books full of sticky notes and highlighting and she stared at her computer screen for hours.

But the words wouldn't come. She had ideas, but no thesis. No coherent story for her paper. She had no thread to pull that would unravel into a line of thought.

Except the uneasy suspicion that there were things the Empire didn't want her to know. But that was silly. Every government has secrets. It doesn't mean the government is immoral. No government can operate with complete transparency. She knew that. She wasn't so naive that she didn't understand the need for secrecy. Sometimes.

But why had she heard nothing about forests in the last few years? Surely someone would have mentioned forests, or woods, or rivers, or something. Not busy waterways like the Anacostia and Potomac, but a real river, with fish and rocks and maybe even a waterfall. The images in her mind were hazy and dreamlike, but she knew they were real.

Where had the book gone? Why did Dandra deny it? Aria was sure Dandra knew which book she meant. But why would she lie about it?

*What if he'd died?*

He had died, of course. No one could live with those injuries. No one could evade the IPF, much less when injured so terribly. Maybe they'd found him and taken him to a hospital. *But that's not what they intended.*

She bundled up against the cold and went out. A walk would clear her head. Or perhaps give it more to think about. More questions might lead to answers, or connections between questions, which might be almost as good.

She considered turning toward Connecticut Avenue, where her friend Amara lived. But this was an alone kind of walk. An alone kind of mood.

Aria looked in the shop windows as she passed. The familiar up-scale clothing boutiques and trendy bistros didn't interest her. Fashionable mannequins modeled outfits she couldn't afford on her graduate student stipend. Only the restaurants and coffee shops were open this late.

She considered a hot drink, perhaps tea to break with her coffee tradition, but decided against it. The shops looked small and cozy, but the bleak weather suited her mood better. She had warm boots and a hood against the coming snow. She pushed her gloved hands further into her pockets and continued on.

There were few others walking the streets; they all looked like they were headed somewhere in a hurry. *Maybe they're smarter than I am. It's miserable out here.* But there was traffic, the bluish headlights and red taillights of electric cars meandering through the commercial district. A door opened briefly as a man entered a little bistro, and she heard laughter from inside.

Without meaning to, she found herself near the river. The edges were just crusting with ice; it was barely below freezing. She turned southeast, with the river on her right, and followed it morosely.

Had she caused his death? Had the IPF caught him? Why had they hunted him anyway?

Was it her fault?

She wondered if Dandra's shop was open this late. Probably not. *Should I tell her what happened?* Aria headed to the bookstore anyway, not looking up until she was nearly to the door. Then she stopped in surprise.

The lights inside were off, of course; that was as she'd expected. A handwritten note taped to the inside of the glass door said *Closed until further notice.* That was odd. She peered in, but the streetlights behind her barely illuminated the interior. Nothing looked unusual. The row of tiny tables near the coffee bar at the front was neat and clean; behind it the aisles of books could barely be seen. Shadows cloaked the bookshelves and tables, but nothing looked out of place.

She ran her hand along the icy handle and finally turned away. Maybe Dandra was ill or something. At the bridge, she looked to her right across the undergirding. She almost walked past, then a barely perceptible movement caught her eye and she froze.

There, forty feet above the water, was a dark form on the metal. Well out of the light, the dim shape was scarcely visible, but it was in the same place she'd seen him before.

It was impossible. He was dead. He had to be. Anyone would have died, wounded like that.

But she stared anyway, trying to make out the shape. Was it a person? A dead body? *His* body? She glanced up and down the street and saw no one.

It took only a moment for her to decide. She slipped down the dark, wet slope toward the base of the bridge. The ladder rungs were high, and she had to jump to reach the bottom one. Her glove slipped and she nearly fell, but she caught it again and kicked hard against the metal piling until she could lunge upward for the next one. Finally she got one foot up high enough to climb the ladder the normal way. She was breathing hard, and she stopped at the top to catch her breath and look across the girder. The supports were arched, making room for the ships that traversed up the Potomac River.

From this angle, it was clearly a man's form. He lay on his back with his feet toward her, one leg dangling off the edge toward the water. He was barefoot and completely motionless.

She edged toward him on hands and knees. The girder was wide, perhaps three feet, but the water was far below and very cold, and it made her nervous to be so high. She tried not to think about the height. Closer. *Breathe, Aria.* She focused on her hands as they moved, dark gloves against dark metal. At least the girder was flat. Even without an angle to it, the metal was slippery in the damp.

When she glanced up again, he was sitting, leaning forward with one arm resting on his knee.

"Why are you following me?" His voice was soft. "I've done nothing to you."

"I wasn't following you. I was walking, and I saw a shape here. I wasn't sure it was you." She edged a little closer. "I was worried. You were hurt, and the IPF..." her voice trailed away. "I thought they meant to help you at first." She frowned.

He huffed softly, a short hard sound that might have been a laugh. "They never mean to help us."

Aria tried to see him in the darkness. His form was shadowy, and she could see only the pale, angular shape of his face, his arms, and his bare feet. Closer. "I wasn't looking for you, but you're hurt. It's freezing out here, and you don't have any shoes. Let me give you mine. I have more at home. They're boots, and they're too big for me anyway. They ought to fit."

She sat back and started to pull at her laces.

He reached forward and stopped her with one bare hand. "I'm fine." There was a hint of warmth in his voice now, and she met his eyes.

He swallowed and looked away first, glancing back toward the empty street beyond the steep bank. "Thank you for your concern. It is unusual."

She stared at him. "You must be freezing. You have no coat either?"

He looked back at her. "No." He rested his left hand against his stomach and shifted with a wince.

She stared at his hand. It was bandaged with

what looked like torn strips of one of his dark shirts.

"Are you healing? Who are you? *What* are you?"

He laughed softly. "Dandra told you not to ask questions you don't want to know the answer to."

She stared back at him. "How did you know that? You were gone."

"I hear many things." He smiled at her, teeth very white in the darkness.

"What maps did you want?"

He cocked his head to one side, staring at her with cold suspicion. "Who do you work for?"

"What?"

He lunged at her, caught her by the throat, and flipped her on her back. He knelt by her and whispered with icy menace, "You ask a lot of questions. Who do you work for?"

She shook her head, unable to speak against the pressure on her throat. Tears squeezed from her eyes against her will. "No one," she gasped. Mouthed. The words were inaudible, and she stared at him, willing him to believe her. Her heart thudded wildly.

He let her go and sat back. He was breathing as hard as she was, and he pressed his bandaged left hand against his stomach. He glanced past her toward the street again.

She wiped at her eyes. Her gloves were wet, and the chill stung her cheeks. "I was just trying to help you. Why do you keep assuming the worst? I don't even know what you mean." She wanted to go, but curiosity kept her. And compassion.

He leaned back against the vertical support, and this time his pain was more obvious. He

40

stared at her for a long moment, then looked back toward the street again. "You should go. If you're not one of them, you won't want to see what happens next."

"One of who?"

"Them." His eyes flicked toward her face again, and she blinked at their cold intensity. "Hunters."

"Hunting you?" She let her confusion be obvious. If she didn't know what he meant, perhaps he would trust her a little more. The wind gusted suddenly. It caught her hood and dragged it backward, and she tugged at it, shivering.

"They can track you, you know." His blue eyes watched her for a reaction. "You're leading them to me."

She frowned at him. Was he mad? "No. They can't. They wouldn't. *Why?*"

"Trackers. They're in almost everyone. Except for my people." The cool blue gaze rested on her, gauging her reaction before moving back toward the street again.

She glanced back toward the street too. "Why? Where? *How?*" She shivered, and this time it wasn't only because of the icy wind.

"I believe you. That means you have a choice." He pressed his bandaged left hand hard against his stomach and stood, with a soft huff of pain. He leaned back against the vertical support and looked at the opposite shore of the river for a long moment before looking back at her. "You can leave the tracker in and follow their rules. Go back to your life. It's the easiest way. Safest."

He glanced over his shoulder again thoughtfully. "Or you can let me remove it. There's no go-

C. J. BRIGHTLEY

ing back. You're out of everything. No job, no school, no electricity, no money. You're invisible. And hunted."

She swallowed. "What happened to Dandra?"

He watched her face. "What do you mean?"

"Her shop is closed until further notice. What happened to her? Did you tell Petro?"

"No." His voice was flat, as if he didn't really care whether she believed him.

"Why should I leave my life?" She wondered that she was even considering it. But then, it wasn't so great, was it? A school she didn't enjoy. A thesis that made her question everything she remembered. A boxy little apartment that she'd tried unsuccessfully to make cozy. A family that consisted of fragmented memories. A few school friends. No one close, not anymore.

"I didn't say you should." His voice was soft, and she glanced up at him. He was watching the street again, and she studied him for a moment in the dim light. Lean and hard. *Like a soldier*, she thought again.

"What are you?" she asked again.

He glanced down, meeting her eyes. "There's not much time. Make your decision."

"Do it."

He knelt suddenly in front of her. "You're sure? There is no changing your mind, afterward."

She swallowed. "I'm not giving up much."

He studied her for another long moment, then nodded once. He pulled a shirt from his rucksack, nearly invisible in the darkness. "Cut a strip off this." He pulled a knife from his belt and held it toward her, hilt-first. She stared at it. Eight inches long, sharp on both edges and narrowing to a needle point.

"You're going to cut me." She pulled her gaze away from the blade to stare at him.

"Yes. You said you wanted it out."

"Will it hurt?" She felt her breath coming short. The cold air burned her lungs, and she shivered again, pulling her coat closer around her chest. As if that would protect her, if he wanted to kill her now.

He snorted softly. "Yes."

She took a deep breath and felt her heart thudding. She forced herself to take the knife from him. The blade was razor sharp, but cutting the fabric into a usable shape was hard in the darkness. He reached out with his good hand to help her stretch the fabric taut. She tried not to think about what she was doing. It was crazy. *She* was crazy.

"Take off your coat and pull up your sleeve. Right arm." He set the knife down beside his knee.

She pulled off the coat and put it behind her, shivering harder. It was getting foggy, and though the wind had lessened, the cold still cut through her thick sweater to her bare skin. She pushed her sleeve up just above her elbow.

"More. No, take it off completely." He glanced over his shoulder at the far shore, then back at the street nearest them.

"It's freezing," she whispered.

"I'll be fast." He was still searching the street, cold blue eyes flicking down the long stretch of road and resting for a long moment on something. She turned to look over her shoulder as she pulled her right arm out of the sweater sleeve, but didn't see anything. She pushed her arm down and out the bottom of the sweater, keeping the rest of it on.

The thick knit bunched around her throat and she pulled at it, trying to keep as much covered as possible.

"Lay down on your coat. And get your phone out."

She lay back, shivering. *Aria, you've officially lost it. This is insane. You're on a bridge with a crazy man with a knife, and you're about to let him cut you. No, you asked him to cut you. What is wrong with you?*

He moved forward, still kneeling, his bare left foot on the edge of the girder, his right knee beside her ribs. He bent to look at her arm, eyes intent. *What will it look like? I don't know why I believe him, but I do.*

He reached out and ran his hand along her upper arm, fingers cold as the metal, and she gasped at the chill. He prodded at one spot, then brought his bandaged hand up to the place and held her arm down firmly. "Don't move."

The warning was unnecessary. The knife flickered in and out so fast she barely had time to gasp at the sudden pain. He pressed, and she bit her lip to keep from crying out. Then it was done. He held a tiny metal object up for her to see.

"Hold it." He dropped it into her hand and wrapped the strips of cloth around her arm. She stared at the tiny metal capsule, the size and shape of a grain of rice. The wound burned, but not as much as she'd expected.

"What does it do?"

One handed, he had a hard time tying the bandage, gripping one end in his teeth, and she helped with her left hand. He moved his right hand to cup icy fingers against the back of her neck, sliding up into her hair. She shuddered. He cocked his head, eyes half-closed as if he was concentrating. Then she blinked. A red light appeared on his shoulder, wavered a moment, and then shifted to his head.

"Move!" He jerked her upward and behind himself. "Around the upright, now."

A shot cracked, and he jolted into her. She slammed into the metal face first, stunned. He jerked her left arm, pushed her to the side, his body close to hers. "Around it. There's a step. Drop the tracker and your phone into the water." He sounded like he couldn't catch his breath.

*Around.* Panic rose in her throat and threatened to choke her. His bandaged hand on her shoulder steadied her as she put her booted feet on the ridge that circled the upright.

He followed her to the other side. He was breathing hard, unevenly.

"You're hit."

"Yes." He coughed, a short hard cough. He caught her arm again, kept her in the shadow of the upright. The laser caught the underside of the bridge and moved slowly away, then back toward them. Searching. Floodlights blazed in the darkness, flaring up at them and across the water. "You dropped the tracker? Phone? Good. Wait here for at least an hour. There's a coffee shop three blocks north of Dandra's." Another cough, nearly a groan. "Called Franco's Fuel. Go there. Stay in the shadows. I'll find you." A pause, then, "Don't go home."

Then he stood, visible, and took a few steps into the clear. He stood in the cold floodlight until the laser veered toward him, then stepped off the girder. A shot rang out, then more, following him down. He landed feet first with a barely audible splash. She heard boots running across the bridge to look for him. She huddled in the shadow of the wide metal girder.

More searchlights flooded across the underside of the bridge, and she shrank even further into the tiny shadow. She could hear them talking, though some of the words were indistinct.

"Which one is it?"

"Unknown. The human was Aria Marie Forsyth. Birthdate August 19, 2061. Age twenty-four. Address 19 McKenna Walk, North Quadrant. Lives alone. Currently enrolled in Historical Studies at City Central University. No family."

Aria had to bite back a cry. He was right, they were tracking her. But why? Hearing her life summarized like that, it seemed so small. So sad.

"Did it kill her?"

"Unknown. Probably. She dropped first. We didn't have the lights up yet."

"You didn't hit her, did you?"

"Unlikely. The reading was cold."

"Could have been her jacket, if it's thick. Insulation could mask the body temp."

"Could be. I think I got it though."

"Search for her body too. Either way, she's dead."

"Unless… no. Never mind."

"You think it knows about that?"

"No."

They searched the shoreline. She shivered as she counted them, her teeth chattering in the cold. Nine spotlights downriver. Four upriver. They tilted up toward her again, moving slowly across the undergirding of the bridge, and she held her breath, her knees pulled into her chest as she stayed out of the light. She tucked her hands inside her sleeves and hugged herself. Her arm hurt, a throbbing pain that burned against the cold, pulsing in time with her heartbeat. She felt the bandage gingerly with her left hand. He'd been inhumanly fast. *If I'm the human, what is he?* And good with his knife. The cut wasn't as bad as she'd expected. He'd been efficient. She tried not to think about the shot that had slammed him into her. The sudden rush of air from his lungs at the impact.

He didn't deserve to die. He'd been hostile, yes, but could she blame him? As much as they wanted him dead, it was no wonder he was suspicious. *They called him an 'it.'*

The spotlights moved slowly down the river. She heard dogs barking, IPF dogs on leashes. Big ones, though not like the beast he'd killed. She closed her eyes, feeling suddenly exhausted. The cold of the metal stole through her clothes and took her strength. *No. If he's still alive, somehow, I need to meet him. How long has it been?*

She glanced cautiously around the upright. The searchlights were distant now, and as she watched they moved farther down the river. Searching. Would they come back? She waited a while longer to be sure, but heard nothing aside from the hum of the city. A dog barking. The quiet lapping of the water beneath her.

She took a deep breath and pushed herself up to stand against the upright. She pressed her back to it and glanced at both shores. No one was there now. No one to see her.

She felt for the ridge with her foot, slid behind the upright, and eased onto the girder on the other side. She paused, half-expecting a searchlight to flare in her face. Nothing happened, and she crept forward, using the glint of the streetlights on the edge of the girder for a guide. She slid each foot forward carefully. They hadn't noticed his rucksack, which he'd left on the girder. She pushed it ahead of her, advancing on her knees now. She felt around the top of the girder, unable to see whether he'd left anything else. Nothing.

She found her coat. It was damp inside now with the misting rain, but she put it on anyway and then slipped the strap of the rucksack over her shoulder. She crawled to the end of the girder and felt for the ladder. It was darker here under the overhang, and her heart was in her throat as she swung her legs off the girder and felt for the ladder rungs. She climbed down as silently as she could, and swung from the bottom, trying to judge the distance before letting go.

She landed with a jolt, falling to one knee, then pushed herself to her feet and trudged up the muddy slope toward the street. It was still empty, and she wondered how late it was. She hadn't worn a watch.

Aria paused at the top, under a streetlight, then thought better of it and moved to a shadow. *Last chance. Last chance to stay out of it.* She took a deep breath, and began walking.

ARIA KNEW FRANCO'S FUEL, but she didn't like it. Their coffee was always over-roasted and bitter. The storefront was distinctive, though, which made it a good place to meet. She took a circuitous route, uneasy now about being followed. *Which is stupid, because the tracker is gone and no one saw me. But it won't hurt to be careful.* She came to it from the north, slipping through the shadows. She stopped across the street and crouched in the shadow of a hedge.

She jerked in surprise when he put an icy hand over her mouth.

"Follow me." His voice was only a breath in her ear. "Be silent."

She nodded and he let go. She trailed him down an alley barely lit by the faint reflections of streetlights on windows on the main road. Then another turn into pitch blackness. He took her hand in his, and she could feel the cold even through her gloves. Another turn, then the soft swish of a door opening.

"Steps down." His voice was barely audible. He closed the door behind her, then took her hand again, guiding her down the stairs. Then through what seemed to be tunnels, the air cold and still. She could hear his breathing, a catch in each breath, though he made no other sound. She could hear her own too, over the thud of her heartbeat and her quiet footsteps. He coughed, a short hard sound. Another turn, and another. Then another door. He put his hand on her shoulder and guided her through, then stepped through himself and locked it. He moved away from her, and she waited. A light flared, and she blinked for a moment in the brightness.

They were in a small room, perhaps ten feet by twelve. There was a camping cot pushed against one wall. A lantern sat on a worn table, and the man stood just to the side and a little in front of it, nearly silhouetted. He studied her for several long seconds while she tried to see him against the light.

"Where are we?" she whispered.

"Under the East Quadrant." His voice was low, but he didn't whisper, and she took it as a sign that they were safe. He looked at her a moment longer, then stepped back from the light. "Sit." He nodded toward the chair.

He leaned against the table, half-sitting on the edge. He took a deep breath and coughed once, hard, and then again, leaning forward as it shook him.

"I'll ask a favor," he said hoarsely.

"Sit down. Or lay down." She reached forward to help him and he drew back, blue eyes on her face. "You're hurt. What do you need?" She glanced around the room. There was nothing here, nothing that could help him.

He studied her face one long moment, then drew the knife and held it toward her, hilt first. "The bullet is in my right lung. Dig it out. It's poison."

Her mouth dropped open. She backed away, shaking her head. "No. You'll die. You're dying now. I can't..." *I can't believe you're still standing.*

He coughed again, doubled over with his right hand braced on his knee, still holding the knife, and his left held to his stomach. Harder and harder, he coughed and could not stop for a terribly long minute. He gasped and swallowed hard, took a deep breath, wiped the back of his mouth with his hand. It came away streaked with blood.

He stripped off his shirt with one quick motion and dropped it to the floor. Around his waist was the bandage made from his pants. He'd cut off the extra fabric and the knot was against his left side, the fabric pulled wide across his stomach, black and stiff with blood. The caked blood had softened in the river water, leaking dark down to soak into his damp trousers. He picked up the lantern and put it on the floor, then knelt with his back to it.

"Find the bullet. It must come out." He held the knife toward her again. "There's not much time." He bent forward, coughing so hard he couldn't speak.

Aria pulled off her gloves. She took her coat off and tossed it at the chair.

She took the knife from his hand, which tightened convulsively as he coughed. She moved around behind him and covered her mouth, suddenly nauseated. The bullet had hit just below his right shoulder blade. Blood soaked his shirt and now pulsed out in a slow rhythm, streaking his pale wet skin. The hole was as large as her thumb. Scratches and bruises crossed his back, probably from the fight with the vertril, she imagined.

"Can you lay down?" Her voice was hoarse.

He almost fell forward, caught himself with his right hand, and lay on the cold stone floor, jerking as he tried to control the coughing.

"Do it. Don't be afraid." He coughed again. "Break a rib if you have to. Get it out. It must come out." Then he was racked with coughing, so hard his knees jerked beneath him and his face scraped against the floor.

She took a deep breath. *Do it. It's not going to get any easier.* She pressed her left hand hard against his back, the muscles alive beneath her fingers. She stabbed the knife in, trying to push the nausea away. He gasped beneath her and dug his fingers into the floor. She shifted the knife to her left hand and pushed two fingers inside. His flesh and blood were cool, though not as icy as his hands, and the sudden shock of that made her blink in surprise. He truly wasn't human, despite his looks. A human would be warm, hot, even. Didn't they say "hot blood" when they described a human bleeding? He was definitely cool.

Farther. She could feel nothing that might be a bullet. She felt the strong solidity of bone, the rib cage, and how the hole passed between two of the ribs into the lung. She pushed, and her fingers moved wetly through and wiggled in the emptiness inside. He jerked beneath her. She was lightheaded and queasy at the thought of what she was doing, but she pushed the feeling away.

"I'm going to break it." Her voice felt like it came from someone else.

He nodded once.

She raised the knife and slammed the hilt downward. Not hard enough. Again with two hands, and there was a nauseating crack. He jerked, eyes shut. He spat blood onto the floor near her knee and coughed again. *Quickly now. He said there isn't much time.* She pushed her hand in, fingers reaching past the broken ends of bone. She closed her eyes. Looking at it only made her want to vomit, and she felt more confident as she operated by touch alone. She had a little more play now, and she felt around. She leaned onto her left hand as he twitched and jerked, coughing more weakly, choking on his own blood.

*There.* The bullet was large and had flattened a little as it hit the front ribs and lodged against the bone. She could feel the layers of tissue sliding against each other as she pushed. She could barely grasp it between her index finger and middle finger, at the very extent of her reach. She pushed a little farther, and he made a small, choked sound. There. She had it. She drew it out, paused to get a better grip on it, and then all the way.

She caught her breath, chest heaving like she'd been holding it for hours. "I got it. It's out." She put it in front of his face.

He was still. Eyes closed. She sat back and stared at him. *No. Not after that. You can't die now.*

His back rose and fell, the slightest hint of life. Barely anything. She cast about for something to stop the bleeding and found only his shirt. It was soaked with blood and river water. Maybe he had another? She dug through the rucksack frantically. Six books. A blanket. A smooth, rectangular stone. Socks. One shirt. A pair of soft black shoes, which he was inexplicably not wearing in the frigid weather. She folded the socks and cut the shirt along one side, then knotted it around his chest so the socks made a thick pad over the wound. He didn't move.

She stepped back and stared at him. It wouldn't help the internal bleeding, which was doubtlessly worse than what she could see.

She'd wrestled with his limp body and he hadn't twitched. He kept breathing though, and that alone was enough to prove he wasn't human. His blood smeared her hands and arms. Spread onto the floor. She swallowed bile again. She wanted to throw up, but she wouldn't. No. Not now.

Should she put him on the cot? It had to be better than laying facedown on the stone floor. But moving him would be challenging at best, and would probably injure him more. She folded the remains of the shirt and slipped it under his face. His lips were open, and a slow trickle of blood dripped from his mouth. She wiped it away. She pulled the blanket from his rucksack and draped it over him.

That looked a little better. The blanket hid the worst of the bloodstains, all but the spot near his face.

Now what? The room was nearly empty. She sat on the cot and stared around the room, then back at him. She wanted to rub her hands over her face, but thought better of it when she looked at them. The blood dried slowly, darker in the corners of her nails and her cuticles.

*What have I done?*

# CHAPTER 3

His skin was as pale as marble in the dim lamp-light. Her own skin was only a little darker. Her friend Amara had teased her, told her she ought to be in skin care commercials, but Aria knew she was being kind. Everyone had good features and bad. Her skin was beautiful, but she was too petite for the current style. Too angular. Her mouth was well-shaped but too wide. She didn't mind it when she looked in the mirror, but she wasn't the kind of beauty that advertisers or movie producers wanted.

He was. Or he would have been, had he been human.

She frowned. Hunted, he'd said. Hunted by the IPF, apparently. Were there other hunters, too? Why?

She rubbed her hands over her face. They were dry now, at least, and the blood had rubbed off with a little effort. What time was it? She'd been up for hours when she left her apartment, and it had been hours since then. It must be close to morning. Her eyes felt gritty. She sat in the chair. Her boots were wet, and she kicked them off, but her socks were still damp. She shivered and tucked her cold feet under herself in the hard wooden chair.

She leaned forward and put her head on her arms. Her eyes drifted closed.

Aria woke with a jerk.

His cool blue eyes were resting on her face. He hadn't moved, still lay on his stomach on the floor.

"How do you feel?" she nearly whispered it, and the sound of her own voice nearly made her jump in the thick, cold silence.

"Alive." It was a croak, and he closed his eyes for a moment. Then he looked at her again with a faint smile. "Thank you."

Her stomach rumbled, and she smiled awkwardly. "Sorry."

One corner of his mouth quirked in amusement. With a deep breath, he pushed himself up to sit on his heels in one quick movement. In the deafening silence, his gasp of pain was terribly loud. He paused then, eyes closed, fist pressed to his mouth as he slowed his breathing, controlling the pain.

Then he looked at her again. "Where is it?" He was hoarse, and the whisper sounded painful to her ears.

She knelt and found the bullet on the floor. He looked at it in her hand but didn't touch it.

"They can't track that one." He had to stop to

breathe.

"Why don't you lay on the cot? I'll help you." She knelt in front of him and offered her arm.

He hesitated, then leaned on her for an instant as he stood. "You'll need food."

"I can get some later. What do you need?"

He was white as ice, and he shivered suddenly as he stood there. He ran his right hand over his face and through his hair. It stuck up afterward, and she thought suddenly that he looked both younger and more tired than before. "How long have we been here?"

"I'm not sure. It's probably morning."

"We should move."

"You're in no shape to go anywhere."

He swayed as he stood. "I think you're right." His voice was distant, and he blinked dazedly before taking an unsteady step toward the table. She half-caught him as he crumpled, let him down to kneel on the floor.

"You wait here. I'll go get food. What do you need?" She tried to make her voice certain, strong, competent.

He sagged against the leg of the table. "There's a butcher shop on Dumbarton Street." A deep breath. "It's not far from the ladder we came down. Called Bryson's. Tell him you're picking up Owen's order. Get what you need first, if you're short of money." Another deep, painful breath. He coughed once and wiped blood from his mouth. He looked at the smear across the back of his hand thoughtfully and licked his lips. "Take my knife. Don't show it unless you have to."

"I'll help you to the cot."

"I'll be fine. Don't take long. They'll be looking

for you." He held her eyes a moment with his cool blue gaze. "Take the lamp for the tunnels. Go on, then."

She frowned, but nodded. She slipped out, leaving him kneeling by the table in the dark.

The tunnels were more confusing than she'd realized. She paused at yet another corner and wondered whether she'd be able to find her way out at all. Finally she found a ladder and crept up. It ended at a doorway, and she pushed it open a crack, peeked out, and then slipped through. She tested the latch, and guessed it wouldn't lock behind her. She closed it, and then tried it. It opened again almost soundlessly. Good.

She wrapped her coat around herself against the chill. It was late morning, the sun bright overhead. She didn't know exactly where she was, but it felt familiar. She walked quickly, cautiously, trying to be aware of everything without looking like she was nervous. At the next corner there were vendors gathered, mostly paper and cigarette carts. Olive Street, though not a section she frequented. She turned left, and in less than a block found a grocery store.

Bread. Cold meat. Cheese. A bag of apples. *What else?* A pack of five black short sleeved shirts. A large pack of matches. Some lantern oil. Two bottles of water. She went to the front to pay.

The man raised his eyebrows. "Men's shirts?"

She shrugged. "A friend asked me to pick them up."

"Hm." He gave her the change, and she felt his eyes on her as she left. She walked left out of the doorway, away from the direction she'd come.

She circled the block, trying to see if anyone

was following her, and then started a larger circle, looking for the butcher shop. Finally she saw the sign. It was small, the kind of ethnic shop favored by poor immigrants hungry for a taste of home. Not that there were many of those left these days. The man behind the counter eyed her suspiciously.

"I'd like to pick up Owen's order." She tried to sound confident.

"Owen?" his accent was strong, and he stared at her again, not moving. "You know him?"

"Yes." She bit her lip. "He asked me to pick it up for him," she added when he didn't move.

"Hm." He kept a suspicious eye on her as he finally moved toward the back. He opened a large refrigerator and pulled out a paper bag with a small white receipt stapled to the top.

"Four dollars."

Good. It wasn't too expensive. Still, if she couldn't go back to her apartment, she'd run out of cash soon. She handed the bills over and he pulled off the receipt before he slid the bag across the glass countertop. It was heavier than she'd expected.

She took an indirect route back toward the ladder.

Down. She'd blown out the lantern at the bottom, and she felt for it in the darkness, careful not to knock it over. She lit it and then went back through the tunnels, counting the turns. Finally she found the door, proud of herself for not having gotten lost.

She turned the knob quietly and slipped inside. He lay where she'd left him kneeling, curled on his side, facing away from the door. She set the lantern down, almost silent, and watched him a moment. Soft, shallow breaths. He was shirtless still, even in the cold, and she could see the lines of his ribs, the hard muscles of his back disappearing under the makeshift bandages, the curve of his shoulder into his neck. If his hair had been longer, it might have formed ringlets, but it was cut short on his neck and just a little longer on top. The hair-cut was uneven, as if he'd done it himself.

She stepped forward to put the bag on the table.

Swords in hand, he spun up into a crouch so fast she didn't even see him move. He stared at her a moment, then stood straighter, breathing heavily. He sheathed the swords. "Don't startle me."

She swallowed, her back pressed against the door. "I'm sorry."

He steadied himself against the table. "Did you have any trouble?" He coughed and closed his eyes, pressing his knuckles against his mouth.

"No. I brought your package." She set it on the table along with the other two bags, put his knife next to it, spread out the food and looked at him. "Sit down."

He eyed the spread and then her. "You'll want to eat first."

"There's plenty for us both."

"I'm not eating that. Go ahead." He picked up his knife and moved away to sit on the edge of the cot. He inspected the knife blade carefully, turning it this way and that to catch the light. Satisfied, he slipped it into the sheath on his belt and leaned forward to rest his elbows on his knees.

He watched her as she ate. The bread was a little mashed, but she made a sandwich anyway. She turned the chair so she could look back at him.

"So your name is Owen," she said finally. "That's good to know. Seems like we should know each other's names by now." He stared at her wordlessly, and she ventured, "I'm Aria. Aria Forsyth. Do you have a last name?"

"Not in English."

She blinked. "If you're not human, what are you?"

He ran his right hand over his face again. "What do you think?"

She studied him, and he let her, watching her face as her eyes moved over him again. Lean, athletic. He looked human.

"How old are you?" she asked suddenly. It was so hard to tell. No lines at the corners of his eyes or beside his nose. Yet that light touch of grey just at his temples.

He smiled, just a faint wry twitch of his lips. "Now that's cheating." She held his eyes, and he said, "Two hundred seventy-three."

She blinked. "That's impossible."

He only smiled. "Eat. Or if you're done, tell me. I'm hungry too."

She ate the last of her sandwich in three large bites and stood, still chewing. She opened her bottle of water belatedly and took it with her as she moved to the cot.

He stood at the table and opened the sack to pull out a large paper bundle. He unwrapped it with an unreadable glance at her, leaving the paper sticking up so she couldn't see what was inside. She heard the crinkle of the thin butcher shop plastic inside the paper. He drew his knife.

A few quick slices, and then he sat, half-turned so she couldn't see past his shoulder.

"Are you eating it raw?" Aria said in disgust.

A pause. "Don't ask questions you don't want to know the answer to."

She took a drink. "What is it?"

He swallowed. "Don't ask questions you don't want to know the answer to." Another bite. He licked his fingers.

She stood indecisive for a moment, and finally moved closer. He didn't move, though he shot a glance over his shoulder at her. Closer.

A bloody mass cut into cubes lay on the plastic from Bryson's butcher shop. His knife lay beside it, still red.

"By the emperor," she breathed. "What is that?"

He picked up two cubes and swallowed them, one after the other. "Pig's heart."

"That is revolting." She stared at him in horror and then back at the heart.

"Says the human." Another cube. "What do you think I am?"

She backed away to stand at the door. Her mind whirled. "I'd say you were a vampire, but that's absurd. They don't exist."

"I am not a vampire." He didn't look at her.

"But what else is cold to the touch? And eats blood?"

"I'm not eating blood. I'm eating a pig's heart." He enunciated clearly, then stopped to cough again.

"I don't know."

"Have you heard of elves? Fairies?"

"They're small. And they live in the forest or something. And they have wings."

He ate another bite. "Incorrect. You humans

have long since forgotten the truth of the Fae. We are not miniature. We do not have wings. We do not fly. Vampires, elves, fairies… they're partial shadows of the old memories. We're both closer to human and more alien than you imagine."

She felt dizzy, watching him eat the bloody cubes. "Do you kill humans? Do you *eat* humans?"

He choked, coughed, steadied himself on the edge of the table. She waited, her hand on the doorknob. But no. He'd had plenty of opportunities to hurt her that he hadn't taken.

"No," he said finally. He gazed at her with weary amusement. She was starting to read his subtle expressions; they weren't obvious, but this one was as clear as any. "Like humans, we are capable of choosing cruelty. But we are not monsters."

He studied her. "If you're afraid, you can leave. But it's not safer out there." The amusement had faded, leaving only weariness in the set of his shoulders. He finished eating without looking at her. He folded the bloody plastic into the paper, then carefully folded the whole bag into a neat packet, which he slipped into his pocket. He leaned forward, still not looking at her, his head drooping. Then he straightened, as if he'd remembered something. He opened the other water bottle and rinsed his right hand, the water falling to the floor. He shook the water off with a quick flick of the wrist and then drank deeply.

She watched him warily.

"How did you escape them last night? They searched the riverbank."

"I swam."

She frowned. That didn't really answer her

question. "Upstream?"

He nodded once.

"I saw the lights upstream too."

He nodded again.

"What did you want the maps for? From Dandra?"

He reached over to the pack of shirts and held it up to her. "Thank you." A quick cut of the knife slit the plastic wrapper and he pulled one out and over his head. Then he stared at the table for a long moment before looking at her again. "We need to move. It isn't safe to stay in one place for so long."

"What did you want the maps for?"

He stood without answering. He tugged the shirt hem down farther; it had gotten caught on the knot of the bandage around his waist. He leaned his right hand on the table and stood still, resting. Then, slowly, one-handed, he packed everything in his battered rucksack.

"I'll carry it," Aria offered. She picked up the blanket from the floor and folded it, then put it on top and zipped the pack closed. She slung it over her shoulder. He didn't protest.

"Blow out the lantern." His voice was a little hoarse.

He led her through the door, his hand cold in hers. Silently they walked. She heard the faint brush of fabric on the left wall at long intervals, and realized he was touching it with his bandaged hand. Right, left, down a long gentle slope, left again, and up some stairs and around a corner. More walking. Downward again. She was thoroughly lost. She couldn't even guess how far under the city they were. Twenty feet? A hundred feet? The tunnels were cool and dank, but not wet.

"Where are we going?" she ventured.

His *shhh* was barely audible.

She followed him in silence for several more minutes. Down again.

"Where are we going?"

"Quiet."

"No. I want to know where we're going!" she jerked her hand away from his. "I've followed you without question and I'm done. I want to know where you're taking me." Her voice echoed.

He grabbed her wrist and pulled her along, nearly running now. "I'll tell you when we're out of the tunnels." His own voice was much quieter.

She yanked her wrist, but she couldn't escape his iron grasp. There was a sudden sound from behind her. Growling.

Owen jerked her forward and shoved her to the floor. Then it was upon them with a roar that filled the tunnel.

Aria covered her head, scrambling backwards. *I'm dead!* It would kill them both. He was in no shape to fight and she had no weapons, not that she knew what to do with them if she'd had them anyway.

The battle was over in a moment though. She heard him breathing heavily. A cough. The soft sound of his sword being sheathed. Then he grabbed her hand and pulled her to her feet. "When I tell you to be silent, it is not only for my own sake." Though the words were only a whisper, she could hear his anger, and she nodded. He pulled her along, jogging through the tunnels with barely a hesitation at each turn. Then up a very long flight of stairs. He had to stop and cough in the middle, doubled over and leaning against the wall. She helped him as he stumbled upward, still coughing, and then he steadied himself and pulled her on. Suddenly he stopped at a ladder on the side of the tunnel, which continued ahead of them.

"Here. Climb up first."

She obeyed, scrambling up the ladder quickly. At the top the hatch was like a manhole cover, a round metal plate so heavy that she strained to open it. He climbed up farther, his body pressed against hers, to shove it away with his good hand. She clambered through, and he followed her. He pushed the cover back over the hole one-handed and remained kneeling, breathing heavily. In the dim light, she could see he was splattered with blood, a dark streak across one cheek and into his hair.

"Is that your blood?"

"No."

He coughed, bowed so his head nearly touched the ground, and wiped blood from his mouth again. He straightened painfully and wiped his bloody hand on his pants.

"It's not much farther," he said finally, when he caught his breath.

Her breath fogged in the cold; his did not. The concrete floor beneath her knees felt icy and unwelcoming. She looked around. They were in a vast, dimly lit room filled with boxes and machinery.

"What is this place?"

He didn't answer. He struggled to his feet, and she offered him a hand belatedly. He wound through the aisles and found a set of open metal stairs, which he followed upward to the next floor, high above the first. *Some sort of warehouse? But where is this?* Then down a long hallway to a room at the end, with windows on two sides.

He closed the door and locked it, then went to the windows and looked out. "Here. We can rest here." He sank to the floor, sitting with his back against the wall, a little uneven so his right side didn't quite touch. He leaned his head back, eyes closed.

"Are you going to live? You shouldn't be alive at all." She came to sit by him.

He huffed softly, as if he wanted to laugh but didn't quite have the strength. "Oh yes. Always have so far."

The smooth skin of his neck moved as he spoke. "We're hard to kill, we Fae. They know how, though. Getlaril bullets. A few other ways. They're doing research. Testing." He opened his eyes to look sideways at her. "Test. Evaluate. Refine. Test again. They experiment." He coughed.

"That's what I want the maps for. Government maps. The secure facilities. They have test subjects." He grimaced when he said it, a twist of the lips. "Of course they won't be noted on any map I could acquire, but with a power grid I could figure it out. Or water lines. Or security checkpoints. A clue. I've been trying to make my own, but it's slow going." He coughed again, licked the blood off his lips without seeming to notice. "You'll be useful. They have sensors that sense Fae blood. They're expensive and hard to make, so they don't have many, but I've found a few. Found a few possible testing sites."

"You want to use me?" Aria felt her voice squeak with fear. Then outrage. "You want to use me to go where you can't? You'll get me killed!

You wanted to use me all along!" She rose to her feet and stared down at him.

His voice was hard. "I told you to leave me alone. You didn't. So I gave you a choice. I did you no wrong." The effort was too much, and he was convulsed by coughing again. He struggled to his hands and knees and retched onto the floor, spitting bright red blood.

Unable to maintain her anger in the face of her guilt, she knelt beside him. "What do you need?"

"Time." He caught his breath and sat back on his heels. His chest heaved. If anything, he looked worse than before. He glanced out the window. "We're safe here for a while."

Aria stood and looked out the window as well. The view matched her mood. Overcast and chilly, with a hint of bitterness.

"What about the vertril?" she asked suddenly.

"What about them?"

"You said they can kill you. Humans, I guess. Can a vertril kill you?"

"No. A vertril will incapacitate a Fae, but not kill. I'd lay there until they came to fetch me for their experiments." He shifted to sit slumped back against the wall, one leg crooked up and the other stretched out.

She wanted to ask him more, but she hadn't realized how bad he looked in the darkness and dim lamplight. Now, the clear cold light streamed in through the windows and washed over him, and she bit her lip. White as marble, streaked with blood from head to toe, blood in the corners of his mouth, bandages soaked with it. A bruised knot stood out dark at the edge of his right eyebrow. "Should I leave you alone?"

He sighed. "Please."

She stood at the window, watching the city. It had a good view, such as it was. Near the river, with only shorter buildings between her and the shore, so she could see the wide expanse of cold grey water. The bridge was to the north, and she could see only the far end of it, blocked by the peeling metal window frame. Below, the streets were busy but not frantic, the efficient speed of the shipping district. There were few horns from the electric vehicles below, not too much noise actually. Not like the commercial district, closer to her apartment, which hummed and clattered and honked and roared.

Probably no one had even reported her missing yet. She didn't have class today. Amara might have called, but if she didn't, she wouldn't notice anything amiss until Aria didn't show up to class tomorrow. *You know, that's a sad commentary on my social life. Or my life in general. No one to notice that I've been missing for how long now?*

But the authorities knew already. They thought her dead. She wondered when Amara would find that out. Or her professors. Would Dr. Corten question it at all?

How would it be reported, anyway? Aria Forsyth, missing. Aria Forsyth, killed by a vagrant. Killed by a fairy? She glanced at him again. He didn't look like something the word *fairy* might describe. Fairies were small, glowing sprites, with wings, who loved nature and water and such. *Fae* sounded a little more fierce. That word suited him. She rummaged in her mind for the old stories. He'd mentioned fairies, vampires, and elves, as if the legends overlapped. She'd thought they were

69

quite distinct.

He didn't drink blood, but he was definitely carnivorous. She applied the word carefully, trying not to think about the pig's heart. It was still bloody, and she suspected it had been delivered that way upon request. *A little extra blood, please. Like frosting on a donut.*

Vampires. What did vampires fear? The cross. Garlic. A stake through the heart. Elves. She didn't know much about elves. Tolkien's elves were beautiful, cultured, and strong, but she wasn't sure that was the kind he meant. That concept was so recent, and the older lore tended more toward impish little devils, troublemakers, and pranksters. That didn't seem to fit him either. Fairies. She couldn't remember what they feared. Iron? She thought vaguely of the Seelie Court and Unseelie Court of the Fairies, but couldn't remember what they were. She did remember that fairies were said to be amoral, rather than immoral, outside the laws of human interaction. Something about a blood tithe to the underworld? Not that she believed in the underworld. But she hadn't believed in fairies either.

She took off her still damp boots and socks and laid them to dry on the floor. Then her coat. She glanced at Owen. He hadn't moved, his eyes closed. He might have been dead but for the faint movement of his chest as he breathed. She turned away and pulled off her sweater. She tugged at the bandage around her arm and finally pulled it off with a preemptive wince. The wound was small and clean, a narrow slit scarcely the length of her thumbnail, and it had already started to heal. A thin film of skin showed dark red over the cut, with smudges of dried blood around it. She pulled her sweater back over her head, unfolded the bandage and spread it out.

She wanted to be angry with him, but maintaining it was hard. He'd jerked her away from a bullet that would have killed her. Sure, it was meant for him, but he could have saved himself more easily if she wasn't there. He could have run across the bridge long before they'd arrived. He *could* have used her as a shield, if it came to that.

True too, the fact that she'd been the one to bother him. The one to find his apartment and try to break in. Twice. The one to see him on the bridge and hold him with her questions, even as they tracked her to him. She hadn't known, but he had.

He had reason to be angry with her, not the other way around.

A slight sound caught her attention.

Eyes closed, he sang. Barely audible, under his breath, he sang. The tune rose and fell, wove into a tapestry, repeating itself in layers that seemed to stay in her mind after the sound had faded. The words weren't English. She wasn't sure all the words were composed of sound at all. But in her mind, she pictured a forest, a green and vibrant forest, filled with mist and the sound of things growing. A rushing stream, water cool and clean and fresh as morning. And Owen, stepping one bare foot into the stream, kneeling, not minding the water soaking the ragged hem of his pants, bending to drink from one hand, graceful as a deer.

She blinked and stared at him across the room.

Craggy mountains of stark stone rose behind

hills so green they hurt her eyes. A forest, the trees old and rich with history deep enough to merit their own history books. Textured bark and wood. Lichen, cool blue-green. Yellow-green moss cloaking rounded boulders. Water flowing over smooth pebbles. This time he stood, one hand resting on a tree trunk, head bowed slightly and eyes closed. He opened his eyes and looked straight at her. Blue eyes clear and cold as a winter sky.

She shook her head and blinked, stared at him again. He lay as before, motionless but for the slight rise and fall of his chest.

Did his song give her the vision? She tried to tell herself that was impossible, but nothing in the past two days had been normal.

Aria spent hours staring out the window. Thinking. She ate another sandwich. She looked at Owen occasionally, but he never moved. It got dark, and she lay on the floor. It was cold and uncomfortable, but at some point she fell asleep.

SHE BLINKED at the ceiling. It was light again, and by the angle of the cool shadows, the sun had been up for some time. She stretched and sat up, expecting to feel terribly sore, and was surprised to feel refreshed instead. She closed her eyes and stretched her shoulders again. *Best night's sleep I've had in a long time, actually. Strange.* She'd had odd dreams. She couldn't remember them clearly, only the impressions they'd left. Green forests. Running water. A feeling rather than a memory.

A movement caught her eye and she glanced over to see Owen shift. He rose without looking at her and stood at the window. His motion was stiff, painful, but he didn't cough. His bare feet made no sound on the thin industrial carpet as he moved to look out the other window.

"Good morning," she ventured.

"Hm." The answer was noncommittal.

She sat up and hugged her knees. "Do you know the test subjects?"

"Yes."

She swallowed. "What are they doing with them? I mean..." she wondered if there was a way to say it diplomatically. "What exactly are they trying to find out?"

There was a long pause, and he didn't look at her. "We don't know yet," he said finally.

This too, she had wondered about. "We? Are there many of you Fae?"

Now he looked at her over his shoulder, a long, thoughtful look. Finally, he said, "Not as many as there were."

She took a deep breath. "You sing beautifully."

She might not have noticed the smile, if she hadn't been looking for it. A slight twitch of one corner of his mouth, as if he were amused rather than complimented.

"Do you need another pigs heart? Because I'm getting low on food and you didn't have dinner last night." She tried for a light tone, and felt it fall flat between them.

"Not yet. Soon." He turned to look out the window again for a moment before unwrapping the bandage from his left hand. He flexed the fingers, made a fist and then spread the fingers wide with a wince. He cradled it in his other hand and sat on the floor, eyes closed.

And he sang. *Leaves rustling in a summer breeze,*

*light streaming through like beams of gold.* She was lost in it.

She blinked and stared at him again. He looked down at his hand and flexed it again, turned it over and rubbed it fiercely with his right hand.

"May I see?"

He held up his hand toward her. It was whole, strong and pale and perfect as his other hand.

Aria knelt in front of him. "May I?" She nearly didn't wait for his nod before reaching out and holding his hand in both of hers. It was unscarred, the skin smooth and white over the fine strong bones. Cool to the touch. "Does it hurt?" she whispered.

"It's a little sore still. But it works."

"How did you...?" She didn't know what to call it. Heal? The word was too innocuous for what she'd seen. "The bone was broken, wasn't it?"

"Several were. The singing helps." He did not elaborate.

She suddenly realized she was still holding his hand, peering at it inches from her nose like he was a lover. Or a science experiment. She dropped it and scooted away from him on the floor. "I'm sorry." She frowned. "What about your other injuries? Can you heal them too?"

"Yes. But I'm tired. It takes effort. And time." He took a deep breath, and she realized he was fighting exhaustion already.

"Is there something I should do to help?"

He studied her face, cool blue eyes not giving her any hint of what he was thinking. Finally, he said, "Why were you at Dandra's?"

She blinked. "Researching. For my thesis. I'm studying history."

74

His eyes remained on her, evaluating. She shifted uncomfortably, and the silence drew out.

Finally, she asked tentatively, "Are you really that old?"

"Why would I lie about that?"

"You probably remember everything I'm trying to research then." She smiled.

He glanced away, and said softly, "I remember a lot of things."

Aria swallowed. "My thesis is on, well, it was going to be on how things have changed since the Revolution. I was trying to narrow down my topic, because it seems like so many things have changed. And I found this book, someone's memoir. No one important. He talked about the forest, and the wind in his hair when he rode his bicycle as a child. I remembered riding my bicycle down the sidewalk in the sun, and the trees." Her voice trailed away as she watched Owen for a moment. He was staring off into the distance somewhere past her shoulder. "Are you okay?"

He nodded.

She continued tentatively, "Well, I spent probably two hours reading that book at the back table, and I meant to go back to it. I went back the day I saw you asking about maps, and it wasn't there. I asked Dandra about it, and she said she didn't know what book I meant. But I know she did. It made me suspicious, I suppose. Like someone didn't want me to read about the past. But I'm a history student! That's what I'm *supposed* to be studying. None of my professors even seem interested in history at all." The more she thought about their lectures, the more irritated she became.

"I wouldn't expect so." His eyes focused on her

with sudden intensity. "It challenges them."

She licked her lips. "What do you mean?"

"They live in a world of propaganda. Easy untruths that hide the tragedy of what they have lost. Of what they have done. Of what they are even yet doing. No one wants to face their own sins." His voice didn't rise, but he leaned forward just a hair, and she caught her breath. "You are a threat, if you wish to know the truth of history. It's one of many reasons they hate us. Because we remember."

He leaned back, and she took an unsteady breath. He could, indeed, be intimidating when he chose.

He rose to go look out the window again, flexing his left hand. "We're safe here until at least tonight."

Aria watched him for a long moment before eyeing the food thoughtfully. "Do you think this is still safe to eat? It hasn't been refrigerated, but it's pretty cold in here." She poked at the meat, and then finally made another sandwich. It wasn't appealing, but she ate it anyway.

He remained by the window, eyes on the grey scene that spread out before him.

"Why do you like the bridge?" she asked. "I can't remember much about fairies or elves or vampires. But I thought fairies were afraid of iron."

He turned his cool gaze on her. "It's old. Everything is new here. This city is made of plastic and concrete and steel, most manufactured in the last hundred years. It has no soul. The bridge looks new but the pilings and girders are original, from 1929. I'd prefer rocks and trees, but there aren't many of those around here."

"You can feel the age?"

He hesitated, as if searching for words. Finally he said, "It's like plugging in your car, but not exactly. I don't run out of battery without it, but it gives me strength."

"Why didn't you sing and heal yourself earlier?" she frowned. "I mean, from what the vertril did, before they shot you? And why did you say I wouldn't have seen a vertril?"

He took a deep breath, already tired, and she regretted her words.

*No. If I'm stuck in this with him, I need to understand. I need to know what we're doing, and why. And what might kill me while I'm doing it.*

"Vertril are drawn to Fae blood. They were engineered to hunt us, and they have no interest in humans. Most humans never know they exist. They're tracked too. If one is injured or killed, or even excited, the IPF won't be far behind. But in the tunnel, it could crush you without noticing as it leapt at me."

"Why didn't you sing?" She tried vainly to think of a word to describe it.

"They were close by. Sometimes when they're searching, they have sensors that can locate..." again he seemed to consider the words. "You'd call it magic, but the term isn't entirely accurate. Magic is something outside the laws of nature. The Fae word is *megdhonia*, which translates to something like 'use of the in-between.' The in-between being," he stopped and closed his eyes, took a few deep breaths to steady himself. "The in-between being the spaces between this possibility and that possibility. The laws of nature permit many possible outcomes, of which one comes to pass." Another deep breath. "We can push our own energy into those spaces to direct the outcome."

She blinked. "Do you know the future, then?"

"No."

"How do you heal? What possibility is that? It seems impossible."

"Only when you look at the whole. Each small part is possible. That this bone will be strength-ened and set back into place is one possibility among many." He stopped to catch his breath, and she waited.

"I'm sorry I ask so many questions. I just want to understand."

He slid down the wall to sit leaning against it again. He leaned his head back, eyes closed. "If I'm to ask you to help us, it's only fair that you know what we are. When I sing, it helps focus my energy into those spaces. And I ask for strength from El." His chest heaved like he'd been running.

"Are you never cold?"

He huffed softly. "Cold is nature. Nature is nothing to be afraid of and bundle up against. Not for us." Another pause, and he flexed his fingers again.

She stood and looked out the window as well. Today there were more boats in the river, a barge easing slowly beneath the bridge flanked by two tugboats, as well as smaller vessels speeding around them.

"Do you remember the beach? Do you remem-ber forests? I didn't before, but now I think I went hiking once, with my father. I didn't remember until you sang, but now I'm sure I've been in a for-est before."

"Yes."

His answer was so soft that she knelt beside him.

"You remember? What was it like? When was it?"

He held her eyes with his own, and this time she had no trouble reading the aching sorrow. "It was very beautiful. And it has been a long time."

"Is that why the book disappeared? It had dates. I don't remember, sometime in the early 2050s I think. Not long before I was born."

He sang, eyes on hers, voice as soft and clear as a summer breeze. The sound wrapped around her, layer upon layer, clean and thin and sweet as clover. It wove, up and over and underneath. *Running laughing through the warm humid air, sunbeams breaking through the leaves. Flowers in his hair. Drinking from the stream, water cool and fresh, running between his fingers soft as silk.*

"Yes. I remember."

THEY STAYED ALL DAY. Aria wrinkled her nose at the meat and decided it was inedible, but she ate the last of the bread and apples and cheese for lunch. She found a restroom down the hall with working water faucets.

"What books do you have? If we're going to be here all day, I need something to occupy myself."

He nodded permission for her to look without rising.

She unzipped his bag and set them on the table, aware of his eyes on her. The first had been blank, now nearly filled with page after page of neat, small writing. She wanted to read it, but wasn't bold enough to flip through while he watched her so intently. She wasn't even sure it was all in English.

The next was older, the well-worn leather cover dry and crumbling slightly at the binding. The paper inside was nearly translucent, though stronger than it looked, and it had been carefully wrapped with a long strip of leather to keep it from coming open. She frowned at the cover. There was a symbol and a line of text in some language she couldn't read.

"What is this?"

"A Fae epic translated into Old Irish."

"Old Irish?" she frowned. "What is that?"

"I learned it when I was young, from my grandfather." He smiled slightly at her confused look. "He thought everyone should learn to speak the human languages. That was the one he thought most relevant at the time."

She set the book aside to look at later. She held two others up for him to identify.

"A book my grandfather wrote about his childhood. And a history book."

She glanced at him. "And these?"

"Histories."

*Histories of what?* She studied the covers. Old, though not as old as the epic. The languages appeared to be different, though she couldn't read any of them. She didn't even recognize the alphabets. She took them to the window for better light. "What languages are these?"

"Fae dialects."

She glanced at him again. "Do you mind me looking at them?"

He sighed, his eyes closed again. "No."

She opened one book and paged through with

careful fingers. The books were well cared for but obviously old and she bent closer. "Was this handwritten?"

"Yes."

The script shifted between writing so ornate it nearly formed pictures, characters and lines flowing like water through and around each other, and something slightly more akin to English cursive, though the letters were unfamiliar. One page caught her interest, and she followed the curves. "This is beautiful." Her voice was only a whisper. "I meant to find something to read, but this is art. Can you read this?"

"Yes." His voice was tired, but tinged with amusement this time.

"How many languages do you speak, then?"

A pause. "Eleven? It depends on whether you count several of the dialects as separate languages or not." He shifted against the wall, eyes still closed.

Aria studied his face. The bruise near his eyebrow had faded slightly, though it was still visible. He'd washed the blood from his face and hands that morning and changed into a new, clean shirt. The pants he'd washed in the sink; he'd reappeared in the doorway after a trip to the restroom and dripped his way back to the spot beneath the window. Now they were damp, as was the carpet beneath him. If he'd been human, he'd have been shivering in the unheated warehouse; Aria was, despite her thick sweater and coat.

He sang again that afternoon.

The sound rose around her like saplings, green and fresh, shot through with golden sunlight. She saw him kneeling again in the stream, cupping the clear water to his face, running wet fingers through his curling black hair. He looked up at someone on the other side of the stream, though she couldn't see who, and smiled suddenly, a flash of white teeth and a bright, clear smile like that of a boy given an unexpected compliment.

She found herself staring out the window at the grey twilight, her forehead pressed to the glass. *And who wouldn't want that, instead of this? This city is all cold, unfriendly people in cold, unfriendly rain and dreariness. Even when it's not winter.*

Owen rose and stood next to her for a moment. "We should go soon."

"Where? Do you have a plan?"

"There's a human population that will take you in. They have no trackers. It's a hard life, but they find the freedom worth it. I will take you there tonight. They have connections. They can get you outside the city, if you wish."

"I thought you wanted to rescue the test subjects."

"I will. But I won't ask you to join me. It's dangerous, and it's not your fight. I was wrong to try to use you." He inclined his head slightly, and she suddenly realized it was a sort of bow.

"I have nowhere to go." She took a deep breath. "I have no family. I may as well help you."

She flinched at his sudden hard look.

"This is not a may-as-well. This is my family. This is my people. I may die trying, but it is worth it. If it's not worth death to you, I don't want you." His eyes blazed.

She swallowed hard. "I will help you."

THEY MOVED to another hiding place in the middle of the night. Owen, a little steadier on his feet, led her to a tiny brick building that echoed with the faint sound of traffic from the street. A drizzling rain began to fall just as they stepped inside.

"Where are we?"

"The Summerhouse. It's one of the oldest buildings left standing." Owen stopped to catch his breath, leaning against the icy brick for a moment. He led her to a fountain and bent to drink from it, cupping the water in one hand. Then he slid down to rest against one wall, legs bent before him.

"There's no roof." Aria stared at him. "It's raining. And freezing cold."

He blinked at her slowly. "Is that a problem?"

"For me it is." She shivered in her coat, wishing she'd thought to bring a change of clothes on this unplanned adventure. Every inch of her felt grimy.

He pushed himself to his feet and led her through a little archway into a tiny enclosed room. He pulled the blanket from his bag and handed it to her. "Use this."

Aria nodded uncertainly, and he sat down in the doorway, head leaned back against the brick. She finally curled up on the brick floor, wrapped tightly in the blanket. She slipped slowly into a comfortable doze, warmer than she'd expected to be.

Hours later, she drifted into wakefulness, surprised at how cozy she felt. Her arm, crunched beneath her on the hard floor, wasn't cramped or cold. She watched Owen through half-closed eyes for long minutes. He sat in exactly the same position, head dropped back against the brick, hands resting loosely in his lap. The late-morning sun barely broke through the misty haze to light the empty room behind him.

*Why do I trust him?*

The question flickered into her mind, and she couldn't answer it, but she knew she did.

They stayed in their new hiding place all day. Aria paced restlessly a few times, trying to keep warm. Owen went out once, leaving her to hide, and returned with a hot coffee, water, and a sandwich from a street vendor for her. He didn't eat himself, and spent the rest of the time resting, motionless against the brick.

"What are we waiting for?"

"Nightfall."

# CHAPTER 4

ARIA CROUCHED in the darkness beside Owen. "Now what?"

Owen's eyes flicked past the gate into the darkness beyond, and then back to the guardhouse. "Talk to the guard. Try to distract him for as long as you can."

Aria gaped. "What? I'm not good at that kind of thing! I'll be arrested!"

"Possibly. More likely they'll throw you out." His eyes flicked over the gate again.

"What about my tracker? Will they know it's gone?"

"Unlikely. Most of the guards don't know about them either, so the sensors aren't part of standard equipment."

"What are you going to do?"

"Best you not know, in case you're arrested." He turned to her, blue eyes oddly bright in the dim light. "Last chance to back out. I'll hold no grudge."

She took a deep breath. "It's wrong, what they're doing." She nodded firmly, as much to convince herself of her courage as to answer Owen. If he could do his part while still in pain, she could do this simple thing.

"Approach from the street there." He pointed off to the left. "I'll meet you at the coffee shop across from Bryson's afterward." He paused, then added, "It might be a while."

She nodded again, and they slipped back through the shadows. He left her at the edge of the road and disappeared into the darkness.

She took a deep breath. *What makes you think you can act, girl?*

Her shoes crunched on broken glass as she approached the guards. "Hello!" It wouldn't do to surprise them.

"Hold." One of the three guards held up a hand. "Identification, please."

"I don't have it. I'm sorry." She spread her hands regretfully. "Well, you see, I haven't been home all day, and I didn't plan on coming here. But I'm working on a project for school and hoped you could help me." She smiled up at the stern guard with her most innocent expression. She could do that one well; she'd practiced it on her teachers when she was younger.

"What do you want?" He was cautious, alert.

She hesitated and looked him over. His nameplate read Ballard, but she wasn't sure how to read the insignia on his uniform for a correct title. "I'm compiling information on the education and background of security and police forces. Do you have a moment? It won't take long."

Ballard frowned at her. "Government analysts are well aware of our background and credentials."

"Yes, sir, but this is for a school project." She smiled again, thankful for once that she looked younger than she was. "We're looking at commonalities in background in people who are motivated to serve in particularly patriotic ways. It's inspiring, really. It would be very helpful if I could hear your story and how you came to work here." Her heart was pounding, but she kept her voice light and cheerful.

"Hm." The guard stared at her for another long moment. "Come into the guardhouse."

The other two guards shifted position in front of the gate as she stepped into the tiny room. Ballard stepped behind a desk, eyes on her. "What's your name?"

"Aislin." The lie surprised her, as did the name itself. *Where did that come from?*

He frowned and studied her again. "What do you want to know?"

"Where did you go to school? What did you study?"

"You're not ready to take notes."

She blushed. "I have a very good memory."

"North Central Community College. Majored in legal studies and criminal justice."

She smiled. "A double major! That's a lot of work. Is this what you planned to do when you graduated?"

His eyes flicked over her shoulder to watch the

other guards pace slowly outside. "Not exactly. I hoped to be at Quadrant Headquarters and eventually work up to the President's staff. But it's a good starting point." His voice had warmed a little in response to her friendliness.

*He's too terse. I need to get him talking.* Aria tried for a question that might have a longer answer. "Were there any specific experiences that inspired this career path?"

He hesitated and glanced out the window again. The other two guards appeared unconcerned, strolling around in the clear area in front of the guardhouse. "Not exactly. But my uncle—"

The phone rang and Aria jumped.

Ballard picked up the phone. "Front gate."

Silence. His eyes ran up and down her, cool and professional. She glanced at the walls of the guardhouse, trying to look unconcerned.

"Understood, sir." He hung up the phone. "Remove your coat and shoes and anything in your pockets. Step through this."

"Why?" She hung back.

"Colonel Grenidor wishes to speak with you." His expression was closed, not giving her any clues about what would happen next.

She frowned, trying to look innocently confused. "I don't need to bother a colonel. I'm interviewing security personnel, not military officers."

"It's not a request."

She hesitated, but finally took her coat off. Maybe it would buy Owen more time. Barefoot and coatless, she felt vulnerable. The contents of her pockets looked forlorn on the smooth desk surface. A gum wrapper. A key ring with three keys on it. A few slips of paper with notes to herself about groceries to buy and research she was no longer doing. She stepped through what she assumed was a metal detector. He frowned at a screen behind the desk.

"Remove your socks and belt."

She swallowed, trying not to look nervous, and stepped through again.

He frowned at her, but she thought hopefully that his expression looked more thoughtful than suspicious.

"Do you have a shirt on under your sweater? If so, remove your sweater."

"I don't."

"I'll have to frisk you."

"Okay."

He ran his hands along her body in quick pats, up and down both legs, inside and outside. She would have blushed, but it was over so quickly she didn't have time to be embarrassed. *Very professional.*

He nodded for her to walk through the screen again.

"Hm." He glanced at her again and she could almost see the mental shrug.

He made another call. "I need an escort at the front gate. Thanks."

Then, "Wear this at all times." He handed her a badge that she clipped to her jacket. She put her shoes back on, toes icy from the cold concrete floor.

They waited in silence. After several minutes, the rear door opened and a young officer near her own age met her. "Come with me." He didn't return her smile.

They crossed a large empty space paved in concrete, a line of spotlights against the high wall marching away to each side. Lights flooded the front and corners of the building, a massive six-story structure with a grand entrance. Her escort led her to a side door.

Bland white hallways led deeper into the building. Her escort paused several times to glance at the signs posted at each corner.

"This building is huge. Do you ever get lost?" Aria asked.

"Not anymore. The room notations are pretty logical for the most part. Floor, corridor, hallway, room number. Corridors are more or less north-south, hallways east-west. But there are a few out-liers." He led her down a staircase. "Here."

The door was one of several in a row with or-nate wooden frames and embossed nameplates. She knocked, her heart in her throat.

"Come in."

She turned the knob and entered. The escort waited for the colonel's nod before he took off down the hall.

Aria closed the door behind herself, buying time for another deep breath. Then she turned and smiled.

The man was middle-aged, the beginning of a pot belly just showing beneath his crisp uniform. He stood to greet her with a firm handshake and nodded to a chair. He glanced at a stack of folders and adjusted them slightly to align with the edge of the desk.

Aria sat, her knees together and her hands tucked between them. She forced herself to sit back and try to look relaxed.

He smiled at her coolly. "So. Aislin. An inter-esting name."

"Thank you, sir."

He continued looking at her, unhurried and thoughtful. "How did you come by it?" he said finally.

"My mother thought it was pretty." She smiled innocently.

"You were asking the guard questions. Why?"

"I'm doing research for my thesis."

"Your thesis?"

"Yes, sir. I'm doing research on the Revolution. What makes people want to serve in patriotic ways? I'm interviewing security personnel, but it would be very helpful if I could get your perspective too, sir."

His skepticism was clear, his dark eyes amused. "An interesting story. I'll humor you for now. Have you any particular questions?"

Aria was sure her panic showed on her face. She stammered, "Well, not exactly. I'm just beginning my research so I haven't gotten that far yet."

"Do you always interview people without pen and paper?"

"No, sir. I'm sorry I'm not more prepared, sir. I do have a good memory though, and I'd be happy to show you the final draft to ensure I don't get any of the details wrong." She tried for a confident tone despite her nerves.

He licked his lips and gazed at her thoughtfully. "I graduated from the Army Academy in 2065 with degrees in biology and psychology. My first assignment was in the technical arm of the 91st. Subsequent assignments focused on research in nonstandard biology and alternate models of sentience." He watched her face as she frowned.

"Nonstandard biology?" Her confusion wasn't

feigned. "Like mutations?"

"Something like that." Again, a neutral gaze on her face.

"And alternate models of sentience? What does that mean?" She tried to look innocently interested. "Robotics?"

He smiled slightly. "More like cultural studies with layers of psychological and sociological terminology on top."

"Hm." She frowned. He wasn't giving her much to work with. "What was your most interesting project?"

He glanced down at something in his lap, fiddled with it, and then looked up again with a slight, amused smile. "When I was at the 70th, we did a study on the Cherustin people in the Himalayas. They believe that the spirits of their ancestors can be heard in the wind. Not too surprising, I suppose, since the winds howl through the mountains there. The spirits are believed to be trapped in nets left out for the purpose, and carried with them to each new campsite to be set free to guard the living. Interesting, but not entirely bizarre. What was more intriguing was how the ancestor spirits were enticed to provide their protection—"

The phone rang on his desk. He picked it up after one ring, his eyes remaining on her. "Yes?" His mouth tightened as he listened for a short moment. "Yes. Thank you." He set the phone down and smiled at her coolly for a long moment before continuing. "Oh yes. The ancestor spirits. Their cooperation was bought with a sacrifice of blood. A chicken, a goat, it didn't really matter, but they wanted fresh blood every night."

She nodded, her eyes wide. "Really?"

"At first we dismissed it as superstition, but one clan, about twenty adults and some children, had grown tired of the cost. They asked us for our opinion. We encouraged them to refuse the tribute, in hopes that they would move toward modernity. The next morning, we found every member dead."

She swallowed. "How did they die?"

"Their throats were mangled, the bodies nearly drained of blood." He was watching her closely now. "Several had their hearts ripped out; they were missing. We presumed the hearts were eaten."

She swallowed hard again. "Did you find out who did it?"

His eyes rested on her face, dark eyes unreadable. "We had ideas. No proof."

A knock sounded on the door and she jumped. "Come in."

Four soldiers stood in the hallway, tall and imposing. "Sir."

He smiled at her across the desk, eyes cool and inscrutable. "Thank you for a most interesting diversion tonight, Aislin. These men will escort you to your cell. You are under arrest."

She shot to her feet. "For what crime? I've done nothing!"

"Attempted infiltration of a secure facility, and for aiding and abetting a criminal in the same."

One soldier jerked her arms behind her back and secured her wrists with plastic handcuffs. She felt herself breathing too quickly, on the verge of panic, and forced herself to slow down. *Think.*

"I don't understand! I don't know what you're talking about."

She tried to meet his eyes but the soldiers forced her into the hallway. The soldiers walked her down the long corridor and around a corner, down a long flight of stairs and through several more hallways before reaching a sturdy metal door. Inside was an empty room. They left her there and the door clanged shut behind them.

She stared about the room. The floor was hard linoleum tile laid over concrete. The walls were concrete, painted a grim industrial grey with a stripe of patriotic gold around the top. The ceiling was also concrete, twelve feet above her. A fluorescent light fixture flickered in the middle of the room, far out of reach, but otherwise it was an empty box.

She turned in a circle, trying to push down the fear that made her breath come too fast. What were they going to do? How long would she be trapped there?

Through the door she could hear the indistinct sounds of footsteps at long intervals. She kicked the door a few times, but nothing happened.

No one came to check on her, no one shouted through the door. Her shoulders burned and her hands cramped at being bound behind her for so long.

Aria eventually sat in a corner, her legs propped before her and her bound hands in the space behind her. She would have thought it impossible, but she dozed. Hours passed interminably, and the only way she could judge time was by how thirsty she was and how much her arms ached. They passed from ache to raging fiery pain, back to a dull ache, a worrying numbness, and returned to fiery pain that settled in as if for a long stay.

The door opened and her head jerked upward. Colonel Grenidor and four different soldiers stood in the hallway. Grenidor entered and waved the soldiers to stay in the hallway. He left the door open, as if he did not fear any escape attempt. Aria struggled to her feet, leaning against the wall for support. *Of course he doesn't fear an escape attempt. I can barely stand up.*

He stepped closer and looked down at her from arm's length, studying her face. She tried to look up at him without looking afraid.

"Why would you help him?"

She blinked. "What?"

"Why?" He stepped away from her to pace thoughtfully. "If you know what he is, why would you help him? I assume you know. Perhaps that is an erroneous assumption." He glanced at her, as if giving her an opportunity to interject.

She remained silent, and he continued, "I speak of the intruder last night, of course. The one who used you as a distraction while he attempted to infiltrate the secure area. You know him. What is he to you?" His voice remained cool, curious.

She sighed. "I don't know what you mean."

He spun on his heel and stalked toward her, eyes hard on her face. "Do you not? I grow tired of your lies, Aislin, or whatever your name is. I have no interest in you. I am prepared to let you go without bringing charges against you. Except..." he let his voice soften as he walked away, then whirled back to bark, "Who is he?"

She swallowed and glanced around the room again. "I don't know." That was more or less true. He'd told her very little.

"But you know *what* he is." His eyes remained on her face. "You know he isn't human."

She swallowed again. "Um."

His eyes bored into her and she looked down. "Yes, you do. You know at least some of what he is. Do you know how many people he's killed? Of course not. Foolish girl. You think because he has a pretty face he can be trusted. You think because he hasn't harmed you yet, that he won't." He stepped back to look her over, his eyes running down her body. "You won't be useful forever. Tell me his name. Tell me what he's trying to do. And I'll let you go."

She pulled herself up and shifted her shoulders, wincing at the pain that shot down her arms. She didn't have anything to say, but clenched her jaw and stared back at him. *Why am I being defiant? I don't owe Owen anything except perhaps pity.*

He smiled at her, a small sad smile. "Still loyal, aren't you? For no reason you can define. He's good at that, I hear. Inspiring loyalty." He turned on his heel and walked out, and the door closed behind him with a click.

The lights stayed on. The hours passed. Her shoulders burned. Her eyes felt gritty and she dozed again, slumped in the corner with her head resting against the cold concrete wall. Her tongue grew thick and swollen from thirst. She wanted to cry, but was stubbornly unwilling to let him find her with tears on her face.

The line of light under the doorway flicked out, though the lights in her room did not. *Nighttime? Again?* Later it came back.

The door opened at long last. Grenidor stood in the hallway flanked by soldiers. He entered and she pushed herself up, more weakly this time. The effort taxed her, and she leaned against the wall, trying to catch her breath and stifle the whimpers that rose unbidden at the pain in her shoulders. Grenidor stopped at arms length and raised his right hand toward her. He held some sort of device, and he glanced from its small screen to her and back to the screen.

"Interesting," he said at last.

"What?" It irritated her that her voice sounded so pathetic.

"How did you find it?" He pinned her with his eyes.

"Find what?"

He stalked closer, and she shrank back against the wall. "He told you, didn't he? He removed it. This is problematic. It means I can't release you, regardless of what you tell me." He sighed, as if it bothered him.

"Why not? What are you talking about?"

He stared at the screen for a long moment. "What is your name?"

"Aislin."

"Your real name." His eyes flicked to her face.

"Aislin."

He sighed, staring at her as if perplexed and saddened. "You'll need water soon. It's been almost two days. I hate to do it. You're human, and that makes things different. But I need to know who he is and who he's working with, and I can't let you go back to him." Then to the soldiers, "Transfer her to a solitary cell in Block 3. Give her no water until she tells me her name, his name, and those of any associates."

"Yes, sir."

The soldiers entered the room and pulled her forward. She stumbled along between them without resisting. *What harm would it do to tell him?*

The cell was much like the first room, the same color and shape, the same cold concrete. One of the soldiers stood in front of her for a long moment before they left. "Ma'am, are you ready to talk?" His voice was quiet and calm, devoid of feeling.

"No."

He nodded and stepped out into the hallway, closing the heavy metal door behind himself. This room had a single metal bench bolted to the floor. She sat on it, staring at the floor near her feet. *Truly, what harm would it do? I know so little, what harm can it do to tell him?*

But they didn't come back for hours. She slumped to the side on the bench and finally lay down, face pressed into the metal to take the pressure off her screaming shoulders. It didn't work, and the position grew more uncomfortable until she struggled up again and slid to the floor in the corner.

She woke to the door opening.

Grenidor stood there again. He looked more rumpled this time, the uniform slightly less crisp. He pulled her to her feet, hands on her upper arms. His grip wasn't cruel, but the touch woke her muscles to agony that brought tears to her eyes.

He stepped back. "Tell me. What's your name? What's his name? And who are you working with? I want names."

She sniffled. "I want water first. And my hands free."

Grenidor nodded to a soldier behind him. The

soldier stepped forward and used wire cutters on the plastic handcuffs. The soldier looked at her for a long moment as she hunched forward, trying to hide the tears of pain. Everything in her arms burned as the blood flowed sluggishly through aching muscles and joints. She bent her elbows and hugged herself, wiped angrily at the tears that welled up.

"You're horrible." She finally looked up at Grenidor. "You're a horrible person."

The soldier handed her an open bottle of water, and she closed her eyes as she drank. The water tasted of plastic, but she didn't care as it slid down her dry throat. She drank and drank, opening her eyes to shoot a reproachful glare at Grenidor. She emptied the bottle, the water cool and heavy in her empty stomach. She felt suddenly dizzy and almost stumbled. The soldier caught her arm, and she pulled away with an angry jerk.

"Names. Now."

She sniffled again. "I'm Aria."

"Aria what?"

"Aria Forsyth," she muttered.

"And him?"

She swallowed. "Owen."

"Owen what?"

"I don't know."

He reached out to grasp her chin and pull her face up to stare into her eyes. "What is his name?" His voice was low and angry.

"I don't know!" She jerked away. "I don't. He never said."

"Who do you work with?"

"Nobody. We haven't seen anyone. He hasn't mentioned any names at all."

"*Where* is he?"

"I don't know!"

He frowned at her, gauging her honesty. She stood warily, shoulder blades against the wall. She wrapped her arms around herself again, muscles screaming with pain. She flexed her fingers, wincing, and he scowled suddenly.

"You are useless," he muttered. He turned on his heel and ushered the soldiers out. One of them turned a quick, unreadable glance toward her before they closed the door and locked it again.

This time she couldn't keep her composure. She pounded on the door and screamed.

Her screaming didn't last long, and she faded into sniffling sobs, slumped weakly against the metal door and finally to her knees on the cold floor. She bowed forward, resting her head on the floor. Her back and shoulders throbbed, she was still thirsty, and now her stomach felt both queasy with exhaustion and aching with hunger. She fell asleep curled on the floor near the door, arms around her head.

She woke with a start and scrambled back from the door. It clicked as it was unlocked and eased open, more slowly than before.

One soldier stood in the doorway. "Come with me."

She swallowed. "Now what?" She tried to keep her voice confident, but it cracked.

He glanced at her face with a faint frown. "Can you walk?" He held out one white-gloved hand for her.

She hesitated, but grasped it, and he pulled her to her feet and steadied her when she swayed.

"Come," he repeated. He kept one hand on her

upper arm, firm but not harsh, and guided her out into the corridor, where he locked the door before leading her down the hall. He stopped at an intersection and looked around, then pushed her forward again.

"Where are we going?"

"Quiet."

Even that answer gave her hope. If he wanted to be quiet, perhaps he wasn't doing what he'd been instructed to do. She barely dared hope.

Down a stairway until they were perhaps one floor under ground level and through another long hall. Aria felt that the last week had been nothing but long concrete halls with metal doors. They walked to the end, then up another stairwell. This one went up five floors. She had to stop and catch her breath in the middle, dizzy with thirst and hunger, and the soldier waited with badly concealed impatience. At the top, she found herself facing another metal door.

The soldier opened it and guided her out. It was a clear twilight, the stars just beginning to show in the cold sky. Her coat had been left in Colonel Grenidor's office days before, and Aria shivered, the wind cutting through her sweater and stealing away her pathetic warmth.

They were on a concrete walkway on the fourth floor some eighty feet from the perimeter wall. The soldier gave no signal that Aria noticed, but a thin cable sailed over the railing near them and tightened with a jerk. The soldier clipped a harness around Aria and pulled her upwards as he clipped it onto the cable.

"Over now." He helped her climb over the railing, where she balanced on the edge precariously, gripping the cold metal railing with numb fingers.

She looked down into the indistinct blackness and her head whirled.

The soldier grasped her arms for a quick moment and put his face close, his cheek brushing against hers as he spoke into her ear. "Tell Owen my debt is paid." With one quick movement he pulled her hands off the railing and pushed her away.

She bit back a frightened shriek as she sailed through the air.

Strong arms caught her just before she would have crashed into the top edge of the wall. Aria felt dizzy and sick with exhaustion, and she wasn't much help as Owen pulled her up and over the wall.

He breathed into her ear, "Put your foot here and hold on." He bent to slip a loop of rope under her foot, then straightened again, holding onto her until she got her arms around his neck and shifted toward his back. She tried not to choke him, feeling awkward with her face and arms pressed against the hard muscles of his shoulders. His skin was cold, and when he turned his head, she felt the soft brush of his hair against her face. He tugged on the cable twice, and it loosened. He pulled it quickly across the lawn and up the wall, then dropped it to the ground below.

Her heart lurched into her throat when he descended. He wasn't wearing a harness; he only held on with his bare feet and hands wrapped in the rope. He descended quickly, nearly a fall, but slowed at the bottom to let her land gently.

"Stand a moment." His voice was only a breath in her ear, and he climbed again. The rope fell down, and he jumped, landing in a crouch beside her. He coiled the cable and put it over his shoulder, then looped the rope over it.

"Can you walk?"

She nodded, and he took her hand and led her away, slipping silently away from the wall. But in less than a block, she stumbled, her head spinning. He caught her up with one arm behind her shoulders and the other behind her knees and quickened his steps to a soundless jog. Her head jostling against the cool hardness of his chest, she felt suddenly as if she must be dreaming. *It all feels so unreal. This must be a dream. Not exactly a nightmare, because if so, I should have woken sometime while I was still imprisoned. You wake up when you're terrified, right? I was terrified, and I should have woken up. But something unreal, certainly.*

After some length of time she could not determine, he opened a door and went into a darkened building. Her eyes were closed, but she had the feeling of a small, closed space, and then another door into a slightly larger room.

He let her down gently onto a blanket folded on the floor to make a pallet, then knelt in front of her. He lit an oil lantern and she blinked. The space appeared to be a bookstore, with shelves lining the walls and forming aisles.

"What do you need?" His eyes met hers.

She swallowed, her tongue thick in her mouth. "Water." She hated that her voice sounded like a croak. But then she rearranged the thought and felt angry with him. "Did you know? Did you know what he'd do?" She tried to rise, and he caught her wrists with his cool, strong hands.

"Sit. I'll bring you water. Wait." He waited until she nodded before he stood, graceful as a cat.

In a moment he reappeared with three bottles of water. He opened one of them for her, then he disappeared again, coming back into the tiny circle of light with a loaf of bread, a block of cheese, a pack of fresh raspberries, and a plastic box of fresh spinach. He knelt again and opened the spinach, berries, and bread, then began cutting the cheese into neat cubes with his knife.

Aria drank, too intent on the water to voice her anger. Or whatever she felt. Anger, curiosity, relief, fear, all mingled together into a hysterical jumble that finally overflowed into tears. She leaned forward and covered her face with her hands, shuddering. After a long moment, she felt one cool hand resting on her shoulder.

She raised her head to sniff and wipe at her eyes. "I'm sorry."

He arranged the cheese cubes in a line on the plastic top of the spinach container. "I owe you an apology. I did not expect they would arrest you."

"Why did they?"

"I believe either Colonel Grenidor or others noticed that you had no tracker. The guards at the gate did not have the sensors; it would have been someone at a higher security level inside the facility. It seems Colonel Grenidor has become more suspicious of late."

She hunched forward, holding the water bottle tightly in one hand while she reached for the cheese. "I think he hates you."

"I imagine so." Owen did not seem surprised, and she wondered at that. "I had some unexpected difficulties and was detected earlier than anticipated. I am sorry you suffered for it."

She sat up, catching his eye. "Are you? Can I believe you? He didn't say exactly. But he gave me this story about the ancestor spirits someplace that cut the hearts out of this tribe." She felt hysteria rising again and bit back a sob.

She closed her eyes and pressed her lips together. *Breathe, girl. Breathe. It's over, and you're safe. More or less. With a heart-eating inhuman thing that rescued you from a man who might have been any Revolution hero. This is so confusing.*

"He wanted to know your name," she continued. "And mine. And who you were working with." She watched his face.

"What did you say?" His face showed nothing, as neutral an expression as she'd ever seen.

"Nothing at first. After three days? I think it was three days of no water, I gave up. I said you were Owen, I was Aria Forsyth, and I didn't know any associates. Also I didn't know where you were."

"'Tis little harm. They'll know your name and that you're not dead, and that you were helping me, but they would figure that out eventually anyway." He pushed the raspberries toward her. "Eat."

She stared at him. "So, was it worth it?"

"Eat."

"Did you find out anything useful? Because I hated it, but I'd hate it even more if it was pointless."

"Yes. I thank you." He rose and stepped back from the light. "Stay here and rest. I will return. There is a restroom through that door. Go nowhere else."

She wanted to scowl at him, but he was already gone.

SHE WOKE to his touch on her shoulder.

"Are you well?" He knelt beside her.

She sat up, rubbing crust from her eyes and nodding. She had no idea how long she'd been asleep.

"There is someone here you should meet." He looked up into the darkness beyond the lamplight and she followed his gaze.

A boy stepped closer to stand just inside the circle of light. He studied her with cautious eyes, lips pressed together. He glanced at Owen for a long moment, then back at her. He was barefoot, clothes ragged, and circles ringed his wrists and ankles, as if he'd been wearing shackles, deep blue bruises edged by green, with angry red marks over the top. Her wrists were irritated by the plastic handcuffs, but the slight chafing she'd suffered seemed trivial in comparison. He was painfully thin, with dark circles under his blue eyes. She swallowed. Who was this child? He appeared to be perhaps eight or ten, but if he was Fae, that guess meant little. Ghostly pale, with dark hair that fell into his eyes.

He made a gesture with one hand and shook his head at Owen.

Owen said something, and she looked at him in surprise, her mouth dropping open. *That must be one of the Fae dialects.* The language reminded her of a mountain stream, flashing in the sunlight. It sounded old, somehow, but also as fresh as spring, unhindered by the passing of time.

The boy shook his head again, this time with a

plea in his eyes and an unhappy set to his mouth. He looked from her to Owen and his shoulders dropped.

He stepped forward and knelt close in front of her, sad blue eyes on her face. Owen lifted the lantern so it lit the boy's features clearly.

"This is what they are doing to us. Among other things." He touched the boy's shoulder with a gentle hand, and the boy opened his mouth wide.

He had no tongue.

The bottom of his mouth was empty, except for a wide patch of pale scar tissue and a ragged pink nub. Aria stared, then closed her eyes and covered her face as the horror hit. A child! He was only a child.

The boy closed his mouth and turned away, hiding his face from the light. He made more signs to Owen, hunching his shoulders and rocking on his knees. Owen said something softly, and the boy bowed his head to the floor, hands stretched out toward Owen.

Aria watched, her eyes filled with tears. Owen placed his hands on the boy's head and leaned forward, singing quietly.

This time she saw the forest and the two in front of her at the same time, as if the two images were layered like the music. The sound wove around her, over and under and through her bones, green and gold and silver, clear as water. Layer upon layer, each note hanging in the air while the others rose.

It was hours before Owen's voice faded.

He was tired, his hands trembling as he stroked the boy's dark head. The child might have been asleep, kneeling with his face pressed to the ground for long moments in the silence. But then his shoulders jerked, and he let out a soft wordless cry, shuddering. Owen pulled him up and wrapped his arms around the boy's shoulders, pressed the boy's face into his shoulder. Owen's eyes, too, were closed, and in the lamplight she saw tear streaks on his pale cheeks.

At last he let the boy go. The child brushed at his cheeks and kept his face turned away from Aria. He slid back from the light and sat with his knees pulled up to his chest.

The silence drew out. Owen turned to her, un-ashamed or unaware of the tears on his face, and let his cool blue eyes rest on her for a long moment.

"It cannot be healed." He ran his hands over his face and through his hair. "It has been too long, the wound too severe." His hands were still shaking, and he clasped them behind his neck, stretching his shoulders with a wince. "This is what I did, while you bought me time. Colonel Grenidor was distracted trying to figure out why you had no tracker. Despite his diversion of soldiers to that task, he had more sensors than I anticipated, and I was detected quickly. I could find only Niall before I had to flee." His eyes flicked to the boy as he said the name. The boy hesitated, then nodded once.

Owen straightened with a deep breath. "Niall was captive nearly two years. He's endured much. Since we are not human, the researchers think nothing of inflicting inhuman cruelties upon us. All in the name of scientific discovery, of course." His voice was low, but Aria flinched at the cold anger in his voice.

"His family is still captive, as are others. I thank you for your help. I owe you a blood debt." He turned his blue eyes on her.

She swallowed. She glanced across at the boy again, and her heart clenched at his pale, frightened beauty. "You owe me nothing. I had no idea we humans did things like that. Not today. I thought we were past such cruelties."

Owen snorted softly, then rose and stepped back from the light. She could tell he paced only by the faint movement of air behind her; he made no sound. At long last, he stopped and knelt beside her again, facing her squarely. He said softly, "A Fae blood debt is not a thing to be tossed away. I thank you for your generosity. It is unusual and much appreciated. Yet I count myself in your debt. Niall is my nephew, and my subject, and currently my heir. He is important, and I will sacrifice much to keep him safe."

"Your subject? Your heir?" She latched onto the words as if it would keep her from drowning in his eyes.

Niall twitched. He was looking at Owen as if surprised, and he shook his head when Owen glanced at him. Afraid? Owen spoke softly in Fae, and Niall bit his lip and stared at her for a long moment.

"It doesn't matter now. But it might someday. He's a child, and my kin, and I'll not have him harmed more."

He reached for his rucksack. "Rest. Niall has information that will take some time to piece together. Then we can talk."

She pulled her knees up to her chin and watched them. Owen pulled several blank notebooks and cheap pens from his rucksack, as well as the small notebook she'd seen before. He flipped it open to what appeared to be a list, though she realized now that the language wasn't English, and handed it to Niall.

The boy read through it with tight lips, then began at the top. He wrote something next to many of the names in a tiny, neat hand. From her vantage point, she couldn't see it, but assumed it must be in the same language. It took nearly ten minutes for him to finish, as he flipped deliberately through several pages, pausing to think occasionally before writing. Near the end he wrote for several minutes, adding something to the bottom of the list. Owen let him write without comment, glancing at the pages at long intervals. He wrote in one of the blank notebooks, and when Niall finished, he set it aside.

Owen took the notebook and sat close to the lamp, Niall standing over his shoulder. His eyes ran down the pages, and at the end, he let out a long breath. "This many?" He leaned forward and let his head drop into his hands.

Niall stared over Owen's shoulder at Aria with a distrustful look.

"What is it?" Aria asked finally.

"The names of those I knew were missing. He's noted those he saw, and when, and how badly they were harmed." For the first time, he seemed unsure, staring down at the notebook. He leaned forward to put his head in his hands again, and after a long moment Aria slid closer. She reached out to touch his shoulder, and Niall struck her hand away angrily. He glared at her, putting himself between Owen and her.

"I'm sorry." Her voice was unsteady in the face of his blazing blue eyes. "I was just trying to be sympathetic."

He let out his breath in a low, wordless growl that seemed to fit his expression.

Owen caught his wrist and held it, speaking softly in Fae. After a long, trembling moment, Niall crumpled to the ground, kneeling in front of Owen and bowing his head. Owen sighed, stroked the back of his head with one hand, and spoke to Aria.

"Please forgive us. Niall is protective. There are so few of us left. That," he took a deep breath, "that is the problem. We are too few to attack by force, even if that was our goal. And I've never wished for war with humans. But I see no other option except extinction." He raised his eyebrows, still staring at the book. "Which, to be honest, is not very far off."

She knelt beside him. "Tell me. How bad is it? What can we do?"

"We? You're still with me in this, after what Grenidor did?" He glanced up at her.

"After what they did to him, how could I not be?" She gestured at Niall.

Owen ran his hands through his hair again. The lamplight caught his face for a moment as he closed his eyes, and she realized how beautiful he was. And how exhausted. His hands were still shaking as he rested his elbows on his knees.

"Were you hurt again? And had to heal yourself?"

He shrugged. "It's no matter." He shifted to face her, resting his hand on Niall's head for a moment. The boy curled into a ball on the floor and Owen smiled sadly. He lowered his voice.

"We don't procreate the way humans do. The mechanics are the same, but a Fae child cannot be conceived by accident. There are songs that are required from the father and mother. Removing a Fae tongue makes the victim voiceless, yes, but for us, it is also castration. It is an unprecedented act of war."

Aria swallowed.

"Yet it is a war we cannot win, and one I have no desire to pursue. I do not hate humans, only the harm they do to us." He sighed. "And we are beset. I have perhaps," he glanced at the notebook again, "one hundred? At most? One hundred, scattered across the continent, who are still free and could fight at need. And children to protect."

Niall shuddered, still curled on the floor, head covered by his arms. Owen leaned forward to look at his face, and smiled sadly. "It's good he's asleep. He'll need to eat soon. As will I."

"What were you writing in the other notebook?"

"Questions for him. He's in no condition to answer them now, though."

Aria swallowed. "Since I'm in this, and I can't read your notes, will you tell me? And I need to know what Colonel Grenidor meant by that story about the ancestor spirits. I need to know everything."

Owen nodded, and she felt guilty all over again when he pushed his hands through his hair, which was already sticking up, then rubbed them hard over his face as if he were trying to stay awake. He pulled the notebook closer to him and nodded that she should sit next to him. The lamp lit the page with the flickering yellow glow. It didn't surprise her that his handwriting was neat and precise, each line perfectly level, though the letters were fluid.

"I won't go through all the names, because most will mean nothing to you. Niall added another thirteen names to those I was aware of. This is his father. He was alive three months ago, but then they were separated for testing. His mother, my elder sister, was last seen six months ago, when she was moved to another testing facility, possibly for," he hesitated, then said quietly, "reproduction experiments. Their younger son, Liam, was killed when they were captured." He stopped, and though his voice had not wavered, he bowed his head a moment and closed his eyes. Aria felt her own throat tighten with emotion, and she reached out a hand and laid it on his arm.

"This is my father's name. He was last seen alive two months ago but was transferred to a solitary confinement area. I can imagine why." At Aria's glance, he said softly, "My father is not the sort to let his people be abused without a fight. I'm sure he's caused all manner of problems for them. And paid for it, no doubt." He took a deep breath. "This is a childhood friend. She was moved to solitary confinement around the same time my father was. This is a friend as well. He died as a result of an experiment on drug toxicity." He took another deep breath and let it out slowly, moving his finger to the middle of the next column of names. "This is my younger brother, Cillian. He was last seen alive nearly six months ago, when he was moved to an enclosed compartment for testing infectious diseases."

Aria felt something break inside her, and she

leaned forward to rest her forehead on his shoulder, one tentative hand on his back. "I'm so sorry," she whispered.

There was a long silence, and finally he said softly, "You had other questions, did you not?"

She pulled back so she could see his face, watching him in profile. "What did Grenidor mean by the ancestor spirits story? Was it a lie? Does it have anything to do with Fae?"

He waited so long to answer that she wondered whether he meant to at all. "I've heard a similar story before, but I don't know the Fae of that area. Fae have long preferred to remain unseen rather than walk among men. Some have good reasons, some less so. Some men are superstitious and invent malice and monsters where there are none. And some Fae enjoy the power to make men afraid. If I had to guess, I would imagine that there was one, perhaps two, turned Fae who thought it amusing to play with the tribe for a while and eventually grew tired of their game. But there are other things than Fae and men in the world, and I could be wrong."

She took a deep breath. "So a Fae could have done it." *It's not as though people don't do horrible things too. You've already seen the evidence. We even do them to each other.*

"It is possible."

"He also said," she hesitated, but pressed on, "he said I was stupid to be helping you. Naive. He asked if I knew how many you'd killed. And said that just because you hadn't hurt me yet didn't mean you wouldn't; it only meant I was useful for now." She swallowed, trying to read his expression.

"And you believe him?" He stared at the floor in front of his crossed ankles.

"I'm not sure. Should I?"

"What do you think?" Still he kept his eyes on the floor, and she wondered suddenly if it was out of consideration. Surely by now he'd realized that it was hard for her to think when his eyes were on hers.

"I believe you're helping your people. I know you could have hurt me and you didn't, and you rescued me from Grenidor. But how many people *have* you killed? And why?"

"I do not dwell on the exact count." He spoke slowly and precisely. "I've been alive a long time, and most of that time has not been idyllic. All have been for reasonable cause. Most were trying to capture or kill me, or other Fae. One I surprised in the middle of his attempted murder. Grenidor sees us as dogs, and dogs who bite deserve to be put down, regardless of what the human does to the dog first. I believe we have a right to self-defense." He sighed, leaned forward to look at Niall's face for a moment before lying on his back with his hands clasped behind his head. "You are free to go if you wish."

"All of them were self-defense?"

"All were for reasonable cause." His eyes were closed now, and he turned his back to her, lying on his side with one arm curled under his head. "Believe what you like. I must sleep now."

She stared at his back. *Why did I even ask him? He's given me no reason to fear him, and Grenidor is a monster. I don't doubt there's more to know, but I owe him an apology. After he rests. After I rest.*

She rubbed her eyes and wrapped herself up in

the blanket on the floor, then reached out to turn
down the lamp.

# CHAPTER 5

ARIA WOKE to the feeling of being stared at. The lamp was turned up again, and she blinked for a moment before she realized that Niall was sitting on the other side of the circle of light, his blue eyes on her face.

"Hello," she said tentatively. "My name is Aria. I don't think I said it last night. If it was night."

His eyes flicked away and then back to her before he nodded.

"You understand English, don't you?"

He nodded again. She sat up. He looked a little better after sleeping, the dark circles under his eyes fading. The red rings and underlying bruises around his wrists and ankles were much fainter too. Owen's singing had helped, then, though it couldn't heal his tongue.

"Where is Owen?"

His mouth twitched, and then he picked up a notebook and pen and wrote. He turned it to show her. *You should refer to him as Lord Owen.*

"Oh." She considered a moment. "I'm sorry. He didn't tell me." Those blue eyes on hers seemed a little softer. "I'm sorry about what they did." He stared at her, and she felt suddenly that she was being measured.

*He went to get food.*

"Good. I'm hungry, and I bet you are too." She smiled, trying to lighten the mood, but he merely stared at her. "When did you last eat? Well, how often do you normally eat? Owen, I mean Lord Owen, didn't seem to need to eat every day." The title felt awkward and strange in her mouth, but she thought she would oblige him until Owen came back and made his wishes known.

*Normally we eat every three or four days. They fed me once a month.* After considering her face a moment, he added, *Grenidor lies.*

"Did you hear us last night?"

*Only the part where you accused Lord Owen of being a murderer.* He wrote the words with irritated force, then glanced up at her again.

"That's not what I meant! I just wanted to hear the truth." She was going to keep justifying herself, as thin as the words sounded, but he started writing again.

*Grenidor is one of the directors of the experiment program. He devises the tortures that are inflicted on our people.* He turned the paper around so she could see it with an angry flourish, then stopped to add, *If you cannot believe Lord Owen's word over*

*Grenidor's, you are the stupidest human I have ever met.*

She winced. "You're right. It was stupid. I'm sorry, and I owe him an apology."

He scowled at her, only slightly mollified.

"How old are you?"

*78.*

She blinked. Yes, that would be right. If Owen looked about thirty, but was 273, this child looked something close to a third of that, eight or ten. She shook her head at the strangeness of it. "Where were you born? Do you remember before the Revolution?"

It was his turn to stare at her oddly before answering. *Nearby, outside the city. I remember. Not as much as Lord Owen, because I was young and my parents sheltered me from the worst of it.*

"From the worst of it? The worst of what?"

Another strange look. *The violence.*

"What violence?"

He cocked his head to the side and stared at her for a long moment. He tapped the pen under the word violence, watching her face.

"What violence? There wasn't any violence. It was a bloodless revolution, just a political change. The only fighting was against the Outlanders in the West and South Quadrants, and even that only lasted a few weeks. There was some unrest, competing propaganda for a while, but then it faded as everyone realized how much better things were." She stopped, blinking. The words came from her lips, but they sounded wrong, somehow. False.

She shook her head, feeling as if she stood on the edge of a precipice. "It was bloodless, wasn't it?"

His lips opened as if he wanted to speak, but then he clamped them shut. He wrote furiously, and she read over his shoulder. *No. There was much bloodshed. Do you not remember? Fighting in the streets for years. Many people killed. Some Fae also. Laser guns. Death squads. Getlaril bullets and vertril invented. Trackers. Propaganda war ended with assassinations of journalists.*

"No. No. That's not what I remember." But images flashed in her head. Blood splatters on the asphalt. Rockets. She pressed her hands over her eyes and shuddered. Shivering in the bathtub, hoping it would stop the bullets.

She rocked, knees pulled up to her chest, as memories flooded her, a movie played too fast in her mind, the images running over each other and sounds filling her ears. Running from a fire consuming a building. Her home? A boy clutching her hand. Her brother? Maybe six years old? What was his name? Johann Sebastian. Her mother's attempt at culture, though the family had no claim to musical talent or distinguished ancestors. Her mother's face, beaten and bruised, abruptly yanked away. Her younger self screaming endlessly, throat raw.

She didn't know how long it had been when Owen pressed his hands on each side of her head and sang. The beauty of his song lay over the wounds of memory like gauze, a thin reminder that she was still alive, and that she would recover.

The song slipped through her, quiet but insistent, slowing her racing heartbeat, calming the blood in her veins. It wrapped around her shoulders like a warm blanket.

She blinked, and shuddered, shook her head as if coming up for breath. Owen let her go and sat back, eyes on her face. He and Niall were both staring at her.

Finally, Owen said quietly, "That was unexpected. What happened?"

Niall showed him his half of the conversation written in the notebook, and Owen glanced at her again. "You don't remember?"

"I remember some of it now. It's all disjointed, but I remember." *Blood in the streets, yes, tanks. Soldiers running everywhere. Hiding under my bed. Yanked out by one arm, held up while...* "It's the trackers!" She caught her breath again at the memory. *They put it in then. I was maybe 15? Terrified as a child in a nightmare. It hurt. A lot. But it faded, and then so did everything else.*

"What?" Owen and Niall were watching her with identical expressions of wary curiosity. "What about the trackers?"

She trembled as the memories kept falling into place. One little piece here, a jagged edge there that lined up with that other one. She forced herself to answer, "The tracker. I think it made me forget. It was all foggy. Everything was different. But now I remember."

"Remember *what*, exactly?" Owen asked.

The memories jostled with each other for space in her mind, recent and distant connected with each other by threads of thought or a feeling. *Desolation. When my house was burned, desolation, and when Mom died, too. Johann. Is he alive? No. Yes. Maybe? I can't remember. I think he's gone. And Dad died. I remember that. On the carpet in the living room. One of the soldiers shot him, when they came to put in our trackers, because he fought so hard, punched a soldier in the face.*

121

"Everything. It's so jumbled. But I remember now." She blinked at them. "They put in the trackers and then everything faded. I forgot all the fighting. I forgot everything. I didn't even remember—" a sob rose up in her throat. "I didn't even remember I had a brother! His name was Johann." She leaned forward to bury her face in her knees, and felt Owen's cool, gentle hand rest on her shoulder for a moment. She couldn't face him, not now, not with everything so fresh again in her mind. She couldn't face anything.

But while one part of her mind parsed through the memories, placing them in a logical order, another part listened to Owen and Niall.

*Johann was younger there, so that one must be earlier. Mom has less grey in this one. That was when I was studying for the spelling bee, which was in sixth grade. This was when we went camping by the river. Johann fell in, because he was being a little scamp and running across the fallen tree. Mom warned him so many times! This was when I was studying for the college entrance exams. Dad was dead by then. Mom was dead. Johann dead? Or gone?*

Owen spoke first in Fae, but shifted to English, and she imagined that he did it on purpose, knowing she might be listening. "Here." The crinkle of paper and plastic told her he had been to the butcher shop. Somehow the thought of the pig's heart did not horrify her the way it had before. *Strange what you can get used to.* They knelt beside the lantern, a cardboard box acting as a makeshift table.

Silence but for the almost inaudible sound of thin wet plastic, and then Owen spoke as if he were answering a question. "I have heard nothing about it from the other humans. But we keep our distance. I have not spoken to Gabriel in nearly three years."

Another pause.

"No. We have both been occupied with our own pursuits, that is all. I don't believe he blames me. He shouldn't."

A long silence, and she looked up to see Owen shaking his head. He sighed heavily and stared at the bloody plastic before him. He said something in Fae, and Niall shot to his feet.

The boy stood trembling in the lamplight, paced away and back, away again, then threw himself onto his knees before Owen with a wordless cry. He was shaking his head, tears running down his face.

Owen put his hands on the Niall's shoulders and spoke softly, urgently, but the boy struck his hands away and shook his head, his eyes never leaving Owen's. The tears glistened on his cheeks.

*Arguing. Niall refuses to accept something Owen said.*

Owen's voice softened still further, and he seemed to be pleading. His straight, strong shoulders slumped a little, and he closed his eyes against Niall's wordless plea. Finally, Owen nodded once. Niall caught one of Owen's hands in his own two smaller ones and pressed it to his cheek, kissed the back of Owen's hand and then pressed it to his forehead.

The silence drew out, and Owen finally rose, tousled Niall's hair once, and stepped back to disappear into the shadows.

Niall remained on his knees, his blue eyes rimmed with red. He glanced into the darkness and then stared at the floor.

"What just happened?" Aria finally whispered to him.

He looked up at her as if he'd just realized she was there. After a long moment, he picked up a notebook and slid toward her. He wrote slowly as she read over his shoulder.

*Lord Owen wanted to take me to the Old Country. He says it is safe there, and I can find refuge with some distant relatives of my mother. He would return to pursue the fight alone. I begged him to let me stay with him.*

He hesitated, then continued. *I am afraid for him. He has been alone too long in the concrete and steel, and he has lost hope. If Gabriel still hates him, I see no hope for us. Lord Owen has no one to sing for him, as he sang for me, and no one to heal the wounds he has suffered.*

She swallowed. Niall looked up at her, his eyes brimming with tears.

"What can I do?" she murmured.

He studied her for a long moment. *Do you know Gabriel?*

"No."

He sighed.

"What about the trackers? If I didn't remember, perhaps no one does. Would it matter if more people remembered? Do the others who removed them remember?"

He blinked at her, then shrugged. *Gabriel is the leader of the human resistance. He should know.* Another pause, then, *He is dangerous.*

Wonderful. She hesitated, then shrugged herself. "Everything is dangerous, though, isn't it?"

He glanced at her again, and a slight, sad smile quirked his lips.

"You look like him, you know. Like Lord Owen."

His eyes widened and then he smiled. *Thank you. I would be proud if I were like him someday.*

"Will you take me to see Gabriel?"

His mouth twitched, and he hesitated. *I cannot leave Lord Owen without letting him know. It would be cruel at this time. I doubt he will let us go without his protection.*

Another hesitation, then, *He needs to rest first. He gave all his strength to me and needs a few hours.*

Niall left the notebook in front of her and rose to slip into the darkness.

OWEN PACKED his rucksack and wordlessly led them up through a trapdoor in the ceiling, through several connected attic crawl spaces, down another trapdoor, and into the back of a small clothing shop. Three horizontal metal bars lined one wall, the third only a few inches below the ceiling, all filled with hanging clothes.

"Wait here."

He slipped through a door and reappeared in a few moments with a middle-aged woman close behind him. She flipped on the lights and stared at Aria thoughtfully, as if she already knew what was going on.

Owen frowned again. "It's a lot to ask, Margot. I'm sorry."

She shook her head with a quick wave of her hand. "You know it's nothing. I owe you, Owen." She patted his arm with quick affection, then walked around Aria thoughtfully. "Take off your clothes."

"What?" Aria blinked at her.

"You look like a fugitive. Streaked with blood and dirt and smelling like a sewer. You can't be seen like that."

Aria glanced at Owen and Niall, and Owen nodded for the boy to follow him as he moved to the front of the shop.

Margot gave her an odd look. "Don't want him to watch?"

Aria shrugged. "It's just awkward."

Margot chuckled. "You're so young. I'd give my right arm for him to peek at me."

Aria blushed. It wasn't that he wasn't attractive. It was just *awkward*. Besides, he ate bloody pigs' hearts. She covered her embarrassment by asking, "Why do you owe him?"

"I found myself in the wrong place once. It would have gone badly, but he escorted me home." Her odd tone made it clear there was more to the story, but she didn't want to tell it. She gazed at Aria a moment longer, then turned to peruse the racks of clothes. She pulled out a few pairs of jeans, a couple pairs of boots, and three shirts.

"Try these."

The first pair of jeans fit so well Aria blinked in surprise. Slim fitting and fashionable, they somehow made her feel more confident when she looked down at herself.

"And now the boots." Margot watched her as she slipped her feet into the soft, flat boots, the jeans tucked inside. "Yes, those will work."

Aria caught sight of herself in a mirror propped in a corner. "I look good."

The surprise in her voice made Margot smile.

"You need to blend in, stylish but not eye-catching. Practical clothes, because heaven only knows what you'll be doing. Try this shirt."

It was a form-fitting turtleneck in a deep teal, warmer than she'd expected. A sweater went over it. Margot draped another turtleneck over her arm.

"Take this one too. Here, let me fix your hair." Margot pulled a brush from her purse and ran it through Aria's brown curls.

"Come." She led Aria out into the main part of the shop, where more neat racks of clothes filled the floor.

"Here you are." She presented Aria to Owen and Niall as if pleased with her work. Aria had completely lost track of time in the interminable darkness of the bookshop and tunnels, and she was surprised to see the clear light of early afternoon.

"Thank you, Margot." Owen inclined his head.

"She looks good, don't you think?" Margot prompted.

Owen's eyes flicked up and down with disinterest so obvious that Aria felt a little stung, despite her determination not to care. "Yes, thank you, Margot." His eyes shifted toward the windows at the front of the shop.

Margot frowned at his profile. "Be careful, Owen."

He smiled slightly, just a twitch. "You know I am."

She snorted. "Don't get yourself killed. Or worse."

"I'll try." The quirk of his lips held no humor.

With that he slipped toward the door with noiseless steps. Niall followed, and then Aria, who glanced back at Margot with a grateful smile. The woman lifted one hand in a quick wave and smiled, but her eyes were grave and worried.

Owen led them block after block. Aria was surprised to see him stay in the open so long, especially during the day. No one seemed to notice him though. His shirt was new, but his pants were worn and threadbare enough to stand out in this prosperous section of the city. Though the afternoon sun slanted into the shop windows, it gave little warmth, and forlorn patches of melting sleet remained in the shadows. His short sleeves and bare feet, and those of Niall, should have caused some remarks, or at least second glances, but people brushed by without seeming to notice them at all. *Interesting. I wonder how he does it. He's not invisible, since I can see him and no one actually bumps into him. He's just unnoticeable.*

Down a narrow alley and back out into the sunlight of a broader street. This time he crossed and entered what appeared to be an old hotel. He stopped just inside the door, Niall and Aria pressed against his back. He spread his arms to keep them from advancing past him.

"I request entrance and an audience with Gabriel." His voice wasn't loud, but it carried in the open lobby.

Aria peered under his arm to see a white marble floor with several threadbare red rugs spread across it. A dark fireplace loomed at one edge, with worn leather chairs arranged for conversation. A balcony loomed to their right. No one was visible.

There was no sound at first, but then a door opened at the far side of the lobby, on the first floor. There was movement in the darkness beyond, and a glint of light on metal.

"What do you want?"

"I will speak with Gabriel directly."

"You'll tell me your message or you won't see him at all." Irritation tightened the voice, and Aria heard a soft, metallic click.

Owen paused, then said, "Eli. Do you hate me so much?"

A bullet cracked the stone above Owen's head. He didn't flinch, but Aria did, her heart racing.

"Get out!" the man shouted. He advanced just enough to show himself pointing the gun at Owen's heart, eyes narrowed.

Owen murmured, "Please wait outside."

Aria swallowed, unable to move for a moment. Niall took her hand in his small cool one and led her outside the door and just to the side, where they waited with their backs pressed against the stone.

Aria closed her eyes and tried not to listen. Her heart thudded in her chest, and she jumped at another shot. Then there was silence.

Niall peeked around the corner, then pulled her through the door again. Owen spoke softly to the man, who held a pistol in one hand dangling by his leg. He looked at Aria and blinked slowly, then at Niall.

"Yes. Yes, I will take you." He blinked again and shook his head, as if coming up from swimming. He looked back up at Owen. "That's not fair, you know."

Owen smiled faintly. "You have a gun, Eli. I have a human and a child with me. I don't want anyone hurt."

Eli scowled at him, but without much rancor

this time. He waved the pistol as he talked. "Fine. Fine. I'll take you. Give me your weapons, though. I need to show I did my job. More or less."

Owen unbuckled his sword belt without comment and handed it to Eli, who slung it over his shoulder. He drew his knife and handed it over, hilt first.

"Come on then." He pulled the door open and led them down the hallway. At one intersection, he shouted, "Need someone on guard." At an answering shout, he continued on, then turned to go up a long flight of stairs. Halfway down another hall he stopped at a nondescript door.

"Wait here. I'll go in first." He chewed his lip nervously for a moment, then opened the door without knocking, slid inside, and closed the door again before Aria could see anything of the interior.

They waited. Owen seemed to be listening, but Aria couldn't hear anything.

The door opened suddenly. "Come in."

Owen stepped forward and a shot cracked, deafening Aria. Owen staggered back, almost falling into the hallway. Aria caught him by one shoulder as Niall leapt forward and threw himself in front of Owen with a wordless shriek.

Owen shook himself free and lunged forward to catch Niall by his shoulders and jerk him back. He pushed Niall to the side, behind the shelter of the wall, and stayed upright, leaning against the doorframe and blocking it with his body. Niall trembled beside Aria, and she put one hand on his shoulder.

Owen growled, "I was not to blame for that, and you know it."

A deep voice answered, "You were. You should be glad I used lead and not *getlaril*. Why are you here?"

Owen raised his left hand to his chest, and then dropped it back to his side. Blood smeared his fingers.

"We had an idea. Wanted to test it." He paused and raised his hand to his chest again. "It might help you. Might help us both." He turned to catch Aria's eye. "Stay here." Then he closed the door in her face.

They heard the low murmur of voices for a while, then a long, disconcerting silence. Then voices again.

Finally the door opened. Eli nodded them in, his face guarded.

Niall rushed to Owen, who was sitting in a threadbare chair. His black shirt couldn't hide the spreading dark stain from the wound, approximately where his heart would be if his heart were on the right side. He pressed his left hand to it, his fingers red.

Niall closed his eyes and rested his forehead against Owen's knee.

"Aria, Niall, this is Gabriel. He is the leader of the human resistance. Gabriel, Aria is human. Niall is my nephew. You've met before. He's been imprisoned for the last two years." Abruptly he looked down at Niall and said something in Fae. Niall looked up at him with a skeptical look and hesitated, but finally rose to stand at Owen's shoulder, a small, stern protector.

Aria and Gabriel studied each other cautiously. He looked older than Owen did, perhaps forty-five or so, with grey liberally sprinkled in his brown hair. A little thick in the waist, but still fit, perhaps a former soldier. Cautious eyes, irritated, but not afraid. He still held a pistol, though it wasn't pointed at anyone at the moment.

She tried to smile. "Hello."

Gabriel did not return the courtesy. "Why are you with this creature?" He gestured toward Owen with the gun.

Aria frowned. "Because I want to be. I trust him more than I trust you." The words came unbidden, but she knew they were true.

To her surprise, that provoked a slight smile from Gabriel. "Huh." He rummaged in a drawer of the desk and tossed a rag to Owen, who folded it and pressed it to his chest.

"You remember things now?" He nodded to another chair.

She sat, with a glance at Owen, who had closed his eyes. *He's really caught it lately. Even for someone, something, as tough as he is, the last two weeks have been rough. How much is my fault?*

"Yes."

"Tell me." He leaned forward.

She raised her chin. "Not unless you put away the gun and get him a proper bandage."

Gabriel stared at her, then smiled tightly. "Done." He nodded to Eli, who left the room. Gabriel put the gun in a lower desk drawer and closed it, then clasped his hands on the tabletop.

"I take it you're not afraid of him then." She was proud of how her voice didn't waver.

"No."

"Then you shouldn't have shot him."

Gabriel raised an eyebrow. "I don't need to defend myself to you. You came to tell me something. What is it?"

Aria looked at Owen.

He blinked slowly, as if dazed, then said quietly, "Tell him."

"He removed my tracker about a week and a half ago. I didn't notice anything different at first. Yesterday I was talking with Niall, and he asked whether I remembered the violence." She shook her head, the images rising again.

Eli entered at that moment, and she watched while he handed a roll of gauze and medical tape to Niall. The boy positioned himself between Gabriel and Owen as Owen pulled off his shirt. She couldn't see the wound itself as Niall worked on it, but she did see Eli wince with involuntary sympathy.

"I didn't. He was surprised, and prompted me, and everything seemed to come flooding back. It's all jumbled now, but I'm putting things in order. I remembered a lot. I'd forgotten I had a brother." Her throat closed with sudden emotion, and she stopped, unwilling to cry in front of him. "How my father died. Things like that. I remembered when they put the tracker in."

Gabriel studied her, and she wished she could read his expression.

After a long moment, Gabriel asked, "Eli, did you ever have a tracker?"

"No."

"Hm. Nor did I." Gabriel tapped his fingers together as he thought. "Do you know the memories are true?"

"Yes." Aria blinked at him. *What kind of question is that?*

He glanced at Owen and said, "You know he

could have changed them. He has that power."

"I did not." Owen's voice was low but clear.

"Can I believe that?"

Owen put out one hand and moved Niall aside so he faced Gabriel squarely. His bare chest was streaked with blood, but the bandage was taped on securely. He leaned forward slightly, and Aria shivered at the cold fury in his quiet voice. "Have I ever lied to you, Gabriel?"

Gabriel swallowed and looked down. "No." The denial was soft, ashamed. "No, you have not."

After a tense silence, Eli ventured, "The only one I know who had a tracker was Aaron."

Gabriel sighed. "Hm."

Aria wondered what that meant. Niall pulled a clean shirt from Owen's rucksack and helped him put it on. It didn't conceal the blood streaking both their hands, though.

Gabriel gazed at Aria thoughtfully for a long moment before standing. "You should see him. You will understand why I find this difficult to believe, and more difficult to plan around."

Aria nodded and rose. Owen stood too, only to stagger into the desk, barely catching himself with both hands on the edge. Niall glared at Gabriel as he tried unsuccessfully to get Owen to lean on him.

Gabriel paused, halfway to the door, and glanced back at Owen. "You're not up to your usual."

Owen shook his head, blinking dizzily. "No."

Gabriel led them down the long hallway and down a flight of stairs, then another. Owen stopped at one point to lean against the wall, eyes glazed, and Gabriel waited three steps below, neither impatient nor sympathetic at the delay. Aria offered her arm to Owen, but he shook his head, only resting one hand on Niall's shoulder as they continued downward.

Beneath the hotel was a cavernous room that had once been an underground concert hall. The chairs had been removed, though numerous small holes remained to show where they had been bolted to the concrete floor. The floor dropped toward one corner in deep arcs, with a larger flat area at the bottom. Groups of men and a few women were scattered across the open space, sitting or laying on bedrolls. Some were cleaning weapons, some reading, and others talking quietly with each other.

At Gabriel's entrance two sentries straightened to attention, then relaxed.

They wove through the groups of people to a door at the far side. Aria tried not to stare, but they caught her attention. Everyone looked tired, worn. Most were between thirty and forty-five, and nearly all had the bearing of soldiers. *Who are these people?*

They went through another door into a darkened hallway, and Gabriel stopped at a door.

"We've been calling him Aaron, but we don't know his name. We think he might have been a journalist. He was caught in the middle of a battle between us and the Rev Forces. He lost his arm and nearly died. We saved his life, but his mental state has never been stable since. He might be mad. He's a liability, but we've done our best by him. It was partly our fault he was injured, and you know what they do to cripples. Most times he's not violent, but he's unpredictable, so we have to keep him contained." He gestured toward the door.

"For his own safety, as well as ours."

They nodded, and Gabriel slipped a key into the lock and opened the door. He peered through the crack before opening it all the way. "Come in." He closed the door behind them.

The man was perhaps forty-five, but he looked older. A worn shirt hung on his thin frame, and greying hair hung ragged over his eyes. He sat on the edge of a cot, rocking slightly, staring at a spot in the carpet some three feet in front of his bare feet. The scar tissue on the bare stump of his right arm glistened in the light of an electric lantern set on a table by the door. He made a low, monotonous moan as he rocked, and gave no indication that he noticed their entrance.

"Aaron, you have visitors." Gabriel stepped closer and put a hand on his shoulder firmly. "Look at them."

There was no change at first, but then the man looked through his tangled hair and stared at them, focusing on Owen for one long moment. "I haven't seen one of your kind in years." He blinked, then his gaze shifted slowly to the far wall, ignoring Aria and Niall completely. "They came!" He shrieked and threw his one arm over his head protectively, hurling himself away from them into the far corner. He shuddered, rocking and moaning more loudly. The sound made Aria cringe.

Gabriel grimaced. "You see. It will be difficult to get many answers from him."

"Let me help him," Owen said.

"How?"

Owen turned to stare at Gabriel for a long moment. Gabriel said finally, "Very well. Shall I stay?"

"If you wish."

Gabriel sat at the end of the cot and leaned against the wall. He gestured to the place beside him, but Aria shook her head, preferring to sit on the carpet with her back against the door.

Owen knelt in front of the man, who flinched away from him, sheltering his head beneath his upraised arm. He spoke softly, and after a minute or so, Aaron relaxed, his forehead resting on his bony knees.

Owen turned to Niall and said something in Fae, which caused Niall to frown.

Then, "I'm trusting you with them, Gabriel."

Gabriel met his eyes for a long moment and then nodded.

Owen placed one hand on Aaron's head and began to sing.

Aria closed her eyes as his voice threaded through the air. Sweet and clear, the song wove up and around her, the words made of sound and rushing water and spring sunlight. She found herself breathing more deeply, slowly, at peace. *Owen stood in the middle of the mountain stream, water rushing past his knees, looking in her direction but not at her. A sudden smile, white teeth in his handsome pale face. He cupped the water in his hands and offered it to someone.*

Hours might have passed; Aria couldn't tell how long it had been. Owen's voice faded, the sound hanging in the air, waiting for the next note. He started again, then stopped, and she opened her eyes to see him crumple. He fell forward, his head hitting the concrete block wall next to Aaron's shoulder with a sickening thunk. Niall pulled his shoulders, and then she caught him too, rolled him carefully to his back. Aaron sat in the same position, head down, unmoving as a statue.

Gabriel stood over them and stared down at Owen's supine form.

"What did he *do*?" He sounded concerned.

Aria might have been gratified at his change of attitude if she hadn't been so worried herself.

Niall waved an irritated hand at him and bent close to Owen's face. He was breathing shallowly, eyes closed, but did not so much as twitch when Niall ran a small hand over his head, feeling the bump that was already appearing at the hairline. He pulled up Owen's shirt to check the blood-soaked gauze, and then studied him again from a distance of about six inches. Finally he went to the rucksack and pulled out one of the notebooks and sat down to write.

Everyone started when Aaron looked up and asked, "Where am I?"

Gabriel answered, "You're in the Resistance Headquarters. Do you remember I've told you that before?"

"Yes. You have. And you are Gabriel. Who is he?" Aaron looked toward Owen.

Aria answered, "Call him Lord Owen."

Aaron stared at him a moment. "Is he dead?"

"No."

He cocked his head to one side. "I saw him singing in the forest. I remember now. Too much."

"What is your name then?" Gabriel knelt in front of him.

"Joshua Whitemarsh."

"How did you lose your arm?"

"It was crushed. Someone cut it off." He

blinked. "You were there, weren't you?"

"Yes."

Joshua considered Owen again. Aria asked Niall quietly, "What did he tell you before he started?"

Niall was scribbling furiously, but he stopped to write at the top of the page. *He said "Trust me." He also forbade me to use any*, he hesitated, then wrote a Fae symbol. He looked up at her hopefully, but at her confused look he wrote, *"magic" on his behalf. He said I am not yet recovered enough.*

"And you'll obey him?"

*Always.*

He finished the other piece that he was writing and slapped the floor to get Gabriel's attention, then turned the notebook toward them.

*He needs food and time. Silence. Sunlight. Take your conversation outside and give him peace. Bring him food.*

Gabriel nodded. "Agreed." He looked to Aria. "You come with me. There are things to discuss."


SEVERAL PEOPLE STOOD when they saw Joshua emerge from the hallway behind Gabriel. "Look." The curious murmurs were quiet, but in the cavernous space the sound carried.

Gabriel took them to a small alcove with a set of double doors that had been left standing open. He pointed across the hall to several people and motioned them to join the little group. He sent someone to get food for Owen and Niall before they closed the doors and spoke by the light of a flickering fluorescent bulb above a battered conference table.

"Joshua, tell us what you remember."

He took a deep breath and rubbed the stump of his right arm. He began hesitantly, "I used to be married." And there he stopped, staring at the table for so long that Gabriel leaned forward, about to prompt him for more.

Another deep breath. "My wife was killed in the last days of the Revolution. It was an accident; our neighbors next door had been denounced and she was coming home from work when their apartment was stormed. She was caught in the crossfire. I went a little mad. Ran out into the street. I was furious and terrified in equal parts. I'm not sure what I intended to do.

"They put the trackers in by city blocks, because there were so many to be done. We lived in the North Quadrant, near the western side, and were some of the last to get ours. I knew they were doing something strange, but I didn't know what. The reports were vague and spotty. The soldiers had come to our section to install the trackers and caught me then. It's a small metal object, like a pill capsule. After it was inserted, I went back home. I remembered little of my wife's death, barely remembered I'd been married. I scrubbed the blood out of the hallway myself." He stared at the center of the table for a long moment without continuing.

"It didn't bother me at the time. I went back to work. I wrote for one of the science magazines, Nova. But it had been closed for months, and I hadn't had paying work. We'd been scrimping and saving but were close to the end of our money. I was told to appear at the Office for Revolutionary Affairs and given a job in the propaganda office. I wrote pieces for the radio." He stopped again, his gaze distant. "I don't think any of them ever aired. I think they wanted to keep me busy. I worked there for about a year."

"You remembered none of this before?" Gabriel leaned forward intently.

"I remembered blood. My wife's face as she was shot. Tanks. The pain of my arm."

"Do you remember those things now?"

Joshua said, "Yes, but now they're memories, not an ever-recurring present."

Gabriel sat back. "Thank you. We have much to learn from this. Does anyone know anyone else who had a tracker? Ever?"

Silence.

"We'd assumed the trackers were used only for identification and location tracking. But we've wondered why no one seems to remember what happened. We've talked about brainwashing. Drugs. Perhaps the trackers themselves exert some sort of control over the mind."

"What about the delay then?" Eli asked. "Aria didn't have any flashbacks for days, and for Aaron, I mean Joshua, it's been nearly a year."

A woman from the back spoke up. "Joshua had raving nightmares for weeks after losing his arm. We assumed it was a result of the trauma, but perhaps some were actually flashbacks. He might have retreated into a few memories rather than dealing with all of them."

"And now he *can* deal with them? That's strange, don't you think? What happened in there?" This from another man, who looked between Joshua and Gabriel skeptically.

Gabriel rubbed a hand across his face. "Owen sang. I have no problem believing there's healing in that. I'm unsure what to do with the knowledge. If the trackers are exerting some type of control, we should remove them. But that might not solve our problems."

"Why not?" This from a fierce-looking woman who loomed over Aria's shoulder.

"Is it drugs? Is it magic? Is it an electronic signal? If we don't know how it works, we can't counteract the effects of removing it, which may be severe."

"It's not drugs," Aria spoke up. "If so, it would have to be recharged or reinserted after a while. Right? That never happened. It was only the one insertion years ago."

Gabriel tapped his fingers on the table. "We haven't kept up with the propaganda. It's hard to keep abreast of it while keeping our heads down. Does it change? If so, do the trackers update? How? Can that be manipulated?"

Aria thought before she spoke, feeling the weight of their eyes on her. "It does change. At one point I remember Governor Matthias was a war hero, and later he was a criminal and was executed."

"That happens in every war. Heroes and criminals change places all the time."

"Yes, but someone should have said something about the change and his downfall. There should have been new information to change everyone's perception of him. It wasn't like that. It was just that he was favored for months, and then he was, and always had been, a war criminal, and weren't they glad they finally captured him? It was as if he'd never been a hero at all."

"Was it just rhetoric? That can also happen in

war with a powerful regime. No one wants to voice their doubts." This from another man in the back.

"I don't think so. It was as if everyone truly believed it, like the past had changed. I didn't even remember that he'd been cast as a hero until after my tracker came out."

Gabriel grunted acknowledgement. He stared around the table for a long moment. "Think on it, everyone." He rose, and everyone began to file out.

"What now? I can't leave with..." she gestured helplessly toward Joshua's room.

Gabriel frowned. "Joshua, we'll keep you in your room one more night, to be sure you're stable. We'll move Owen out here unless there's an empty room."

Most of the rooms were filled with supplies, but there was one that was nearly empty, only one wall taken up with a ceiling-high row of stacked boxes of military rations.

"I think he'd rather be in here by himself." Aria felt confident stating that much. "And you promised food."

Gabriel gave her a sidelong look. "You're pushy, you know that?"

She gave him a cheeky grin. She couldn't maintain the cheerfulness though, and her shoulders slumped. "At this point, I have nothing left."

Gabriel clapped her on the shoulder. "Help me move him, then come eat with us."

When they opened the door to Joshua's room, Owen lay in the same position she'd left him, as white as death in the stark electric light. Niall had moved the lantern closer and was writing in the notebook. He let her lean over his shoulder, but it

143

did no good; all the writing was in Fae.

*Where is his food?* Niall wrote.

"It's coming. We're moving you to a different room for tonight." Gabriel considered him for a moment, then stepped out the door. A moment later he reappeared with another man, who took Owen's legs. Gabriel lifted him under the armpits and they carried him down the hall to the chosen room, where they laid him on the floor again. His head fell sideways, limp.

Niall followed, kneeling by his uncle anxiously.

Gabriel nodded the other man out, then said quietly, "I'll be back."

He returned in a moment with an electric lantern and a bedroll. "Do you want a bedroll? And one for him?"

Niall shrugged, then shook his head.

Someone knocked on the doorframe, and Gabriel turned back toward them with two paper bags. "Here."

Aria spread her bedroll against the back wall. "I'll be out in a minute," she said to Gabriel. He stepped outside.

The boy's face was solemn, worried, and she finally asked, "What are you thinking?"

He shrugged one shoulder. Aria moved closer and put a tentative hand on his shoulder. He gestured helplessly toward Owen's face.

"There's food if you want."

He stared at Owen and shook his head.

"You should sleep. He would want you to regain your strength. You've been through a lot too."

He twitched his shoulder again, then lay down, curled against Owen's side, his head against

144

his uncle's shoulder.

"I'm going out for a bit, but I'll be back."

He didn't respond, but she hadn't really expected him to.

Gabriel waved to her from a spot on the other side of the theater. She felt everyone's eyes on her as she walked across the empty space, and tried to keep from feeling like she was under examination.

Dinner was a quick affair, but she was pleasantly surprised by the food. After a week of sandwiches, anything hot was welcome.

"This is good."

"Martha does it. She used to be a chef, back when there were such things." Gabriel returned her strained smile. "I'll tell her you said so."

"Why did you shoot him?"

Silence descended on the table.

"It's a long story. For another time." Gabriel stood. "I have work. Sleep when you want. There will be food when you wake up."

# CHAPTER 6

Aria woke to the sound of the door opening. Her eyes were crusty, and she groaned when she shifted. She must have been lying in one position for hours; every muscle in her body ached. *You'd think I'd be used to sleeping on a hard floor by now, but no. It still hurts. Except after he sings.*

She rolled over at Gabriel's startled exclamation. "Peace, Niall. I'm not going to hurt him."

Niall crouched in front of Owen's motionless form, holding the plastic pen like a dagger. He grunted and glared at him before lowering his hand.

Gabriel stepped into the room, leaving the door open. "I came to see if you needed help. More food?"

Niall shook his head, then wrote, *I think you've*

*done enough, don't you?*

Gabriel raised his eyebrows but did not respond. "And you?" he looked toward Aria. "It's lunchtime, if you're hungry. You missed breakfast."

"I'll be out in a few minutes."

She turned her back to Niall and Owen and changed her shirt, scrubbed her face with her hands, and tried to make herself presentable. Not that it mattered.

"How is he?" she asked Niall softly.

He gestured, and she knelt beside him. Owen kept breathing, but that was all that could be said for him. Though no longer so obviously battered as that first night underground, he seemed somehow smaller. Weaker. Drained.

*I feel better now. I could help him, if he would let me.* Niall's frustration was obvious, but so too was his own lingering weakness. Aria reached out with a gentle finger to trace the red ring around one thin wrist, and he slumped.

"He wouldn't want it. You should do as he said."

He nodded dejectedly.

She ate with Gabriel again in a quiet knot of men and women. She had the sense of solemn tension, a mounting feeling of something about to happen, but no one told her anything. When she walked by, conversations stilled. She wasn't part of their team yet, not fully trusted. She wasn't sure she minded.

She wandered back to Owen's room after she finished eating. She thought of it as his room, even though she and Niall both slept there too. *Why do I feel safer with Owen, even unconscious, than in a room*

147

*by myself? In this hotel, that would be creepy.* He hadn't moved. Niall looked up at her bleakly before settling back down with the notebook and continuing writing. He had already filled pages with his neat script.

"Do you need anything?"

He shook his head.

She laid down on her bedroll, still tired. *I haven't taken an afternoon nap in months. Years. A long time.*

Aria woke slowly, aware of the lamp turned up and the soft rustle of paper behind her. She sat up to see Owen's eyes on her.

"Are you well?" he asked.

"I should ask you that."

"Well enough." He shifted with a wince. He sat propped against the wall of boxes, one leg stretched out before him, the other bent. He looked down at the notebook in his lap and flipped the page.

"What does it say?" She slid over to sit shoulder to shoulder with him, not quite touching.

"Niall has answered many questions I had about the testing facilities. The information may be useful when I go in again." He rubbed his chest absently, still reading.

"Did you know Gabriel would shoot you?"

Owen huffed softly. "No. I should have spoken to him before I stepped into the doorway."

"Why did...? How did you...?" She couldn't put her question in the right words. His clear blue gaze on her did not help.

"Why did I what?"

"You frightened us both!"

"I'm sorry. I told Niall to trust me. I did not

expect it to be so frightening for him."

The boy drew his knees up to his chest. He didn't look at his uncle, but leaned in to rest his head on Owen's shoulder on the other side.

"Did you get any useful information?" He looked down at the notebook again.

"Yes. But you should know that. You were in his mind, weren't you?"

"I removed the darkness that covered it. I did not look into his memories."

"You could have, though?"

He turned to meet her eyes. "Yes. But I did not." After a long moment, he leaned his head back against the cardboard and closed his eyes.

"Was it worth it, then? What if we hadn't gotten anything from him?"

"Yes."

She stared at him. "Even if he had no information? How was it worth this?"

"I could give him peace."

In the harsh light of the electric lantern, he should have looked haggard, but she was starting to suspect that was impossible. It caught the grey in his hair and the slow pulse beneath his jaw. Only the slack posture betrayed his weakness.

"So it was altruism?" She raised her eyebrows.

He snorted. "Not entirely. Gabriel is an impetuous child, but he's not without honor. It makes him predictable."

"What?" She sat back to stare at him.

"I bought back his trust. He's a strong ally, but he needed to believe our goals are aligned. An extravagant act was more effective than words."

"So it was an act?"

He gave her a cold look. "No. Act, as in action." After a moment, he let out a soft sigh. "If Gabriel hadn't shot me, it would not have cost so much. I wasn't sure I had completed the task before…" he made a dismissive gesture with one hand. "But Gabriel would protect you. I ensured that before I began." His lips quirked slightly. "I was irritated that he shot me, but it may have been helpful. Guilt is a powerful motivator, and he knows he was wrong."

"How are you now, then? Recovered?" She looked at him skeptically. "What comes next?"

He snorted again. "Not even close. I doubt I could stand right now." He took a deep breath. "I need to speak with him, but after I rest."

"There's dinner for you too." She brought the paper bags closer. "It's been sitting out, not refrigerated. I assume that's not a problem?"

"It doesn't matter."

Niall took the notebook from him and helped him sit up. The boy cut up the pig's hearts and they ate together in silence. Owen stared at the floor, each bite deliberate.

"You think Eastborn should be our first target then?" he asked finally.

Niall nodded.

There was a knock. "Come in!"

Gabriel poked his head cautiously around the door. He considered Owen for a long moment. "We need to talk."

Owen nodded. "Yes. We do." But he did not rise.

Gabriel hesitated, then entered and dropped to sit on the other side of the lantern. "Fine then. Finish eating." His voice was gentler than Aria had heard it before. "How do you feel?"

Owen slanted him a sideways look. "How do you think?"

Gabriel dropped his eyes and waited in silence while they finished.

Niall offered his shoulder to Owen. He leaned hard on it as he stood, blinking dizzily. He nearly fell, and Aria put one hand on his back, but Gabriel moved closer and pulled Owen's arm around his shoulder to support him.

"Come. Others must hear too."

They went again to the alcove. Owen's steps were slow, but he made it to a chair and dropped into it with a sigh. Others filed in and crowded around. There weren't enough chairs for everyone, but Aria and Niall sat on either side of Owen, with Gabriel at the end of the table.

Gabriel spoke without preamble. "Joshua remembered more after he slept. He said that after his tracker was put in, he spent a week in a grey room before reporting for work. Do you know anything about that?"

The image rose in Aria' mind. "I remember a room. I don't know what happened there. I think I got injections." She closed her eyes and pictured it. She hadn't thought about it for years, the memory lost. Now she saw the fresh grey paint, a slight stain on the floor in one corner that might have been blood. A screen at the front. "We watched videos, I think. A lot of videos."

"We?"

"There were about twenty of us in there at the same time. We sat in chairs with our arms and ankles strapped in. It didn't hurt, but we were scared at first. Not at the end though."

"You didn't remember this before?"

151

"No."

Gabriel sighed. "It's not much to go on."

The fierce-looking woman spoke from behind Niall. "So the trackers make people forget? Do they have the technology to affect thoughts and memories that way?"

"No. Not by electronic means." Owen's voice was quiet but sure.

"How do you know?"

"If they could do that, they should be able to detect Fae more easily. The trackers cannot be self-powered; they must be passive. Their scanners have range and can be very precise as far as location, but the trackers aren't much more than product tags. The scanners detect a tracker, not a body. If you don't have a tracker, you're invisible. Only a few secure facilities have the advanced sensors to detect us, and those aren't strictly a technological solution. It shouldn't be that hard, either; just scan for bodies and alarm on the ones that are cold. They have those too, but not everywhere."

Gabriel shot him a sharp look. "Why have you never told us this?"

"I don't recall parting on terms that encouraged me to share information with you." Owen's voice was mild.

Gabriel scowled. "So then what happened in the room? And why the delay? What happened to prompt you to remember?"

Aria answered, "I was arrested and held for several days. No water, hands bound." She took a deep breath. "I'm not the hero sort and it was pretty scary."

Owen said, "She was already troubled by evidence that didn't match her memories. The tracker insertion was associated with these memories, and removing the tracker along with Grenidor's psychological and physiological attack made her more open to reconsidering those memories than she had been before. Then she heard me sing. The song was for healing."

"For her?" Gabriel asked.

"Only later. The first few times were for myself, and after her arrest, the next was for Niall."

"So she benefited by chance?" This from a man standing near the back.

Owen answered, "The song is a tool, not megdhonia itself, but it does carry some power."

Another man spoke from the back. "To clarify, people were detained and received the tracker and a drug cocktail that made them suggestible. Then they were brainwashed while under the influence of drugs?"

There were nods from around the table.

Owen said, "I doubt the cocktail was entirely mundane. They have made more advances in magic in the last ten years than in technology. That could account for the persistent effects."

There was a silence, and Owen added, "There was something in your brain, too. It wasn't doing anything, but I sensed it there. Perhaps it used to affect you."

"What?" Aria's voice cracked. "What are you talking about?"

"I felt it when I removed your tracker. It's inactive. Maybe it's broken."

She remembered the feel of his icy fingers against her scalp that first night under the bridge. "What did it do?"

"I don't know enough to guess. But it wasn't

affecting you. It may have been inactive for years."

Gabriel let out a long, slow breath. "Right, then. Did Joshua have one?"

"No," Owen said.

Silence descended on the table for minutes. Someone whispered to someone else in the back, but no one said anything aloud.

Aria said thoughtfully, "Some people just disappeared."

"Perhaps they couldn't internalize the propaganda they were fed in a way that made sense." Owen answered, his voice so quiet that several people leaned forward to hear him. "Their worldview wasn't malleable enough. They couldn't be manipulated, for whatever reason, so they had to be eliminated."

"So I survived because my mind was weak?" Aria frowned.

Owen smiled slightly. "Call it flexible."

Gabriel leaned forward. "So removing the tracker wouldn't necessarily cause someone to reevaluate the memories. It's more a result of retraumatizing them enough to bring up the memories, and then addressing the brainwashing."

"Perhaps." Owen slumped further in his chair.

"So how does this help us?" Eli asked. "We can't exactly start kidnapping people and removing their trackers, and it sounds like that wouldn't help much anyway."

Gabriel nodded. "And I suspect that if we were the ones to traumatize them, it might be less effective at establishing our position as the good guys."

Owen's lips twitched, as if he wanted to smile. He propped his head on his fist, eyes half-closed. Gabriel glanced at him and frowned. "We'll discuss this more later. Think on our options."

Owen didn't move as they filed out around him, though his eyes drifted closed.

"Are you awake?" Gabriel asked.

He grunted softly.

"You're staying tonight, aren't you?"

He grunted again, an ambiguous sound, but then murmured, "We have more to discuss." He straightened with some effort and fixed his cool blue eyes on Gabriel. "I brought you valuable information. It isn't free."

"I expect not." Gabriel inclined his head.

"I want fifteen of your men with me when I go against the Eastborn Imperial Security Facility next week."

Gabriel grimaced. "Fifteen is a lot."

"If we succeed, it could be important. For both of us."

Gabriel sighed and looked away for a moment, but Owen's eyes did not waver. Finally, he murmured, "You're right. We are stronger together. And I expect your fight and mine are not unconnected."

"Agreed."

DINNER, ANOTHER SILENT MEAL. Aria ate with Gabriel and a different selection of soldiers. *I bet he rotates who he eats with, so no one feels slighted. Savvy, actually.*

"Why didn't any of you ever have trackers?" Aria spoke up tentatively. "I thought everybody got them."

One of the women answered. "We lost the war, but we never conceded. We hid. We didn't know what they were doing, but we knew we wanted no part of it."

Aria frowned at her plate. "I have most of my memories back, I think. There aren't too many empty spots, anyway. But I still don't really remember *why* there was a war. I don't think I ever really understood, even at the time. There was so much propaganda even before the brainwashing, we never really understood which side was which, or what they were fighting about."

Heads turned toward her. "What quadrant were you in?"

"North."

The woman sat back. "Ah."

Aria blinked at her. "What? What does that mean?"

"North Quadrant is the Revolution's home turf. They'd co-opted all the radio and television stations, wi-fi signals, bookstores, everything for quite a while before they made a move openly. You probably got your trackers earlier too."

"Where are we now?"

"East Quadrant. Just barely. But patrols are less frequent here, so it helps. They're still consolidating power."

"So why was there a war?"

"Power. It's always power." The woman took a drink from her canteen. "They wanted the power to tell people whatever they wanted. Arrest and detain people without going through the legal processes, declare war against the Outlanders for no legitimate reason, remake all the infrastructure to their own ends. Medical, legal, political, education, everything. It was like a new regime, except they started before they were held all the power.

We fought back. When people were captured, they disappeared for a time and then reappeared, suddenly compliant. We didn't know why or how, but slowly our efforts fell apart as everyone went along with it."

One of the men said, "The war began before we even realized it. It started slowly. The guns and tanks were desperation near the end, when we'd already lost but we didn't know it yet."

"So you all hid?"

"We haven't given up." Another soldier spoke from across the table.

"Were you all soldiers?"

"No. The soldiers were brainwashed first. A few of us escaped, mostly Special Forces. Tell her." The man gestured.

"I was a journalist."

"Information security."

"Dentist."

"Programmer."

"Orthopedist."

"Middle school teacher."

Aria blinked. They all looked like soldiers now.

GABRIEL LENT HER a book, which she read by the light of the electric lantern. It was easy to lose track of time underground, but she felt tired again quickly. Owen was asleep on the floor, pale and motionless, and Niall had curled up next to him like a forlorn puppy, head nestled against his shoulder.

Aria read the words, but the story was stupid, some crime procedural drivel that meant nothing and didn't hold her interest. Yet the mindless action of reading one word and then the next was soothing, and she put it away with a feeling of gratitude. She remembered none of it, and that was fine. She lay on her back and stared at the wall of cardboard stretching up to the painted ceiling.

Owen sighed softly, the first sound she'd heard from him in hours, and moved his head a fraction of an inch. That was a good sign. More like sleeping, rather than lying half-dead.

She didn't need to sleep again, and the floor felt hard and uncomfortable. But she didn't want to go out into the common area. It was probably night, and they would be sleeping. She turned to lay on her side, eyes drifting closed.

She noticed the movement by the shadow that blocked the lamplight. Owen sat up and put one hand on Niall's shoulder to speak softly into his ear.

"What are you doing?" she asked.

"I heard something. A vertril may have been drawn here. I'm going to check."

He stood and made his way unsteadily to the door. Niall and Aria followed him down the hall.

The theater was lit with numerous lanterns, and most people were up and moving about.

Gabriel waved to them. Owen led the way toward him, and as they approached, Gabriel said, "Something's out there. Big."

Owen nodded. "Give me my swords and I'll handle it."

"You can barely stand. We have guns. Go back to sleep."

"It's a vertril, isn't it?"

"What?"

"Big, wolf-like thing."

"Haven't seen it clearly, but could be. It's trying to break down the door up from the tunnel. We haven't gotten any good shots in. Can't shoot without opening the door. We have a team going around to catch it from the rear."

"Give me my swords. You don't want it to die here. They're tracked too. IPF will come investigate."

Gabriel blinked at him. "What?"

"They hunt us. They have no interest in you. I'll draw it away before I kill it."

Gabriel gazed at him skeptically. "You up for it? We do have guns, let me remind you."

Owen blinked at him slowly. "If you want the IPF on your heads, feel free to handle it yourself. Otherwise, get me my swords."

"Do *you* want a gun then?"

Aria blinked at the offer. Gabriel had shot Owen less than two days ago, and now he was offering to arm him. *That's trusting.*

"No. Vertril are more vulnerable to Fae blades than bullets. A flaw in the design."

Someone came running up. "The door is failing, sir. The team is not yet in position. What defensive measures do you want in here?"

"Get his swords from my office. Immediately."

The man sprinted off.

Gabriel led the way toward the far wall, where an open service door led down a hallway. Eight men were crouched at the far end in defensive positions, staring at a sturdy metal door. Growling sounded from behind it, interspersed with thunderous crashes as the beast threw itself against the door. The bolts for the hinges were sliding back and forth in their holes as the impact crumbled the concrete doorframe.

After another moment, Gabriel handed Owen's sword belt to him. He buckled it on, keeping an eye toward the door. Then he unclasped the scabbard of the larger sword and handed it to Niall with a soft murmur. Niall shook his head, but Owen stared at him a moment and he dropped his eyes.

"Again, I'm trusting you with them, Gabriel." Owen skewered him with a look, and Gabriel nodded.

"Everyone out of the hall except you." Owen pointed at the man closest to the door. "Open the door when I tell you. Don't shoot, just keep out of the way. Close it after I exit."

Gabriel appeared skeptical but nodded to his men to obey. They filed out and closed the lighter service door, then formed a defensive position behind it.

There was a pause, then the far door slammed open with a deafening crack that rang above the hideous growling. A snarl, several heavy thuds, and then silence. After a moment, they heard a knock on the service door. The man closest opened it.

The man on the other side was wide-eyed and slack-jawed. A splatter of blood crossed his face, but he was unharmed. "It's gone," he said at last.

The hallway had two large streaks of blood, and the industrial tile floor was marred by long scratches. The door at the end stood open.

The men closed it silently. Gabriel sent someone in search of heavy objects to barricade the door, and then turned to Aria and Niall.

With forced cheerfulness, he said, "Well, that's

solved then. He'll be back soon, no doubt."

Niall stared at him with tight lips before turning and stalking back to their room. Aria licked her lips and gazed down the hallway at the closed door.

Gabriel considered her. "You know about these vertril? I've never seen one."

"A little. They're scary."


"WHY DID HE leave his sword with you?"

*He said in case it went badly, I'd need a blade.* Niall kept his eyes on the notebook, refusing to look up at her. *I think he should have taken it.*

"I'm sure he'll be fine. He's tough and smart."

*He's only fighting because of me. If he hadn't rescued me, he would have given up.* After a long period of thought, he added, *I did not expect this success with Gabriel. Perhaps there is hope after all.*

"I think he knew exactly what he was doing."

He twisted his mouth in an expression she couldn't read.

Hours passed. Finally even Niall grew tired of their cramped room, and he and Aria wandered out into the theater. Conversations hushed, then slowly resumed. A woman waved to her from a small knot of men and women sitting on the floor near one wall, and Aria led the way toward her.

It was the fierce looking woman Aria had seen earlier. This time she smiled, more friendly. "I'm Evrial. If you want to eat with us, you're welcome to."

"Thanks." Aria tried to smile. "I'm Aria. This is Niall."

"Your friend. He can really handle that thing?"

161

She gazed at Aria with a mixture of skepticism, curiosity, and awe.

Aria forced herself to nod. "He's a little worse for wear right now. But I'm sure he'll be fine."

Niall frowned more deeply. He carried Owen's sword with him, unwilling to put it down, and clutched a notebook under one arm.

"I'm a squad leader for the mission he's leading next week. Do you know what he's planning?" She gestured. "This is my squad. Bartok, Levi, Jenison, and Malachi."

The men all nodded politely, eyeing Aria and Niall with obvious curiosity.

"Not really." She wasn't sure how much she should share. "I assume it's a rescue mission."

Niall wrote quickly and turned the notebook toward Evrial. *We believe Eastborn does not have the advanced sensors to detect our blood. Our chances of success are greater, and if we succeed, it could be important. Also, we have family there.*

Evrial eyed him. "Can you not talk?"

He shook his head but did not explain.

"How many are in the Resistance?" Aria looked around. "This is impressive..." Her voice trailed away. "But the Empire seems really powerful."

"It is," Bartok agreed. He was a little younger than the others, perhaps in his early thirties, his light brown hair prematurely sprinkled with grey. Despite his wiry, athletic figure, his eyes seemed kind and gentle. "We have a safe haven outside the city. A few women and children who escaped the trackers are there. We could take you."

Evrial smiled gently. "What he means is, you don't look like a fighter."

Aria frowned, and Evrial waved a hand dismissively. "Don't be offended. I think we'd all prefer to be back in our old jobs. I was Army, but I was logistical corps. I didn't actually go on ops much."

Levi snorted. "You wouldn't know it. She might have been a drill sergeant in her former life."

Aria smiled. "And what were you?"

"I owned a dry cleaning business." He grinned. "Not too impressive, huh? Compared to these guys, I mean." His wave encompassed Evrial.

"What were you before?" She glanced around the group.

Jenison answered, "A lawyer."

Malachi said, "Management in a small financial firm."

Bartok smiled wryly. "A pediatrician."

"Really?" She eyed him curiously, then bent to whisper in Niall's ear, "Would you show him your mouth?"

Niall shook his head.

"What about you?" Bartok broke the silence.

Aria frowned. "I was a grad student. Studying history. Things didn't line up, and I found a book. It just made me question things."

Evrial sighed. "You don't know how to shoot, do you?"

Aria shook her head.

"If you're going on the mission, you'll need to practice. Better start now." She stood purposefully. "You won't be ready, but if Gabriel says you go, then you go. It's up to him."

The whole squad followed as she led them to

163

the far end of the hall, down a long corridor and into a deeper underground cavern. It had been turned into a training room, with targets stationed at one end backed by thick rolls of carpet scavenged from other areas of the hotel. A jumble of boxes, nets, rolls of carpet, and ropes clogged one corner of the room.

"What's that?"

"An obstacle course. You have to find something in it, or run through it with a piece of chalk and mark all the designated items, or something. Timed. It's an agility exercise, mostly. We do a lot of hand to hand training too, but really, if it comes to that, you've already screwed up."

Evrial and Bartok took charge of Aria's training, beginning with shooting, while Jenison, Malachi, and Levi meandered over to the obstacle course. They put on sound-dampening earmuffs and found a pair that fit Aria. Bartok brought Niall a pair too, which he examined quizzically before slipping them over his head. He settled in a corner with a notebook and the sword across his lap.

Aria focused on the process of shooting. The gun felt heavy and unfamiliar in her hands.

"This is a version of an AR-15. It's semi-automatic, which means it shoots one bullet at a time every time you pull the trigger until you run out of bullets. Aim like this." Evrial demonstrated, bringing her own rifle up to her shoulder. "Line up the sights here and here. Then squeeze the trigger. Don't 'pull' it; everyone says 'pull,' but you really want to use a squeezing motion instead."

Aria went through the motions, putting the gun up to her shoulder and holding the target in her sights. Her arms trembled; and she felt awkward and embarrassed beside Evrial's smooth competency.

The first time she squeezed the trigger, she flinched preemptively. The earmuffs deadened the sound, and the kick was strong but not unmanageable. She frowned down the range at the target. The bullet had left a small hole near the bottom of the outer ring.

"That's not bad, actually. If this is your first time, I'm impressed." Evrial smiled at her encouragingly. "Try again. Don't be afraid of it."

She lined up carefully for each shot. The next five were all in the two innermost circles, an uneven scatter pattern of perhaps four inches.

"That's better." Bartok smiled.

They were patient teachers, and Aria was gratified to find her skill improving. They moved to use a 9mm pistol, which she found more difficult, but Bartok nodded approval at her accuracy.

After an hour, Bartok left the women and sat against the wall by Niall.

He said nothing for some minutes, but finally faced Niall and said, "So you're a Fae, are you?" The sound was barely audible through the earmuffs.

Niall nodded.

"Do you know how to use that?" He indicated the sword.

*Not as well as Lord Owen.*

"Care to demonstrate?"

Niall shrugged but didn't rise. After a moment, he wrote, *For what purpose? Can you teach me?*

Bartok smiled. "I don't know much about swords. I'm a decent shot but that's all. Would you like to try shooting?"

Niall shrugged again, then put the sword and notebook aside and stood. They strode over to the makeshift shooting range. Bartok showed Niall how to check the gun for bullets, how to load it, unload it, sight it, and finally demonstrated how to shoot.

"Here. Start with a solid stance, like this. Brace yourself. It has quite a kick."

Niall sighted down the barrel and squeezed the trigger. Bartok blinked in surprise; the hole was in the dead center of the target.

"Try a couple more."

Niall squeezed off the remaining bullets one after another without pausing. Bartok raised his arm to get Aria and Evrial's attention, then jogged down the range to examine the target. He shook his head and jogged back.

"That's amazing. A half-inch scatter, if not less." He raised his eyebrows at Evrial. "Can you do that? At this distance?"

Evrial looked at Niall. "You've never shot before?"

Niall pantomimed using a rifle, then held up ten fingers, lowered them, then held them up again.

"Twenty times?"

He shook his head.

"Twenty what?" They stared at him, baffled.

Aria guessed. "Twenty years ago?"

He nodded and gave her an appreciative look.

Bartok straightened. "What? You're nine years old! Maybe ten at the most."

He shook his head again and jogged toward his notebook.

Aria said, "Fae age differently. I don't know

much about them yet, but he's actually 78."

They blinked at her incredulously.

*My father said I should know how. He learned with older weapons, where the occasional poor shot was to be expected. He revised his expectations in light of the accuracy of modern guns.*

Bartok blinked at him and let out a soft breath. "I would love to talk to you. I have so many questions."

Niall frowned, and Aria guessed that he wished Owen was back.

She put one hand on his shoulder and said, "He's had a rough time. The Imperial forces had a lot of questions too, and they weren't kind about asking them. I think it would be best not to push him."

Niall looked up at her and nodded. Then he took a deep breath and wrote, *but if my answers can help our mission succeed, I will try.*

Bartok knelt in front of him, and Aria suddenly saw the gentle pediatrician, rather than the soldier. "I don't mean to upset you. I'm curious, but my curiosity can wait. Unlike many of the others, I don't believe all the legends. I'm just interested." He smiled a little, and Niall studied his face for a long moment before giving him a small smile in return. "I'm a doctor, after all. That's what we do. Research."

Niall's face hardened and he turned away with an angry jerk. He pulled the earmuffs off and dropped them on the floor, grabbed Owen's sword, and stalked out the door.

Bartok stared after him, his face stricken.

Aria went after him, nearly running to catch up with Niall's quick steps. "You know he didn't mean it that way."

He did not slow down.

"Where are you going?"

He glared over his shoulder at her.

He paused at the far end of the theater, and Aria stopped at his side and faced him. "What are you doing? Where are you going?"

His mouth was tight, and he glared at her again before finally yanking the notebook out and scribbling, *It has been too long. I am going after Lord Owen.*

"I'm sure he's fine. He would rather you stay here, in safety."

He looked at her scornfully. *There is no safety here for us. If he is hurt, he needs me. I am stronger now and I can help him.*

"Are you?" She tried to keep her voice gentle, reaching for his still-bruised wrist with one hand.

He indicated the sword and raised his chin.

Bartok came jogging up, standing some distance away. "I'm sorry, Niall. I didn't know."

There was a shout from the entrance, and they all turned to look.

Gabriel entered, and behind him came Owen. His eyes caught theirs immediately, and he nodded.

Niall sprinted toward him and stopped suddenly at arm's length. He knelt, bowed his head, and raised the sword in both hands. Owen took it solemnly and clipped the scabbard back onto his belt. Niall rose and bowed, then flung himself at his uncle, wrapping his arms about him, face pressed hard into Owen's chest.

Owen murmured something, and Niall pulled back to grin at him.

"He did it." Evrial had come up behind them, unnoticed.

Aria smiled at Owen too, and stepped closer. "I'm glad you're back. Are you okay?"

"Tired, but yes. I led it on a merry chase for several hours. I killed it close to IPF quadrant headquarters."

Aria noticed now that he had a bloody bandage wrapped around his right thigh. Niall gestured toward it with a questioning look.

"It's not bad," Owen said

Niall pantomimed eating, and Owen smiled slightly. "Yes, please."

Gabriel sent Eli to get food, and Owen limped slowly to the small conference table. Despite his assertion that he was fine, it was obvious his leg was painful. Bartok and Evrial followed, no doubt curious, and Gabriel didn't protest. Owen dropped into a chair and stretched out his leg with a soft grunt. He had blood crusted into his hair near one ear, but there was no visible wound. Niall gestured toward the bandage again, and Owen nodded that he could look.

Bartok also knelt close and turned on an electric lantern. Owen drew his knife and cut the bandage off. Bartok winced in sympathy and started to reach forward to pull the torn fabric of Owen's pants away from the wound, but Niall struck his hand away and shouldered between them.

"Let him see. If they're to help us, they should know, Niall." Owen spoke in English, and he looked down to meet Bartok's eyes. "We are not your enemy. Remember that, though we're different."

Bartok nodded, looking a little confused.

"Agreed."

Niall reluctantly sat back on his heels. Bartok pulled the bloody fabric away from the wound and examined it without touching it. "I need to wash my hands. This isn't sanitary."

"There's no need," Owen said.

Bartok glanced up at him. "You'll need stitches. It's pretty deep. You shouldn't have been walking on it. What happened?"

"I was slow."

"Evrial, would you get the first aid kit? And water?"

"There's no need," Owen repeated. "Just look at it."

"I have."

Niall motioned to Owen hopefully, and Owen studied him for a long moment and then nodded. Niall closed his eyes, one hand on Owen's knee.

*Spring in the forest. Fresh, pale leaves rustled silently in the breeze, dropping their dew. The smell of loam rose, rich and dark. Niall sprinted through the leaves, soundless and light as a deer, laughing. There was music in the leaves, in the sunlight dancing through the waving branches. Silent music.*

"That's enough, Niall."

Bartok sucked in his breath, then leaned forward to pull the fabric aside and peer at the unmarked skin from inches away.

Niall leaned his head against Owen's knee. Owen murmured something to him, and he smiled.

Eli brought a paper bag.

Owen studied Bartok and Evrial in turn, and finally said, "You don't have to watch. But I'm hungry, and it's been a long day already."

170

Bartok stared at him. "Did you do that, or did he?"

"Niall did." Owen reached out to tousle the boy's hair affectionately.

He stared at Owen's leg. "Impossible."

"Improbable. Not impossible."

"But you could have done that too? You're the same kind as he is?" Bartok glanced between them.

"Yes."

"And you limped all the way back here on it because... why?"

"You and the others needed to see."

Niall wrote *Did you discover something? You seem pleased.*

"Yes. I tested the sensors as I ran. I found another facility. It was concealed, and I was unaware of it before. It appeared to have only mundane sensors, perhaps for fear that we can sense the other ones." Owen spread the plastic and cut the pig's heart with quick, efficient strokes. Bartok and Evrial looked on with ill-concealed disgust, but Gabriel had his eyes fixed on Owen's face.

Owen continued, "If we could strike at both within hours, they may not be able to upgrade the sensors in time. I assume the concealment means there is something there they don't want us to find. Perhaps," he hesitated on the phrase, "test subjects. Perhaps something else entirely."

Gabriel stared at him. "That's risky."

With blood on his lips and blue eyes blazing, Owen's smile looked feral. "Yes. It is. Are you afraid, Gabriel?"

Gabriel rubbed his jaw and sat back. He stared at the ceiling and tapped his hands together, and finally said, "You want more men?"

"Twenty-five. Total."

"Why so many?"

"The test subjects will require assistance to flee." Owen's gaze did not leave Gabriel's face.

After a long moment, Gabriel nodded. "Agreed."

Owen smiled again, eyes bright and hard.

# CHAPTER 7

EVERYONE STUDIED the map as Owen drew on it with a stubby grease pencil to outline his plan. It was an old tourism map, thoroughly creased and worn, with tiny holes at the corners of the folds. Gabriel had covered it in packing tape to protect it since maps were hard to come by.

"We'll do this facility on H Street at 10:00 PM. I'll go in first and see what I find. I'll call for Jonah's squad if necessary. Evrial and Geoffrey's squads, Gabriel, Aria, and Niall will provide cover fire from here, here, and here. Dominic and Benjamin's squads should be resting for the mission at Eastborn. I believe, though I cannot be sure, that there are no test subjects held captive here. Other facilities that hold test subjects have non-standard security measures. As far as I know, this facility has only mundane sensors that I can bypass or disable. We will regroup here afterwards and immediately depart for Eastborn.

"The mission at Eastborn will likely be more challenging. It is an extraction effort, not an attempt to destroy the facility. We don't want to kill anyone if we can help it. Most of them are probably brainwashed. But don't let mercy get you in trouble. Niall and Dominic's squad will provide cover fire from here and here. I will enter first, over the wall here. I will radio back the best way in. Jonah, Benjamin, and Evrial will follow with their squads two minutes later. Geoffrey's squad will be split. Two will create some type of diversion here, and the other three will provide cover fire for the rear wall in case the front gate is too heavily guarded. The plan is to go out the front gate, but Geoffrey's squad will have ropes ready in case we need to go over the back wall. Dominic's squad and Niall will move as needed to provide cover as we escape.

"There are sensors here." He marked multiple places on the map, all around the perimeter and several within the complex itself. "They are all mundane. Most of them scan only for trackers, and if you don't have a tracker, you can pass without notice. Some of them are motion sensors. These scan for bodies and will alarm at non-standard body temperature. I can raise my temperature, but not indefinitely, and not without compromising my ability to free the captives. I can also scramble the sensor output, but again, it would compromise my strength too much. I think it best to rely upon speed instead."

Niall waved to get Owen's attention and gestured towards himself. Owen shook his head, but Niall slapped the table and glared at him.

"No, Niall."

Niall wrote furiously in the notebook and turned it toward Owen. Owen straightened and stared at Niall, who glared back at him for a long moment before conceding with a scowl as he dropped his gaze. The humans stared at the map, uncomfortably aware of an argument unfolding that they didn't understand.

Owen spoke again after a moment, his voice even. "The captives are our first priority. They must be freed. Niall will save his strength to ensure that everyone makes it out."

Niall frowned stiffly at the map.

Owen pointed again. "I believe the cells are approximately here, underground. Only the cell blocks have 'magic' sensors and barriers. If we don't find someone with keys on our way in, it may take some time for me to gain entrance. I will need cover in order to focus."

"Could you open the barriers before you go in?" Evrial asked.

"Perhaps. But that will set off alarms as well, and the captives will need our protection as they escape."

Gabriel stared across the table. "What exactly *are* your capabilities, Owen?"

"In what regard?"

"In general. You can disable the alarms from a distance? Could you cause the distraction yourself? Cause an explosion from a distance? Heal? Change memories?"

"Yes."

"Why do you need us?"

"We can do many things, but there are costs. Consequences. Most often they are physical. Given time, I could do a great many things that would surprise you. But I won't have time to rest in the middle of the mission. If I had thirty Fae and sufficient time, we could do almost all of the mission ourselves without leaving this hotel. But I don't." His voice was low and hard.

There was a silence until Gabriel nodded.

Aria asked quietly, "What will I be doing?"

"You will stay behind."

She frowned at him. "I think I could be useful. Apparently I'm a decent shot. And I want to help."

Evrial nodded. "She is good, especially given her inexperience. I'm not sure I'd recommend including her though. If it goes badly, we don't want a rookie panicking."

Aria glared at her as Evrial continued, "I mean no insult, but every squad works together as a team. Inserting someone new into a team right before a mission doesn't typically go well."

Gabriel and the others nodded. Owen studied Aria without expression for long enough that the silence drew out uncomfortably. Aria wanted to fidget, but forced herself to meet Owen's cool blue eyes. Finally he gave a slight nod. "Agreed. You come. You will stay with Niall and provide cover for the front gate."

"When is the mission?"

"Four days. The first one at 10:00 PM, and the second around 1:00 AM, depending on security."

THAT NIGHT, she found herself in the little room with nothing to do before dinner. She'd finished

176

the book Gabriel had loaned her and felt fidgety and nervous. Owen lay on his back with his hands clasped behind his head, staring at the ceiling. His face looked as serene as if he were asleep, though his eyes were open.

"Will you tell me about your people?"

"What about us?" He turned to look at her. His blue eyes on hers made it hard to think straight. Did he know that?

"The Seelie Court and Unseelie Court, for example. I remember the words but I don't remember the legend."

Owen sat up to lean against the wall, legs stretched out in front of him, and gave her a quirky little half-smile. "Those have more to do with human legends than with us. I believe they're a corruption of something a Fae once told a human."

"What is the truth, then?"

"Seelie comes from an Irish word meaning good, and it referred to fairies who meant no harm to humans. Friendly fairies, more or less. The others were dark fairies, malevolent toward humans. In reality, neither type has ever existed as any sort of formal court, or even organized factions. Most of us believe humans and Fae can live at peace." He smiled a little, eyes distant. "Or we used to. As long as we kept to ourselves, the affairs of men had little effect on us. For generations, humans forgot we even existed. That was acceptable. But the technological changes in the last twenty years, and the Empire's interest in us, have made isolation no longer a viable option."

"What about changelings?"

"What about them?"

"Do they exist? Did you ever play pranks like

177

that? Steal human children? Pay a blood tithe to the underworld? Drink blood like a vampire? There are so many legends! Are any of them true?"

Owen raised his eyebrows, and she read amusement in his sidelong glance. "Pranks have been played, yes. I am unaware of any stolen children." His eyes hardened for an instant, and he clarified quietly, "Any stolen *human* children, I mean."

He extended his hand to her, and she looked at it for several seconds before realizing he wanted her to give him the book. He held it a moment then tossed it in the air.

The book became a tiny brown sparrow that fluttered in a spiral, chirping madly, then perched precariously on the vertical edge of the cardboard box next to her ear. Its minuscule claws made scratching sounds as they dug into the cardboard, and it hopped closer. Aria didn't move, barely breathed, as the little bird poked its beak into her hair, hopped onto her shoulder, then her knee, where it turned to face her. It cocked its head to one side, then the other, examining her face with disconcerting intentness.

Aria glanced at Owen, who was watching her with an odd look in his eyes. Her eyes went back to the bird. She couldn't help smiling, and she reached one tentative finger out toward it. It hopped away, but only a few inches, and looked from her to her finger and back again. She could feel the tiny movements of its feet through her pants. She smiled a little more when the bird let her touch its back with her finger, just brushing the dusty brown feathers.

It flew to Owen and alighted on his finger. He

blew at it, and suddenly he was holding her book, which he extended back to her.

She blinked at him incredulously. "Was the bird real, or an illusion?"

"It was real."

"Where did the book go?"

"It was in the bird." He smiled enigmatically.

"Then where did the bird go?"

"It's there. In the book." He smiled a little more, and she suspected his smile was more at her look of consternation than at his own magic.

"I gather that wasn't as taxing as healing?"

"No."

"Blood tithe?" she raised her eyebrows.

"Fool's talk. What underworld do they mean? Hell? Tartaros? Mag Mell? What would the denizens want with a blood tithe, and what use is blood if it doesn't come from those being taxed?"

"Is it strange to live so long?"

He blinked at her slowly, as if he found the question puzzling. "Strange to whom?"

She suddenly felt childish, but came up with another question. "Can you heal humans, or only Fae?"

"Humans can be healed, but it is much more tiring. Your bodies flirt so closely with death, it is difficult to keep it at bay long enough to heal you."

"Why did you want to wait four more days for the mission? I thought you'd be in a hurry."

"I will need all my strength. I'm still tired."

She studied his face in the lamplight. "Does it bother you to wait?"

He drew his swords out of their scabbards and laid them on the floor, then pulled a small, flat stone from his rucksack and began to sharpen the larger sword with long, deliberate strokes. It made a soft, rasping sound that somehow seemed primeval, at odds with the electric lantern.

He was silent for so long that she thought he might not answer, and when he did, his voice was soft. "Yes. But if I act before I am capable, it will gain them nothing, and may cost them much."

She licked her lips and wished she knew how to be comforting. She'd never been good at it, and she didn't know Owen well enough to offer reassurance. He continued sharpening the sword, movements precise and methodical.

Aria offered another question, one she hoped would distract him from unpleasant thoughts. "What makes Fae blades so special?"

He nodded toward the shorter sword. "See if you can feel the difference."

She wrapped her hand around the hilt and lifted carefully. It was heavier than she'd expected, but then she'd never held any other sword for comparison. The metal caught the light, and she ran her finger along one smooth side, avoiding the razor sharp edge. The hilt was forged metal, subtly textured by regular hammer strokes in a repeating pattern. She imagined that it might become slippery with sweat, but Fae didn't seem to sweat as humans did. The guard was a practical crossbar, though it appeared etched or engraved with an ornate pattern on each side. She leaned down to study it; it might have been writing of some Fae dialect, or possibly only a complicated series of swirls and knots and spirals.

"I don't know anything about swords," she said finally. "But it's beautiful."

He glanced up at her as if surprised. "You

think so?"

She nodded. "Is this writing? What does it say?"

He smiled slightly, looking back down at the blade in his hands. "It is an inscription of protection and honor. My great grandfather made it as a child. The blade is quite good, but he had not come into his own as a craftsman when he made it. My father was surprised when I chose it above the others he offered."

Aria sighed and sat back. What would it be like to have history like that? Even now, with her memories back, she didn't feel that sense of belonging. Her mother was a mass of disjointed memories, words, feelings. Baking cookies. An argument. The soft feel of her arms embracing Aria after a skinned knee. Her father, the memories more distant somehow. His laughter. His kindness.

Owen seemed grounded in a way she could only envy.

"You threatened to tell Petro that Dandra didn't get the maps for you. Who is Petro?"

"Don't ask questions you don't want to know the answer to."

"I do want to know."

She stared at him, and he sighed again. "I am not permitted to lie. But you might prefer if I did. Retract your question."

"No." She held his eyes.

His jaw tightened. "Petro is dangerous. I have approached him for information when desperate, but it is a last resort. He does not like to be wrong. When I asked him, he told me that Dandra could get the maps. I doubt Petro lied; that means she didn't tell me the truth. I didn't tell him about her failure." He took a deep breath and let it out slowly. "I was angry, but I am not that cruel. A human should not face Petro's wrath."

"Is he human?"

"No."

"Fae?"

"No."

"Then what is he?"

He stared at her, expression unreadable. "You ask a lot of questions."

"You've told me that before." She smiled at him, hoping for a smile in return, but he merely stared at her as if puzzled.

"Some things shouldn't be questioned. Some answers should not be known."


THE DAYS BEFORE the mission went slowly for Aria. Her stomach constantly churned with nerves. She practiced shooting under Bartok and Evrial's instruction, but then stopped because Evrial said they needed to conserve ammunition. She didn't know how she felt about shooting someone. Causing death. Bartok and Evrial were grim too, and she wondered whether they were as tense as she was.

Owen fought another vertril the morning of their mission, leading it on a long chase before he killed it. He slipped back into the hotel by the tunnel entrance, and Aria felt her shoulders relax when he said none of the blood that streaked his clothes was his.

They ate lunch in their room, and she asked him, "Why did the vertril injure you the first day, but sometimes you seem to have no problem with them?"

"It caught me in the hallway, pinned me against the wall. It's much better to fight in an open space, where I can move and dodge. I was distracted and didn't get into the open in time."

She swallowed, trying not to imagine how terrifying it must have been. "Why were you distracted?"

He raised one eyebrow and stared at her for a long moment.

"I'm sorry."

He smiled, amused by her discomfort. "I should have been paying better attention."

*He said they were tracked, that the IPF would know if they got too excited.* "Why hasn't the IPF found us here? The vertril keep coming."

He gave her another faint, sideways smile. "The vertril are excited when they find that Niall and I are here. I have to make sure they are more excited as they chase me, so the IPF doesn't pinpoint this location."

"You mean you tease them?" *Now that would be terrifying.*

He nodded. "You could say that."

Aria licked her lips. "Why did you decide to let me go tonight? I'm glad you did, but what made you change your mind?"

"I remembered something." He studied her face. "Why did you keep following me?"

*Remembered what?* She shrugged. "I'm curious." She wanted to add, *and you're interesting*, but flushed with embarrassment and stifled the impulse. He'd never looked at her with anything that could possibly be construed as that sort of interest, even when Margot had prompted him.

She blushed even more when she realized his eyes were still on her. His lips quirked in a faint smile as he returned to his lunch.

Her embarrassment turned to irritation, and she scowled at his black curls. "You know, it's not polite to laugh at people."

He blinked at her innocently when he looked up. "Was I?"

She scowled even more as she looked down, feeling his eyes still on her flushed face. Was he embarrassed? At his own rudeness or on her behalf? She didn't feel any censure in his gaze, but neither did she want to look up to try to decipher his expression. He surely read much more in her face than she did in his.

His quiet kindness, his courage, and the ferocity of his love for Niall tugged at her heart. But just because she had begun to care for him did not mean he felt anything in return. She told herself it was foolish. His expressions were human, the quirky smiles that made her heart beat faster. She assumed they meant what they would mean if he were human. But he was *not* human, and it was easy to forget that.

She felt her heart thudding as he continued to study the top of her head.

After a long silence, he said softly, "I'm sorry. I didn't realize."

She glanced up to see his eyes still on her, more serious now. She shrugged awkwardly. "It's my fault. I'm sorry. I'm just irritable. Because I'm nervous." She swallowed and tried to smile. *Play it off. Just because you have a crush doesn't mean he needs to know it. Don't be stupid, Aria.*

His eyes rested on her face, and she had the

184

disconcerting feeling that he understood everything. Then he smiled and said, "First missions are always nerve-wracking. I like to think of all the possibilities and how I will deal with them. But if that makes you nervous, think only of your part and how your courage will enable the mission to succeed."

She looked down again. "Thank you." *For pretending you didn't just watch me embarrass myself.*

# CHAPTER 8

Owen, Gabriel, Aria, Niall, Geoffrey, and Jonah's entire squad wore tiny wireless headsets with microphones that pressed against their throats. Designed for the military back before the Revolution, they still worked flawlessly, but there weren't enough for everyone. They'd tested the headsets that morning and decided on codes. One click of the tongue for yes, two for no, at least when silence was an issue.

The resistance forces had fourteen bulletproof vests. For the first mission, everyone wore a vest except a few of those providing cover fire.

"Do you have a video camera?" Owen asked.

Gabriel and Eli looked at each other. "Yes. Somewhere." Eli found it, an old digital model, with only a few hours of video capability. "It's not much good in the dark. At all."

Owen shrugged. "I'll take a penlight and see what I can get."

The target building was innocuous, more like an office building than a military facility. Aria didn't know what they expected to find inside. The squads spread out to cover each corner of the building. It wasn't large, just one corner of a city block, bordered by trash-strewn alleys to the rear that separated it from the other buildings on the block. The building was older, the concrete facade slightly worn, but not enough to stand out on this street. The windows on the first floor had all been bricked up, but that might have been an older modification. The main door showed faint lines of metal wiring crisscrossing inside the thick glass panes. Despite the protective measures, the inside of the well-lighted lobby was visible to Aria and the others standing outside.

It was clear the building was secure, but it could have been anything from a corporate head-quarters to a bank. Nothing about it was obviously military. The armed guards carried law-enforcement issue pistols and the reception area had metal detectors in front of heavy metal doors. No insignia or logos marked the doors or reception desk. The guards were alert but relaxed, and Aria imagined they were used to long, uneventful night shifts.

Owen stayed some distance back from the building while they got in position. He slipped into the alley and they heard nothing for several minutes.

"Going in a third floor window." His murmur

would have been inaudible to someone standing in front of him, but the microphone picked it up.

Silence.

"Desks. Papers."

Silence.

The silence dragged on so long that Aria would have been worried, except that she could see Gabriel's face beside her. He seemed content to let Owen work without prompting him for a status update yet.

"First floor now," Owen said.

Silence for long minutes.

"Do you want us to come in?" Jonah asked.

"No."

More silence.

The guards chatted with each other. One of them pointed to something behind the desk, and Aria wondered if they had monitors back there, with a video feed of whatever Owen was doing. But what they saw didn't alarm them, and they went back to their discussion. She breathed a sigh of relief, then winced when she heard it over the headset. Everyone else was silent and professional.

"Going to the basement."

After another long silence, Gabriel asked, "Are you finding anything?"

Owen did not answer immediately. "Yes," he said finally. "Is it advantageous or disadvantageous to leave evidence of an intrusion?"

Gabriel's lips flattened as he thought. "What sort of evidence?"

Silence.

"Owen?"

A slight crackle in the microphone. "I'm three floors down now. Reception is spotty. Opinions on evidence?"

"What sort of evidence?"

"Missing hard drives. Dead vertril. Chemical spills."

Gabriel said finally, "Do as you think best."

"Understood." Then, "Losing reception. Remain in place."

It was nearly an hour later before they heard, "All clear. Mission complete."

He met them at the hotel with his rucksack slung over his shoulder, splattered with blood.

"You look gruesome." Aria grimaced at him. "Are you hurt?"

"No."

Inside, he emptied his rucksack on the conference table. Eight removable hard drives, a handful of folders filled with papers, and the digital camera. Then a larger bundle that had filled the rest of his pack. "We can analyze it later. We need to go. It's late." He jogged to his room and reappeared a moment later in a clean shirt. His face was still streaked with blood, and he accepted Aria's offer of a water bottle. He splashed water into his hands and on his face, scrubbed quickly and wiped it off, letting the water fall to the floor.

He spoke while he cleaned up. "The camera is full but I don't know how much you'll be able to see. The basement is huge, the whole city block. I didn't explore all of it, but I got enough. The first basement floor is secure; most of the hard drives came from there. Possibly some sort of planning and intelligence center, lots of computers, conference rooms, secure video links. The second floor down had the chemical work; a number of labs."

He set the water bottle aside and untied the

bundle to reveal a number of glass jars tied together so they wouldn't clank or break. "They're labelled, but I don't know what they do. The names aren't familiar. These three have some non-standard chemical structure. I'll be able to decipher some of their properties, but it will take time. I'd need to study more about human biology before I could guess what they would be used for. These others are mundane, but again, I don't know what they do. If you have a pharmacist among you, you might be able to figure it out, but I assume these are custom-made cocktails so it may not be obvious.

"The third floor underground had a number of vertril of various ages. I killed them. This drive came from a computer on that floor; I'm hoping it contains documentation on them. That floor also connected directly to the sewer and underground rail tunnels."

Gabriel gaped at him. "That's amazing. And I thought windows in the secure buildings didn't open."

"They don't." At Gabriel's perplexed stare, Owen added, "I took it out of the frame. I put it back when I left, but given the other destruction, that was probably unnecessary. At least they won't know how I got in."

Gabriel let out a long, slow breath. "We have much to do."

"Not now. We need to go. If they've discovered the intrusion, the other facilities will heighten their security."

"I don't think they noticed." Gabriel frowned. "How did you do that, by the way?"

"Disabled motion sensors and proximity

alarms. But at least some of the vertril had already been tagged. The tags report on their health, heart rate and such, at intervals. If they haven't already alarmed, they will soon."

Gabriel nodded. "Understood. Ready when you are."

THE SECOND MISSION had Aria's heart in her throat before they even departed.

Owen, Aria, and the squad leaders wore the headsets. The fourteen bulletproof vests outfitted everyone going into the facility except Owen and Jonah. Those providing cover from the walls would go without.

Evrial tried to give Jonah hers, but he flatly refused to take a vest while a woman didn't have one. "The answer is no, Evrial. I know you're a better shot than I am, and it doesn't matter. The answer is still no."

Gabriel silenced them with a look. "We have a few night vision scopes too. Dominic, Geoffrey, and I will take those, unless you want one, Owen."

"No." Owen shook his head.

They made their way to the Eastborn Imperial Security Facility by squads. Owen guided Niall and Aria through the tunnels; the Fae didn't seem to need night vision, and they made no noise as they slipped through the darkness. They climbed a ladder and emerged into a side street, where they kept to the shadows, moving through deserted alleys and darkened commercial zones. Once Aria stopped walking completely, lost in the black night. A moment later Niall's cool hand slipped into hers and drew her forward, around a corner, to where the faint starlight illuminated the alley enough for her to follow Owen again.

They reached the facility, though Aria could see little. All the lights were trained inward and outside the massive wall the shadows were dark.

Owen left her and Niall for some minutes, then came back and murmured, "I disabled the motion sensor at the top of the wall. I'll help you up."

He'd also secured a rope to the top edge of the wall with an eyebolt, which he used to climb up. Aria followed him with some difficulty, and he leaned down to haul her up by one arm.

"Stand here." He'd tied another rope about two and a half feet below the top edge of the wall between two eyebolts four feet apart. Niall followed her, and she felt the rope shift beneath her under his slight weight. It was tight, but with both of them on it, they sagged to the middle. She put her left foot on the eyebolt near her for stability. Owen slithered onto the top of the wall, where he lay motionless. "Can you shoot from here?" He leaned down to whisper the question between them, nearly inaudible.

She nodded and glanced at Niall. The wall was wide enough that he had to stretch to see the ground inside, but he nodded as well. The boy appeared as cool and unworried as Owen did, but Aria felt her heart pounding. The gun felt heavy, the holster dragging at her belt.

Owen murmured so softly she heard him more clearly through the headset than through the air. "The front gate guards have not been alerted."

Clicks told her that the others heard.

"Were these already here?" she mouthed to Niall.

He shook his head, pointed to Owen, and mimed screwing the bolts into the concrete.

"By *hand*?"

He nodded.

Owen waited another few minutes. "In position?" he asked finally. He looked down and nodded to them, then slithered off the far edge of the wall. He dropped to the ground thirty feet below in a soundless crouch and paused a moment.

The inside of the complex was lit by spotlights mounted on the walls and the corners of each building. Aria thought he looked painfully exposed in the harsh light. No alarm sounded though, and Owen crossed the two hundred feet to the nearest building in moments.

He slipped along the wall, a silent shadow, until he reached a utility door. It had no outside handle, but he leaned against it for a moment and then opened it. He reached up to the top of the frame and fiddled for a moment, then disappeared, leaving the door cracked behind him. Still no alarm sounded, and Aria glanced toward the front gate again. She couldn't see the guards from her position, but she would see if they moved into the facility or if the gate moved.

She held her gun tightly, her hands sweaty despite the chill. Her eyes scanned the open space.

In her ear, Owen's voice came through the headset. "Teams in now, over the wall. The door is open. Down the hall, left at the end, down the stairs, right to the end of the corridor. I'll meet you."

Aria glanced to her right. The three teams, fifteen people, rappelled down the wall and streaked across the grass without a sound. She looked back to the front gate. Nothing stirred yet.

Silence for some moments, then Owen said softly, "This is where the alarms start. From here we have three or four minutes at most. Your only concern is getting the prisoners out. I'll handle the rest."

A moment later, Aria winced at the deafening wail of an alarm that blared through the headset. On the outside of the building, floodlights flared to life along every wall, and through the second floor windows strobe lights pulsed red and white.

Aria and Niall kept their guns trained on the guards now visible at the front gate. They didn't move from the gate, though they glanced back at the buildings. Obviously they'd been trained to hold their positions regardless of distractions.

An explosion sounded from a distant corner of the complex. "Distraction one is in progress," Geoffrey's voice said through the headset. "Guards arriving in minutes. How is the front gate?"

"Guards holding their positions," said Dominic. His squad was on the other side of the gate.

Niall motioned to her and she spoke into the headpiece as she figured out what he was saying. "Niall will take care of the guards. Don't shoot yet." She stared at him, trying to read his pale face in the shadows. "Really? Can you do that?"

He nodded. He wore Owen's swords, but she knew he didn't intend to use them. He clicked the safety on his pistol back on, leaped from the rope and disappeared into the shadows without a sound.

A few moments later, she saw a guard disappear. One moment he was there, at the edge of the spotlight, and the next he was gone. Another guard looked for him, stepped closer to the darkness, head raised in curiosity but not worry. That time she saw a small shadow leap at his back, and then he was down, flat on the ground with Niall's skinny body crouched over him. He dragged the guard into the darkness before the two remaining guards noticed.

Aria looked back at the building. The alarm still blared through the headset; it must be deafening inside the building. She heard a dull clank, then Owen's voice.

"El forgive them." He was breathless, though she couldn't decipher whether it was with exertion or emotion. The words made her throat tighten; what horror had he seen to provoke that response?

A sudden crack nearly burst her eardrums, and Aria cried out, jerking off the headset. A moment later she struggled to put it back on, eyes flicking between the building and the front gate. All the guards were gone now, pulled out of sight, and Niall stepped into the light for a brief moment and waved.

"Front gate is open," Dominic said before she could react. "No thanks to our team," he added.

Evrial's voice came over the headset for the first time. "We've encountered some difficulties here but should be out—" a burst of gunfire cut off her last words.

Silence, then several quick shots. "Still coming. Three guards down."

Aria could hear them breathing hard now, and several sets of pounding feet. "Yes," to some question she hadn't heard.

"Clear to exit?"

"Yes."

The door opened and figures streamed across the grass. Harsh white floodlights made the long dash to the front gate painfully exposed, and Aria held her breath as she scanned for threats. She couldn't identify all the figures, but she saw Evrial with a small form over her shoulders, perhaps a child. The others hauled adults with arms slung across their shoulders, the Fae staggering, stumbling alongside the humans.

She didn't see Owen.

"Going back in." Jonah's voice came over the headset, breathless. He'd been one of the first out and she saw him sprinting back to the door, another three men following close behind.

"Going home. Have twelve Fae. We're slow but we can make it. Bartok is staying to help the next group." That was Evrial's voice.

"Understood," Owen said. "Thank you."

Another burst of gunfire from inside the building, longer this time.

"Benjamin's squad is coming out. Cover now." Owen said, his voice composed.

"Time is short. Where are you, Owen?" Gabriel said.

A group of soldiers sprinted around the corner and Aria's heart dropped into her stomach.

The gunfire was even more terrifying as the shots rang out in the cold air rather than only through her headset. Dominic's squad fired at them, and one dropped, but the others found cover in the recessed doorway and began to fire on Benjamin's squad and the Fae they were helping across the lawn.

One of them fell; Aria couldn't tell who, but he

lay there for a long moment unmoving. The Fae sprawled across him didn't move either.

Aria's nerves abruptly stilled as she lined up her shot. The soldiers had cover from Dominic's squad, but she could see them clearly from her vantage point.

One.

Two.

She aimed for their heads, as Evrial had taught her. They were wearing body armor, and a body shot might not even incapacitate them.

Her heart pounded, her throat tight with fear. She could feel herself shaking, but her shots were good. She would deal with the horror of killing later.

The fallen human, whoever it was, twitched. She shot again, though she didn't have a clear shot at the soldier she was aiming for. At least she could make him keep his head down. The man staggered to his feet and dragged the Fae with him in a stumbling run toward the gate. Niall darted forward and all three made it into the sheltering darkness.

"Owen, where are you?" Gabriel's voice came again. "Get out of there. More coming."

"Lots more." Dominic's voice sounded strained.

A loud clang sounded, and Aria looked back at the front gate. Between the front guard post and the rear section, a metal wall had materialized.

Dominic cursed. "Front gate is out of commission. Repeat, front gate out. Go to the back."

Aria stared at the gate. Thirty feet high, the metal gate looked heavy enough to withstand a bomb attack. "Where did that come from?" she breathed.

"Later." Dominic's answer was terse, but she hadn't expected an answer at all. "Moving to the back wall."

Aria debated, but decided she'd be of little use on the ground in the back, unable to see or shoot. Instead, she clambered onto the top of the wall, scraping her stomach and arms in the process. Owen had made it look easy, but she felt clumsy and exposed. On her hands and knees, she hurried toward the rear of the compound.

Jonah's voice came over the headset. "My squad is heading to the back wall. We'll need help getting up the ropes."

"Understood." Gabriel and Geoffrey said together.

Aria continued crawling. More gunfire crackled over the headset. Was anyone hurt?

Owen's voice finally came. "Three down inside. Need assistance at the back door."

Aria didn't know what she could do, and she didn't have a vest. Should she go?

"Assistance coming," Gabriel said.

The lights were brighter here, even more floodlights flaring out across the lawn and edging the concrete wall. Crawling was terribly slow, and she rose to a crouch and ran. The height made her nervous, but her heart was already pounding so loudly that she ignored the trembling in her knees in favor of reaching the back wall sooner.

A door she hadn't seen before opened and figures streamed out. She couldn't identify all of them, but she saw Owen's lean form, without a vest, sprinting across the lawn with someone in his arms.

Gunfire cracked again, but she couldn't see where it came from.

Inside?

Geoffrey's team was hauling both Fae and teammates across the lawn. Aria saw a muzzle flash at a second floor window and sighted toward it. She couldn't actually see her target, but she shot anyway.

Owen disappeared back into the building. "Niall, heal the humans. Bartok first." He was breathing heavily. *Is he injured too?*

Aria reached Gabriel and Geoffrey's squad ranged along the top of the back wall. Gabriel was closest to her; he whipped his pistol up at her face before he recognized her.

Niall was already below her on the ground, bent over Bartok's limp form.

Inside, more guns roared. "Owen, where *are* you?" Gabriel barked.

"Coming." His microphone crackled, and she heard him grunt.

"Squad leaders, check in."

"A all clear except Bartok." Evrial's voice.

"B all clear. Bartok clear." Geoffrey's voice.

Another figure hurried across the lawn, a limp form slung across its shoulders in a dead man's carry. Just to the right of Aria, Gabriel crawled halfway down a rope ladder to help them up.

"This is Jonah. I think C squad is all clear except for me."

"Confirmed."

Silence.

"D squad? Call in."

Silence.

"All clear. Benjamin is injured but he'll live."

Geoffrey's voice again.

"E all clear."

Gabriel's voice again. "Geoffrey, Dominic, Niall, and I will stay to provide cover. Everyone else mission over, retreat safely. "

Aria didn't move. Niall had scaled the wall somehow and was perched between Geoffrey and Gabriel, pistol ready. The door cracked open again.

An explosion boomed from behind the door, blasting it open with a flash of fire and smoke. Aria couldn't see inside the smoke-filled hallway, but the glow told her fire still burned.

"Need help just inside the door." Owen's voice was cool. "Niall, not you."

"I'm coming." Aria didn't have time to think. Gabriel was helping someone else up the rope ladder, and Dominic and Geoffrey were farther away. She slid down a rope and sprinted across the grass toward the door.

"No, Aria. You don't have a vest. Get back."

She was already nearly to the door, and she pulled her shirt over her face as she stepped inside. The hot smoky air burned in her throat, and she squinted to see Owen kneeling beside Jonah. Gunshots sounded in the corridor, and she dropped to her stomach beside them.

Jonah struggled to sit up, his chest covered in blood. "What happened?" he croaked. He felt his chest and stared at Owen.

Gabriel's voice from the headset shouted, "Get out!"

Jonah got to his knees, swaying unsteadily, and Aria realized another figure was slumped beside him. A Fae woman, pale, slim, and beautiful. Her eyes were closed, and blood streaked her clothes. Owen turned to shoot twice through the smoke, then put his hand on her shoulder. She blinked.

"Niamh, you can walk? Get out. All of you."

The woman's eyes focused on Owen with sudden intensity. "You can't go back."

"Get out!" Owen snarled at her. He rose and sprinted back into the smoke-filled hallway.

Aria heard distant shouts. Soldiers.

The woman pushed herself up the wall, barely able to stand. She glanced at the door, then back down the hallway where Owen had disappeared.

"Come. He'll be out in a minute." Jonah pulled her arm. "We need to leave."

She resisted for a moment, but then swayed, near fainting. Jonah pulled her arm over his shoulders and half-carried her out the door, stumbling himself.

Aria watched them until they reached the wall, then turned her attention back to the corridor. A click above her startled her so badly she nearly dropped the gun. Suddenly water rained down on her, and she realized the explosions had set off the fire suppression system. The water was icy, and in moments she was drenched, her sweater heavy as it sucked the warmth from her. It dissipated the smoke, but she couldn't see much through the spraying water. The headset didn't seem affected, but she wasn't sure what effect it would have on her gun.

She couldn't leave, not while Owen was still inside. "I'm still here," she murmured into the headset. "Is everyone else out?"

After a long moment, she heard Gabriel answer, "Yes." She heard grunts and strained breaths

201

as they hauled bodies up the rope ladder. Then Gabriel again, "Get them away. The farther away they are, the better."

An explosion sounded again, just around the intersection in the hallway, and a storm of bullets tore holes in the wall at the end. Aria could barely hear the crackle of the headset over the pounding of her heart, but she stayed in place, pistol trained toward the end of the hall, and Aria waited for Owen to confirm that he was still alive.

Silence.

Then he materialized out of the smoke and water-filled chaos, half-dragging a young man. A Fae.

"Get out, Aria. Run." He stumbled and fell to his knees, the Fae on his back nearly tumbling off. He turned and shot again, then stuffed the gun in his belt. He remained on hands and knees for a long moment, chest heaving. She could hear his breaths beside her and also through the headset, creating a disorienting stereo as she watched him. He was covered in blood; it was hard to see against his black shirt, but the water dripped down his arms in crimson streaks. His black curls were plastered to his head. He'd been shot. She didn't want to count how many times. Five? Six?

"Take him to the wall. I'll follow you."

She struggled to lift the heavier Fae. He was younger than Owen and terribly thin, but still heavier than she was. She got one of his lean arms across her shoulders and wrapped her other arm around his bony hip by the time Owen pushed himself to his feet.

"Can you make it?" Owen asked. "I'll help you."

"Yes."

"Go." He carried most of the young Fae's weight, matching her step for step.

Gunshots cracked behind them, but for a moment Aria thought they might make it.

Then she was facedown in the grass, unable to breathe for the shocking pain.

*I've been shot. So this is what it feels like when you die. I thought it would be peaceful, but it's not at all. Feels like a hot poker.*

She felt cool hands on her back and shoulder, and the pain lessened. Owen.

He lifted her and sprinted. "Need a rope in the corner." Blood from his chest smeared her face.

"Got it."

Gunshots. He stumbled, then leapt upward, grabbing the rope with one hand even as he shifted her to lean against his shoulder. The wall was nearly thirty feet high, and he climbed hand over hand, one foot braced against each wall. Aria jostled against him, too weak to help, too aware to not be terrified. Searchlights flared, sweeping across the wall toward them

More gunshots. Owen grunted and faltered for a moment, grip slipping, before surging upward again. "Gabriel, catch her."

"Coming."

Gabriel caught her arm with one strong hand and hauled her upward, his fingers digging into her bicep.

Owen's voice in the headset. "Everyone get out."

The searchlights found them, and guns roared.

From the corner of her eye she saw Owen fall. His hand brushed against her shoe.

He sprawled motionless on the ground, pale
203

face turned upward.

"You have to get him!" Her voice rose in panic.

More gunfire. His body jerked.

Gabriel pulled her backward and forced her down the rope ladder on the outside of the wall, hand on her shoulder. His voice was in her ears, through the headset and in her other ear as he bent close, running beside her. "We can't do anything. He wants you away."

She strained to hear through in the headset, anything that would let her know he was alive. Gunshots. Muffled shouting. A crunch, then silence.

Gabriel kept one hand firm on her upper arm as he dragged her away. He pulled off her headset and took off his own as well. Aria shuddered, weeping, unaware of the tears streaking down her cheeks.

# CHAPTER 9

THE CONFERENCE ROOM was too small for the group, so they were ranged in rows in the old theater, seated on the cool concrete floor. Aria was in shock, trying to listen. *Remember their names.*

Owen's figure wouldn't leave her mind. Bloodied and motionless, he'd lain there, helpless, while she and the others fled to safety. It was wrong. Her heart cried out against it. He'd healed her with the strength he should have used to flee. Healed the Fae woman. Healed Jonah. He'd told her to go and she'd refused, trying to be helpful. Heroic. And then she'd been shot, and he'd chosen to save her life.

*He chose to. He had a choice,* she reminded herself. *But he didn't. Knowing him, he* didn't *have a choice.*

Niall had healed her completely once they'd retreated to the relative safety of the hotel. The wounds had still been bleeding when Gabriel had pulled her away, but they were superficial, hardly life-threatening. Niall's additional healing had left her with smooth, unmarked skin and no pain, except for that in her heart. He'd completed Jonah's healing as well. Owen had been desperate, giving them enough to escape, saving his strength for the next emergency.

He'd been wise. Everyone but him had made it out.

The Fae sat in a silent group to one side, with the humans facing them. Gabriel and Aria sat in what might have been the heads of the table, if a table had been between them. Niall sat between the Fae woman and Aria, a wordless, trembling bridge between them.

Gabriel spoke quietly, but in the silence his voice carried. "We have little knowledge of Fae. I can plead only ignorance in the face of your accusations. We have never been friendly, I admit it, but we had no knowledge of their crimes and we do not condone them. Your cause is just."

The Fae stared at him coolly without speaking. Finally one said, "Who are you?"

Gabriel smiled tightly, "My name is Gabriel. We are the human resistance against the Empire. We have our own grievances, and our causes align. We did not realize it at first, but we understand more now."

Niamh's eyes flicked to Aria. "Who is she?"

"I'm Aria." She tried to smile, but felt tears spring in her eyes.

Niamh stared at her, watched her as she

brushed unsuccessfully at them.

"Owen was captured because of you." The words were soft, with a tone of both accusation and interest. "And Cillian saved."

Aria swallowed.

The young Fae was Cillian, Owen's younger brother? No wonder he'd been unwilling to leave him behind.

Cillian leaned forward with his elbows on his knees, his blue eyes on her face so intently that she dropped her gaze. He said something in Fae that might have been a question, and Niamh answered just as softly. They sounded perplexed.

Niamh said finally, "We thank you for your efforts on our behalf. We will move on when we have the strength. Tomorrow, perhaps. In the meantime, Cillian will kill any vertril that become a problem." Her tone was one of dismissal. The Fae rose as one, graceful despite their obvious weakness, and retreated to their rooms. Niall motioned to Aria to accompany them, but when Gabriel started to follow, Niall gave him a cool look and shook his head. He was not invited.

The Fae were already seated in a rough circle when she slipped into the room. Several lamps turned down low set on boxes in the corners provided uneven lighting that made it even more difficult to read their expressions.

Niamh motioned to the floor across from her and Aria sat, trying not to feel nervous.

"Niall said you went to help Owen at the end of the fight. Why?" her voice was clear, but softer than it had been in the theater.

"He requested help, and I was closest." Aria swallowed.

"You had no bulletproof vest like the other humans."

"Jonah didn't have one either."

Niamh blinked slowly at her, as if her words had not answered the question. Her blue eyes were as cold and clear as Owen's. Abruptly she said, "He's my younger brother."

Aria blinked. "You're Niall's mother?"

Niamh nodded once, eyes on Aria's face.

Niall had been writing in the notebook and he turned it around so his mother could see. She read, eyes skimming the whole page, and then looked up at Aria again. "Owen has never traded upon his looks, and I doubt he did so with you. If anything, he conceals his beauty, and he is skilled at remaining unnoticed. Why then did you continue following him?"

Aria blinked. "I was curious, I guess. He was acting strangely. He wasn't wearing shoes, and it's freezing outside."

Niamh tilted her head to one side. "You should not have noticed that."

Aria frowned. "I don't understand."

Niamh stared at her for another long moment, then shook her head. "Most humans wouldn't notice, even when we're right in front of them. Perhaps you have some Fae blood in you, however slight." She reached over to draw Owen's sword from the belt that Niall wore. "May I?"

Aria eyed it. "What are you going to do?"

"A small cut only."

"I suppose." Aria held out her hand, trembling a little. Niamh's hand was cool on hers, and she touched Aria's fingertip to the blade gently. Aria winced, but almost smiled at herself; she'd had worse paper cuts. Niamh squeezed the end of Aria's finger to produce a single drop of blood. Then she leaned forward and sucked the blood from Aria's finger.

Aria jerked her hand away. "Ew!" The sensation was bizarre, discomfiting. Personal, invasive, almost erotic in a horrifying way.

Niamh blinked at her with the same faint amusement Aria had seen in Owen's eyes. Then her expression changed. "Hm."

"Hm what?"

She spoke in Fae for a moment, studying Aria with renewed interest. Cillian continued to stare at her, and after a long moment, he answered in the same language.

"What?" Aria asked again.

Niamh said, "I believe you have a little Fae blood. It's distant, but it's there." She paused, as if expecting someone else to speak, but no one said anything. "You know nothing of magic though. Nor have any talents unusual for humans?"

Aria shook her head.

Niamh smiled with a hint of warmth, changing the subject. "These are my people. I am Niamh, eldest of Lord Ailill." She gestured toward the others. "This is Cillian, second son of Ailill." Cillian looked much like Owen. Younger, without the faint touch of grey in his hair, but with the same cool gaze and subtle humor in the quirk of his lip. He was gaunt, with dark smudges beneath his eyes, which continued to rest on Aria with an unreadable expression.

Niamh too, looked like her brothers, or they looked like her. Her features were more feminine, but with the same pale, fine-boned beauty. Her hair had sprung into a mass of black curls that fell halfway down her back. Like the others, she wore what appeared to be cast-off clothing, faded and worn. She wore a dark brown man's dress shirt, a small size but baggy on her thin frame. Untucked, it hung past her hips, half-covering threadbare denim jeans with an incongruous line of pink rhinestones up one leg. Her bare feet were tucked beneath her.

"Siofra." Niamh indicated a younger woman. Equally pale, her hair was straighter and had a hint of red-brown. Her face was softer, and she smiled warily at Aria.

"Ardghal." The Fae man nodded to her, eyes on her face. He was appeared to be in his early forties. Aria tried guess what that meant. Three hundred fifty years or so? He too was gaunt, but he looked strong, muscular beneath his torn, blood-stained shirt. His hair was lighter, a reddish-brown that caught the light.

"Barach." He was also older, not quite so thin but somehow worn looking. Tired.

"Finn." A little older than Niall.

Lorcan. Conal. Aideen. Lachtnal. Tadg. Lonan. Conri. Fearghal. Sabd. Cathal. Aria forgot the names, but she remembered their faces. Tadg, Lonan, and Sabd were children of Niall's age and a little older, with the same hollow-eyed caution she'd seen in him at first. The others were older, ranging from young adults to Conri, the oldest. Aria hesitated to even guess at his age; if he'd been human, she'd have guessed somewhere between sixty and an athletic eighty. His hair was fully grey, and he stooped a little, but his eyes were bright and clear. There were more names too;

twenty-three Fae had been rescued.

Aria tried to focus, but she kept thinking of Owen. How he'd jerked, hauling her upward even while they shot him again. His breath in her ears as his arms strained to lift her high enough. How he fell nearly thirty feet to the ground because he'd made it almost to the top. For her. *'Gabriel, catch her,'* he'd said. Not *'help me.'*

"We need to go back and get him." She looked up to meet Niamh's eyes.

Niamh's lips tightened. "We cannot. None of us has the strength."

Niall paced behind Aria, a quick, agitated rush of air betraying his silent footsteps. He knelt to write in the notebook and showed it to both of them. *He rested before he rescued you. But he had only humans to help him, and you know we are stronger. We cannot leave him there.*

"We will not leave him indefinitely, Niall. But it cannot be for at least a week."

Niall gave a soft wordless cry and looked at his mother. *They will kill him before then. You know they will.*

"We can't, Niall. It isn't possible." Niamh's voice had softened, barely audible, but she spoke in English. She wanted Aria to understand.

*Grenidor hates him. After tonight, it will be worse.*

"Yes, I know. But what would you have me do? Sacrifice everyone to save him? You know he would not want that, even if it could be done."

Niall glanced at Aria and back to his mother, then gestured toward Aria. She straightened, not sure what was happening, but Niamh gazed at her for a long moment.

Aria offered, "It wouldn't be alone. I imagine

Gabriel would help. And I would."

Niall dismissed this with a wave of the hand. *They will not keep him at Eastborn. They will move him elsewhere for interrogation, or kill him immediately. We haven't much time.*

Niamh glanced between them thoughtfully. "What are you suggesting?"

*Everyone should give their strength to Cillian and then go to safety. Cillian, Aria, and I will go to Petro for help.*

Niamh sat back with a sharp intake of breath. "Absolutely not."

Niall stared at his mother, eyes glittering with tears. *I will go with or without Cillian. You cannot prevent me.*

"Leave us, Aria." Niamh's eyes did not leave her son.

Aria slipped out the door gratefully. Her heart felt shredded.

Gabriel beckoned to her from across the room. She picked her way through the bedrolls and rucksacks toward a small crowd sitting on the floor. Aria sat near him, but she couldn't bring herself to look at the group. After a glance at Gabriel, she kept her eyes mostly on the floor, hunched and miserable.

Gabriel looked tired, rubbing his face blearily, but he shook out his shoulders and said, "We're beginning the debrief. I'm not entirely sure what happened and the Fae don't seem to want to tell us right now. Evrial, you go first."

"We went in. No problems at first. Owen warned us about the alarms; the door itself had a sensor that went off when he got close to it. He opened it somehow, magic I suppose.

"Inside was pretty big. The left side had a surgical table and a bunch of equipment. MRI, EKG, defibrillator, all kinds of stuff. It had been freshly cleaned, but they missed some bloodstains. On the right were cages. Rows of them, metal mesh on the front and solid metal sides.

"Owen touched the mesh on one trying to open the lock and it blew him across the room. You probably heard the crack through the headset. He was pretty dazed for a minute but he got the locks open after that without touching the mesh. He said he didn't think it would shock humans, but we didn't want to chance it and pulled the doors open with the handles of some brooms and mops we found. We met the first guards as we were leaving, but my team got the first five out and regrouped outside the front gate." Evrial sighed. "We heard the chaos but didn't see most of it."

Gabriel nodded. "Bartok?"

Bartok rubbed one hand down his thigh, staring at the floor. His voice was quiet when he began. "I went back in to help and got one of them nearly to the door. Then I got shot. It hit the femoral artery, painted the wall with blood. Owen was right behind me, and he did magic, I guess, healed it enough so I wouldn't bleed out. It felt..." he hesitated. "It felt exceedingly odd. I don't think he was focused on reducing the pain, but normally one would bleed out so quickly that the pain wouldn't last long. I think he healed the main artery but left the rest for later. I blacked out, and woke up outside the wall with Niall over me." Bartok's lean face was serious.

"How do you feel now?" Evrial asked.

"A little shaky and weak from blood loss. But there's no pain. The wound itself is completely healed. Niall finished when we got back."

Gabriel nodded. "Jonah?"

Jonah took a deep breath and let it out slowly. "I went to the front gate and then went back in. Owen was somewhere back in the maze of cages. Cells. Whatever you want to call them. Fae were trying to walk, but most of them were in such bad shape they couldn't make much progress. I got one with an arm over my shoulder and hauled him to the front. We rounded a corner and met some guards. They were responding to the alarm, and they didn't expect us that close to the exit. But they got off a few shots before our team handled them. I was in front and didn't have a vest. A couple rounds caught me in the chest and I went down. Smacked my face pretty hard on the floor too, all tangled up with the Fae I was carrying. I blacked out. When I woke, Aria was between me and the door, covering me. Owen was there, the Fae was gone and a Fae woman was lying beside me instead. Niamh. Their leader, maybe. Owen told us to leave and went back. Niamh looked like she might argue, so I grabbed her and we ran to the wall. You know the rest." He rubbed his chest and stared at the floor.

Aria felt her throat tighten. *Owen, how many did you save at your own expense? But this was your mission, not theirs. It wasn't a choice, was it?*

Gabriel frowned. "Why did he go back? He heard me say you were out of time."

Jonah shook his head minutely.

"The last one, the one we brought out right at the end, is his younger brother." Aria couldn't look up from the floor, unwilling to let them see her tears, but she heard Gabriel sigh.

"Benjamin?"

"I got shot on the lawn. I don't remember at all, just running and bam, on my face in the grass, then blackness. I came to on the other side of the wall."

Gabriel said, "I think it was Charlie who got you up the ladder."

One of the men in the back nodded. "Yep."

Benjamin turned to catch his eye. "Thanks."

"Yep. I didn't know if you'd make it. That boy fixed you up pretty well though."

Gabriel ran his hands over his face again.

"Dominic? What happened with the front gate?"

"The guards stayed in their positions even after the explosion in the back. We were considering changing positions when Aria said Niall would handle it. He did. Took them all out without a shot. I don't know if he killed them or just knocked them out. We didn't do anything though, just maintained our positions to provide cover fire when required. The metal gate came up a few minutes later." He shifted. "I don't think it was anything we did directly. Sometimes the advanced facilities have systems where the guards have to check in every few minutes or the ingress point is automatically secured. I'd guess this one was on a five minute timer. A guard swipes his badge or presses a button with a thumbprint reader or something every five minutes. Otherwise the gate engages automatically."

Gabriel's eyebrows raised. "I didn't realize we had systems like that."

Geoffrey shrugged. "Most facilities don't. But the technology isn't new; it's just inconvenient to use on a daily basis. Imagine if cars were always going in and out; the gate would crush a car if the guard mentally checked out for a minute. But if security is important enough, you tolerate a little more inconvenience."

Gabriel sighed. "Anyone have any questions? Comments?"

Silence.

Aria wanted to say they needed to go back to get Owen, but she looked around the room. Without the Fae, what chance did they have?

"Get some sleep." Gabriel stood and waited while everyone meandered to their bedrolls. He shot her a hard glance when she didn't move, but said nothing. He stared around the room, his gaze lingering on the hall the Fae had claimed, and finally walked slowly to the conference room. He closed the doors. A line of white light showed between the doors and the floor.

Aria didn't know how long she sat there. A few lanterns remained lit; some of the soldiers who hadn't gone on the mission remained on watch. No vertril came.

*He had no choice. And no one but Niall seems to think we should, or can, do anything to help him.*

Hours passed. The soldiers on watch went to bed and others took their places. The light under the conference room door remained.

Finally Aria rose, her legs stiff from the cold concrete. She was hungry, thirsty, and shivering, but it didn't seem to matter. She straightened her back, took a deep breath, and walked across to the conference room. She entered without knocking.

Gabriel looked up at her. His boots were on the floor, his sock-covered feet propped on the table and his chair tilted precariously back against the wall. His arms were crossed over his chest.

"We need to go get him." Her voice was flat. "They said Grenidor will kill him within a week."

Gabriel didn't answer, and his gaze slid away from her to the far wall.

"We have to. You know he saved Jonah's life, and Bartok's, and mine. Maybe others. He didn't have to do that." She stepped closer.

Gabriel's jaw tightened. "It was his mission. He knew the risks."

"But they'll *kill* him!"

His gaze flicked back to her. His eyes were red, and Aria wondered suddenly whether it was weariness or whether he'd been weeping. "There are worse things than death."

"Why do you hate him so much?"

His eyes were hard on her face now, angry. "Is that what you think? You know nothing! You've caused enough trouble for us. Go to bed."

She trembled, but she didn't move. "Do you know anything about Petro?"

"No. What is it?"

She searched his face, the lines of tension around his mouth, the tightness of his lips. Angry. Grieving. Frustrated. Doubting. "Never mind."

She turned toward the door and then stopped. "Thank you for pulling me up. You saved my life too."

He grunted. She glanced over her shoulder at him. He stared at the far wall, his face hard and unfriendly.

ARIA LAY ON HER BEDROLL on the floor in the room she'd shared with Owen and Niall. It was empty now; Owen was gone, captured or already dead, and Niall was still doing whatever he was doing. Arguing, most likely.

It was five thirty in the morning and she was so tired every muscle in her body ached. But sleep eluded her for another hour. Behind her closed eyelids she saw Owen's blood-streaked body on the ground, wet curls stuck to his forehead. Saw him jerk as the bullets tore into him. Exhaustion finally won over guilt.

She had strange dreams. Dandra's face appeared more than once, though she couldn't remember the context when she woke up. She dreamed her tongue was cut out. It didn't hurt, but she was terrified, her mouth filled with blood. Later there was so much that needed to be said, important things that should be conveyed, and she couldn't talk. No one would pay attention to her long enough to understand why she couldn't make a sound. She waved a notebook and pencil helplessly, suddenly unable to write. She tried, but the words made no sense, just long strings of meaningless squiggles.

She woke with a jerk to find Niall staring at her. He knelt on the floor in front of her, hollow-eyed and exhausted, one cool hand on her shoulder. She sat up and pulled the blanket around her shoulders. Cillian was crouched behind him.

"What is it?" Her voice felt like a croak, and she wondered how long she'd been asleep. "What *time* is it?"

Niall scooted backward and sat with his legs crossed. He motioned to Cillian to begin and let his head hang down between his shoulders, as if he wasn't part of the conversation.

"About nine thirty. Niall says you would be willing to go with us." Cillian's eyes were bright on her face, so much like Owen's that Aria's heart twisted and she fought back tears.

"Go where?"

He blinked slowly, as if thinking about his words. "To ask Petro for help."

She nodded. "I don't know what he is. But I'll go with you, if you think it will help."

Cillian blinked again and drew back slightly. His gaze swept over her, a long thoughtful look.

She swallowed.

"You should know what we know about Petro before you make your decision," he said finally.

"Owen said some things should not be known." *Why did I say that? I want him to tell me.*

Cillian's lips tightened. "Owen is wiser than I am." He glanced toward Niall and said something, and Niall rose and left the room.

Cillian took a deep breath, and Aria saw again how similar he was to Owen. He had many of the same mannerisms. He looked disconcertingly close to her own age, but she knew he was much older. He was too thin, as if he hadn't eaten regularly in a long time. His shirt had been a white knit with a collar, but it was torn and stained. Through the holes she could see the hard, stringy muscles of his chest and stomach. The dark smudges under his eyes had barely begun to fade. He had no bruises around his wrists or ankles, but he did have a long, livid red scar on one forearm from the inside of the elbow nearly to his wrist.

"Fae are not what you expected, I imagine.

Few humans know anything about us, and most of what they know is wrong. Magic is also inaccurately understood. It is called magic because that is the closest concept in human thought, but the understanding you get from the word is partial and far from accurate.

"Magic is real, like what you call science. Imagine a bubble. The film of the bubble, the interface between the inside and the outside, is what you see as the universe. It encompasses the stars, molecules, time, everything you have ever heard of or studied. Scientific laws, physics, chemistry, etc., they apply only on the film of the bubble. Both the inside and the outside of the bubble are real, but they are not part of this universe, the one that humans inhabit. They are separate, and they are subject to separate rules."

Cillian paused, his eyes on her face. After a long moment studying her, he continued, "Humans live entirely in the film of the bubble. Fae extend a little ways outward, so to speak. Or inward. Direction is an irrelevant concept. This is one reason it is difficult to kill us; only so much of us is present in this universe, and with time and effort we can restore our physical bodies. It is easier with help, and there are limitations, but it is possible. We can manipulate the possibilities and shape the future in ways not possible for humans, using what you would call magic.

"Yet we believe that humans and Fae are closely related. We can interbreed, though for many reasons it is not commonly done. Our physical bodies are very similar, as are our emotions and intellectual capabilities. We feel joy and pain. We love. We grieve.

"It is thought that we diverged from a common ancestor, most likely an early human. While your ancestors were learning how to make fire and sharpen sticks into weapons, a few touched magic. It changed them in ways they didn't understand. Perhaps they studied healing first; it would have been advantageous. Their children found it easier to touch magic, but they became less human. As their control of magic increased, their bodies changed. They lived longer, they bred with each other rather than short-lived humans, and they began their study of magic early. But human newborns and Fae newborns are not as different as you would imagine. We are not human, but we are cousins to humans."

The door opened, and Niall slipped in. He put bags in front of each of them, and dropped to sit to the side again.

Cillian stared at her a moment before opening his bag. "I beg your pardon for eating in front of you. Most humans find it off-putting. But I require sustenance." He cut the bloody heart with his knife, and Aria saw his hand shaking a little as he put the knife aside.

"It's okay." She swallowed. "I don't mind." She pulled her eyes away from his meal and opened her own bag. A thermos that radiated heat, a chunk of heavy, soft bread, an apple, and a bottle of water. "Thank you." She looked up to smile at Niall, who ducked his head politely.

Cillian spoke as he ate. "Petro is different. We live in time, as you do, and we live mostly in the film of the bubble, as you do. Petro does not. We believe that he is from entirely outside the bubble. Sometimes he intersects it. Sometimes, when he intersects it, he chooses to appear human. But he is *not* human. Not even remotely.

"Fae are old. Humans are older, we think. If, as we believe, Petro exists outside of our universe, he is probably outside of time as we understand it. We think, and your science tends to agree, that time is a function of this universe. We know Petro has existed for hundreds of thousands of years, at least. Certainly since before Fae. Probably before humans. Possibly *long* before. We believe he is not bound by the rules we understand, and he intersects this world only when he chooses to, for his own reasons."

Aria frowned thoughtfully.

Cillian ate another bite, licked his fingers, and continued. "Things that one would think would interest him usually don't. He has ignored great sweeps of history, battles, plagues, empires rising and falling. He may have watched, but there was no evidence of him taking any particular interest.

"However, sometimes he follows events and people that one would not expect. We don't know why some things interest him and others don't. He interacts with us very little, and he never explains himself. Sometimes, when he follows a particular Fae or human, he begins as soon as they are born, which seems to support the idea of him interfacing with time differently than we do. Yet we believe he has been surprised; perhaps he does not know or understand the future in its entirety.

"Sometimes he takes action. Sometimes he merely observes. Fae sometimes sense his presence, when he lets us, but humans don't. Sometimes there seem to be several of his kind on earth, but they might all be him. We are only present in the film in one location, where our bodies are. We believe he can touch in one or more than one place at a time. Or none. Sometimes he appears as a human. Sometimes he appears as... something else.

"I doubt it's possible for Fae or humans to threaten him, or even to deliberately interest him. We have no idea what he is capable of. We believe he has a sense of morality, but it is not ours. He is cruel, in that he thinks nothing of killing for his own reasons. But he doesn't seem to take pleasure in it; most of the atrocities in history have been of human doing, not his, and we believe he could do much worse if he wished. He does not appear to be malicious or evil. He requires nothing of us and is usually reclusive."

Aria swallowed.

"He has spoken to Owen more than anyone in memory, but even that isn't much. A handful of times, a few sentences each, in over two hundred years." Cillian's eyes rested on her face.

"What is he, then? Do you know?" Aria's meal was forgotten in front of her, and Cillian nodded to it, indicating that she should eat. She unscrewed the top of the thermos to find a thick chicken and dumpling soup. The smell comforted her.

He licked his lips. "He has been called many things. Petro is a name he gave Dandra once, and Owen used it when speaking with her. Owen spoke to him under the names Conláed and Drake at different times." He watched her face as he continued, "The name you would probably recognize is Dragon, but that generally refers to only one of the physical forms he takes, when he chooses to take a form at all."

Aria swallowed hard. Her throat seemed tight,

and she felt her heart thudding unevenly.

"We need his help if we are to have any hope of rescuing Owen in time. He can supply the energy we need to heal, I think, if he chooses to. The problem is that he has never shown any interest in speaking to any of us. Even to those who can sense magic, he is hard to find. It is possible to sense his location, if he lets us, but if he doesn't wish to speak with us, he will not be there when we arrive."

Cillian's eyes had not left her face. "Although he seems not to care what we think of him, he can take offense, even when none is intended. If he did not want to be sensed, we would not be able to sense him. But we can. He must be letting us, and that may mean he *wants* to speak with us. But it may not. If we approach him too quickly or too slowly, or have misinterpreted the invitation, things will go badly. The opportunity will not come again, either.

"We assume it has something to do with Owen, because he has taken an interest in Owen in the past. However, Owen has also been in danger before, and he has done nothing. We wonder if the difference now is you."

Aria's heart skipped a beat. "Me?" Her voice felt squeaky.

"Have you not wondered why you are here, privy to discussions that humans have not entered for ten thousand years? Why you saw Owen when he wished to be unseen, and why he did not kill you for it? He should have, by logic. I would have. But he didn't.

"Petro once told Owen something that might have been a reference to you. That may have stayed Owen's hand. Or it could have been Owen's unusual beliefs. But it makes us wonder if Petro's invitation is meant for you. We don't know whether taking you to see Petro will increase or decrease our chances of speaking with him or of receiving his assistance. But Owen cannot wait for us to recover normally. They have given me as much strength as they can, and I would not wish to face a vertril, much less infiltrate wherever they are keeping him. We need Petro's help.

"This is our best chance. Our only chance. We need to decide what to do, and then do it immediately. What do you think?"

She swallowed. Her voice failed her at the enormity of the question.

"Is there anything you sense? Do you know something that will help us make the correct decision?"

Aria closed her eyes against the burning intensity of Cillian's gaze. *Do I know something? I know nothing. I feel fear.*

He waited while she thought, patient and silent. She heard Niall writing again, and wondered distantly what he was saying.

She forced herself to begin. "I don't think I can sense things the way you do. I have no secret wisdom or sense that tells me anything. But I know I want to help, and if Petro might be interested in me, then perhaps it makes sense for me to put the request to him."

Niall put the notebook between them. *It is dangerous to seek Petro at any time, and now the danger affects all of us, particularly Aria. Is the blood debt paid? It should have been mine, by rights, but Lord Owen claimed it. The debt was for my freedom. He gave his freedom for her. How does that weigh in the balance?*

Cillian sighed softly. "Only Owen knows the weight of the debt and whether it is paid. Until we know, we are obligated to protect you as if the debt is still in force." He looked up to meet her eyes. "But you can choose whether to approach Petro or not. I do not believe we have the right to prevent you. It is a question of wisdom. Is it the *right* decision?"

Aria swallowed hard. "I will go. I count the debt paid, if that makes any difference."

Niall gave her the ghost of a smile and shook his head.

"You sense nothing? And yet you would take the risk?" Cillian's eyes remained on her face, a hint of disbelief, even censure, in his gaze.

"Yes." She forced herself to nod.

"Then we should not keep him waiting." Cillian stood quickly, then swayed and put his hand out to the wall to steady himself. Niall rose more slowly, one hand braced against the cardboard boxes stacked to the ceiling.

Aria frowned as she looked at them. Gaunt and white as paper, they were both so weak they could barely stay upright. Her heart twisted for them and for Owen, who needed them.

"What?" Cillian asked.

"Is there anything I can do to help you? Before we leave?" She chewed her lip.

"No. Let us go." Cillian led the way out and down the hall into the theater.

"I need to tell Gabriel." Aria stopped outside the conference room, but it was unoccupied. She looked around, but didn't see him, and finally settled on Bartok. He was eating with some others in a small group. They hadn't been on the mission the night before, and Bartok seemed to be in the middle of a quiet explanation.

"I'm going out with Cillian and Niall. We might be back. I don't know when."

Bartok glanced between them. "Are you okay?"

She forced a smile. "Fine. Just terrified. We'll see what happens and whether it's justified."

Bartok frowned and stood. "Do you need help?" He glanced at Cillian again, as if he were the cause of the problem.

Aria shook her head. "No. Thank you. I guess… see that the Fae have what they need. And get some rest." She managed a nod and an unconvincing smile before turning away to follow Cillian toward the front door.

Niall stopped suddenly and wrote, the notebook pressed against the nearest wall.

*Grenidor will extract this location from Lord Owen. They should not be here when the soldiers arrive.*

Cillian nodded. "You're right. We were too tired to consider this before." He thought a moment. "The Hamling Train Station is still secret, isn't it?"

Niall nodded tentatively.

Cillian made his way back to Bartok. "Grenidor is most likely torturing Owen for information before killing him. One piece he will focus on is this location. You should move immediately. It is difficult at any time to lie to or withhold information from a human, and Grenidor is experienced at torture. You have little time."

Bartok stared at him. "You mean go now? With all the supplies?"

"Immediately. We will meet you at the Hamling Train Station. If it is not safe, find somewhere else. We will find you."

"I don't know that location." Bartok frowned more deeply.

Cillian glanced toward the door. "It is likely Gabriel will know it. If not, then Eli should." He held Bartok's eyes and repeated, "You have little time. Move quickly."

Bartok nodded once and Cillian turned away.

# CHAPTER 10

CILLIAN LED THEM out into a bright, cold early afternoon, the winter sun imparting no warmth as it flooded the street. He followed a circuitous path, walking slowly and pausing at each intersection before choosing a direction. Niall did not seem to have any argument, following without a questioning look. Cillian glanced at him once, as if to ask his opinion, but Niall only waited, and after a moment Cillian continued to lead.

Aria shivered, partly from an icy gust of wind, and partly from her thoughts. What if she failed? What if Petro didn't tell her what they needed to know? What if he killed them all?

It didn't matter. She had to try.

"Do you know where we are going?"

Cillian answered, "No. The route is of his

choosing. I know only the next turn."

She frowned, puzzling over that. *So Petro knew where we were. And where we are now. Is this confirmation that he does wish to speak to us?*

Cillian stopped in front of a door. "He is here." He turned to meet her eyes. "Are you ready?"

Aria stared at the door. *Barton & Michel, Attorneys at Law.* The painted lettering was faded and worn. "Why here?"

"It is where he chose." Cillian sounded slightly puzzled at her question. "Are you ready?" he repeated.

She swallowed. "Yes."

The door was not locked. *Would it have been locked if someone else tried it? I should ask him later. But he might not know.* Cillian led them through a reception area that looked equally worn, down a short hallway, and into a tiny library, the walls lined with heavy, leather bound books. A computer sat discretely on a desk in one corner, and leather armchairs clustered in the corner closest to them.

Owen stood in the center of the open space, his hands clasped behind his back. "Good morning." His voice was low, and she heard the smile in it, though his expression was subtle.

Beside her, she heard Cillian's breaths, quick and ragged in the silence. He stared at Owen, his lips pressed tightly together. Behind Niall, the door closed, apparently of its own accord.

Owen did not look at Cillian or Niall, did not acknowledge their existence. He smiled at Aria, his blue eyes holding hers. "Do you love me?"

Aria's heart thudded, her eyes locked on his. *This isn't Owen. This isn't right.* "Who are you?" she whispered.

Owen smiled again, a kindly look in his eyes. "Who do you think?"

She licked her lips. "I've been told you have many names. Which would you prefer today?"

Owen stepped toward her, eyes still on hers. "Answer my question." His voice was gentle. "Do you love me?"

"I don't know you." She raised her chin and forced herself to keep her eyes on his.

Owen stared at her, familiar blue eyes searching her face, head cocked to the side as if he were puzzling out her strange human behavior. He smiled again. Then he was gone, and in his place stood *something*.

Perhaps it was a man. It might have been a young man, with bronze skin, golden hair and laughing golden eyes. For a moment, that's what Aria saw. For a moment, she saw a beast, a lizard with golden scales and glittering green eyes, towering far past the ceiling, staring down at her with an unblinking gaze. For a moment, she saw a woman, pale and voluptuous, sensual lips curved in a smile. Perhaps it was not a man at all.

In Owen's place stood a man of perhaps twenty years old, with brown hair that flopped haphazardly over his forehead. His face was innocent, guileless, but his eyes made her blood chill. Something in them seemed cold as ice. His green eyes roved from her to Cillian, to Niall, and back to her. *Petro. Drake. Conláed. Dragon.*

"You may call me as you wish. It matters not."

Aria felt Cillian's tension next to her, and her own heart beating wildly. Her voice shook. "We have come to request your help. Cillian believes

231

you can help us save Owen." She wondered if he required an explanation of this, or if he already knew.

He stared at her with unblinking eyes for so long that she shifted uncomfortably. *He should blink. It would make the illusion more convincing.* The sudden thought was almost amusing, and it gave her courage.

"Will you help us?" she finally ventured in the face of his silence.

"Why do you wish to save him?"

Aria swallowed. *Why indeed? Because I love him? Because what they're doing is wrong? Because I feel guilty? Because he's their hope? Because Niall trusts me to ask you for help, for reasons I cannot fathom?*

She licked her lips and swallowed a lump in her throat. "Because it's the right thing to do."

He drew back with a knowing look. "Altruism." He stepped away, paced slowly down the length of the room and then back. "You have not convinced me." He met her eyes with a glance so cold she shivered. "Try again."

"Because I love him." Aria blurted the words, not glancing to the side to see Cillian's expression.

Petro smiled a little, a quirk of the lips that might have been calculated to resemble Owen's. "Love. Human love is no concern of mine."

"Why did you ask about it?"

Petro smiled a little more. Aria couldn't guess if he was amused by her efforts or simply mimicking human expressions for reasons of his own. *He's asking because it affects something, not because the emotion matters to him. But what?*

"What are you interested in, then?"

He stared at her for another long moment. "Data," he said finally. Beside her, Cillian twitched, but said nothing.

Aria frowned. "If you're not human, and you're not Fae, and you're older than anything I can imagine, what data could you possibly want? Haven't you seen everything before?"

Petro merely stared at her, his unblinking gaze so intense that she found herself trembling as she kept her eyes on his.

"Are we data points then? Of some sort of study?"

Silence.

"If Owen is interesting now, I imagine he will continue to be interesting in the future. Unless he dies. Then you'll get no more information." She raised her chin.

Again, silence, for so long that Aria began turning over new words in her mind, floundering desperately for another tack. What could Petro possibly desire?

"Why is he so interesting?"

"I require no further information from Owen."

Aria's heart skipped a beat, and she felt her breath coming raggedly. *Then Owen is lost.*

"Where is he?" she asked anyway.

The silence drew out for another long moment, then Petro said abruptly, "He is at the Forestgate Imperial Security Facility in the second basement floor. You will find the gates unlocked at nine o'clock tonight."

"Tonight?" Aria's voice was only a whisper. Shocked that she'd succeeded. Confused. Why had he given in to her request? "Thank you."

Petro did not answer, did not acknowledge the

thanks in word or expression. He merely stared at her, eyes unblinking, and then vanished.

Aria blinked. There was no flash of light, no shimmering, nothing to indicate how he had disappeared. He was just no longer present.

Aria let out a long, slow breath, heart still thudding in her chest. Beside her, Cillian shuddered and turned away from her toward Niall, who had sunk to his knees on the floor, face buried in his hands. Cillian didn't say anything, only knelt beside him in silence, one hand on the boy's shoulder. The other was clenched in a fist that he pressed to his mouth, as if he were trying not to be sick.

"Well, that went better than I expected." Aria finally offered. "Are you okay?"

Niall looked up at her, trembling.

Cillian answered, his voice low. "It was *profoundly* disturbing, in ways you cannot imagine." He took another deep breath and let it out slowly. "We must talk to Niamh and the others." He helped Niall to his feet.

They made their way slowly back down the hallway toward the street. Aria had already stepped outside when she blinked in confusion and turned to look at the door again. The door was an unmarked metal service door, and they stood in a narrow alley. "Where are we?"

Cillian swayed a little and glanced both directions. "Off of Joslin Avenue." He hesitated, then added, "I didn't feel us move."

Cillian led them. Aria watched them worriedly; both seemed so shaken and weary that she wondered whether they would make it back to the hotel at all. She didn't realize where they were until they passed directly in front of Dandra's Books.

"Wait." She stopped. It was still closed, with a note taped to the glass door. Nothing seemed amiss, but she looked again at the note.

"This is different. It's a different note." It was still Dandra's handwriting, as closely as she could tell, and the wording was the same. *Closed until further notice.* But it wasn't the same note. Had she come back and gone away again? It was the middle of the afternoon. The store should have been open.

Aria shaded her face against the glare and peered inside. Everything seemed normal. She frowned. Maybe not. The shelves looked a little less organized than usual. Dandra liked to straighten everything before she left for the night; every book's spine an inch from the front edge of the shelf. Now random books were pulled forward, as if to set them apart from the rest. Aria shook her head. *That's foolish. Of course it's a little disorganized. If she was in a hurry when she left, she wouldn't have straightened the shelves. But why is the note different? And why would she be in a hurry to leave?*

She pulled on the door handle, but it was locked. Of course it was. The store was closed. "Can you open this?" She turned to glance at Cillian.

"For what purpose?"

She could hear the exhaustion in his voice, and she almost shook her head and continued on. *But if something is wrong, we should know. Owen said he didn't tell Petro, so why would she be gone for so long?*

"I think we should look inside."

Cillian reached forward without a word and

placed his hand on the handle. He paused, and then pulled it open with a soft click.

Aria stepped inside, Cillian and Niall following. She walked through the little coffee shop area. *This was where I saw Owen first. What if I hadn't paid attention? Life would be so simple.*

The scents of coffee and sugary syrups were faded, as if the machines had not been used since she'd been here last. She stepped behind the counter. The trash was emptied; Dandra did that every night as she left. The refrigerator that held the cream and milk was still on, and she peered inside. Everything was either out of date, or close to it.

"This is strange," she murmured. "She came back to change the note, but she didn't replace any of the supplies. Why?"

Cillian sighed softly behind her, and she glanced at him. He leaned against the end of a bookshelf, eyes half-closed, shoulders slumped. She thought he might say something, but he only stood there silently, and she moved toward the bookshelf he leaned against.

She slipped down the aisle, looking at the books. There were few empty places; Dandra liked to keep a full inventory with a broad range of books, and books were often stacked horizontally above the vertical rows when she ran out of space in a particular section. The first book that was pulled out caught her eye.

*A History of the Jews.* Odd. Who were they? The next one was *American Superpower: The Rise and Fall of an Empire.* Aria frowned more deeply. The name sounded familiar, and she pulled the book out and flipped it open. The map in the front made her catch her breath. *That's here. When was this?* Copyright 2061, just before she was born. The next book, just a little farther on, was *The Cold War: A New Understanding*. The next was *The Sound of Freedom*. And the next, *Red Rising: The Birth of Modern China*. She covered her mouth with her hand as her thoughts whirled.

*History. Dandra sells history books. Real ones!* If these were true history books, it was probably sedition to sell them. Aria looked around the store again. It didn't look like the IPF had been here; maybe they didn't know yet. But Dandra must have believed she was in danger. Aria moved more quickly now, glancing at each title as she pulled them out and stacked them on a table in the back.

Another aisle. *The Death of Compassion.* That title stood out among the others, and she glanced inside briefly. *Today's world is cold in ways our ancestors could not imagine. We think it is because of the changes in the weather, the changes in politics, but we are mistaken. The coldness is in our hearts, and it has been long in the making.* She put it on top of the stack.

The next aisle had only a few books pulled out, and she moved down it quickly, with only a glance at each title. Her foot fell unevenly as she stepped forward, and she looked down to see a book kicked halfway under the shelf, the title hidden. She knelt to extract it and drew a quick breath. *Memories Kept.* A slip of paper marked the place where she'd stopped reading. *She knew. She left this book for me to find. And the others. She knew I would come. Does she need help? Where is she? Why did I not notice these books before? Was I that out of it? Did any-*

*one else notice them?*

Cillian's voice came from the front of the store. "Have you found what you wanted?"

Aria swallowed. "Yes. We need to take these with us. There's a message in them, but I can't figure it out now. Maybe Gabriel can help. Or Owen. Later." She winced when she glanced at the pile of books she'd amassed.

She found plastic bags with the store logo behind the counter and doubled them, then stuffed them full of books. Five bulging bags, so heavy she struggled to lift two. Cillian stared at her for a long moment, then picked up one in each hand. Niall shouldered the fifth, skinny body bowed under its weight.

Aria tested the door behind them and was relieved that it locked automatically. She trailed Cillian and Niall, stopping periodically to put the bags down and flex her fingers. The plastic bag handles stretched under the weight and felt like wires digging into her hands.

Though the streets were not empty, no one seemed to notice her, and she was grateful. One man actually bumped into her as he walked by, but he neither apologized nor shot her an angry glance; he seemed completely unaware that she existed. *I might as well be a lamppost. Good. Cillian is probably responsible for that too. It's not like you see such a mismatched group every day, struggling under eighty pounds of books for five blocks.*

CILLIAN LED THEM to an entrance to the old subway system. The stairwell down was blocked by a locked metal door; he put his hand on it for a moment and then pulled it open. Aria winced at the rusty screech. If anyone was looking for them, they'd announced their presence. Cillian locked the door behind them the same way.

He led them through the darkness with unerring confidence. Aria followed more slowly, and she lost track of Cillian and Niall quickly. Neither made a sound as they walked, and although the books were heavy, she couldn't hear them breathing. Her own breaths were loud in the thick silence.

Finally Niall came back and grasped the handle of one of her bags and helped her with it, guiding her as he pulled. Aria had the sense of an open space and she pictured them on a small train platform at first, then a long narrow tunnel. Niall's guiding hand on the bag was welcome as she imagined herself misstepping and falling onto the tracks. No train would be coming, but the drop would be six or eight feet to a hard, uneven surface.

They walked for a long time. Aria struggled with the weight of the books, but it was her own decision to carry them. Besides, Cillian was carrying the two heaviest bags, and Niall was helping her. Niall didn't seem to be carrying the fifth anymore.

"Do you still have the other bag?" Aria asked finally.

"I have it." Cillian answered for Niall.

She heard the weariness in his voice and asked, "Do you need to rest?"

"No. We are close."

Her arms were burning and her hands were locked in excruciating cramps by the time they emerged into a larger space again.

Cillian stopped in front of them and spoke quietly. "It is us. Aria, Niall, and me, Cillian."

A lamp flared and he continued forward. Aria grimaced with pain and hefted the books again.

Eli lowered his pistol, darted forward and began to take one of the bags from her. "Thanks." Then she looked toward Cillian. The third bag of books was looped over his right wrist, and he held the handles to the others in each hand. "Help him."

Cillian set the bags down and straightened slowly, flexing his fingers and considering them for a moment before looking up into the darkness. "Come. We must speak to the others." He left the books on the floor and led her past the lantern Eli had left toward another lantern some distance away.

The Fae had claimed the far end of the lower level of the two story train station. Brick ceilings arched high above the second floor. Black train tunnels led in opposite directions; a second floor, reached by unmoving escalators, had tunnels at right angles. The station was apparently long-forgotten, the stained concrete floor thick with dust. The air was cool and stale until she reached the circle of light marking the Fae encampment. A kerosene lantern lit their faces, but the darkness loomed in thick shadows at every corner.

Niamh and the others had been sitting in a rough circle already and Aria wondered whether they had been singing, sleeping, or merely sitting in silence as they rested. *They must have been singing, if not now, then not long ago. This air is fresh, like after a spring rain.*

Cillian motioned her to sit beside him and Aria settled in with her legs crossed between him and Niall. He nodded for her to begin.

Aria recounted the meeting as well as she could, giving her words and Petro's verbatim. She frowned as she thought, trying to remember every detail and every impression. The Fae stared at her in silence until she finished.

She took a deep breath. "I thought you would help, or something. I didn't know you were just going to leave me to it." She tried to glare at Cillian but it faded as she met his eyes.

"We could not." His voice was flat, and he glanced at Niall as he spoke.

"Could not? What do you mean? You could have asked a question or something. I didn't know what I was doing!" Aria's voice rose.

Cillian did not react to her irritation. "We were kept silent. We were not given the choice to speak."

She blinked at him. *What did that mean?* But before she could ask for clarification, he began his own account of the meeting.

"I did not realize until now that Petro did not appear as Owen to her for the entire meeting. To me, and I believe to Niall, he was Owen. The illusion was utterly convincing in ways that a human could not sense. The feel of him was Owen, through and through, down to the taste of his blood. It would have fooled most of you, and in a passing meeting, it would have fooled even me, his brother." Cillian paused, and Niall nodded, eyes flicking up to Aria's face for a brief moment before lowering to the floor again.

Cillian shuddered again. "If he can be so convincingly Fae, how many times has he interacted with us unrecognized? What has he done, and what has he said, that we did not realize were him? And humans can sense so little, he could have done much without being known."

Niamh stared back at him with wide eyes.

Aria frowned. She started, then stopped, and started again. "I don't think so. You said he doesn't seem to want much interaction. Why would he do that?"

Cillian shook his head slowly. "We don't know him. We have no way of understanding what he does and does not want. This meeting was proof."

She waited, watching him as he seemed to gather his thoughts. He flexed his fingers absently, working out the cramps. His wrist still showed the deep lines of the plastic bag handles. *I hope the books tell us something.*

"The change in his appearance was obviously aimed at Aria. Why? He began as Owen, but either did not or could not maintain that deception. He settled on a human form, but showed her a non-human form as well. Was it a test or provocation for her? Or an expression of his limitations?

"Also, Petro answered her questions. Not all of them, but some of them. *Directly.* He has never done that for us. Owen has gained information from him, but it has been difficult, in ways it was not for Aria. He became less evasive as the meeting went on. I don't understand why."

Niamh's eyes rested on Aria again. "And you somehow managed to obtain his location from Petro." Her voice was soft, and her surprise was obvious. "This does not mean it will be possible to save him."

Cillian nodded. "No. He gave a time and said the gate would be open. That is all."

Aria spoke the thought that rose up unbidden. "Do you think he was lying?"

The Fae turned to her as one, but only Niamh spoke. "It is difficult for us to lie, particularly to humans. The consequences are immediate and severe. Unmistakable. We believe it may be more difficult for Petro. At least, we have little evidence that he has lied directly. It is possible for him to deceive, we think; he has given incomplete information that resulted in disaster. It may have been deliberate, but we do not know his purposes in doing so."

Cillian said, "Only to us. We have no such evidence regarding his interactions with humans."

For the first time, one of the other Fae reacted. They had been watching in utter silence, but now Ardghal spoke quietly. "He would know we would explain this to her. It carries risks."

Silence.

"It doesn't matter. We must try."

"What doesn't matter?" Aria was confused.

"Though we believe he spoke the truth, it does not mean there is any chance of success. Petro may be setting us up for disaster. He promised an open door and a location. He did not promise there would be no other interference." Cillian met her eyes, and apparently her confusion was still obvious, because he continued. "It doesn't matter. Because of Owen's position, and what we owe him, we must try. If there was no chance to save him, we could walk away, but knowing there is a chance, we must take it."

Aria swallowed. "Yes. We will."

Niamh looked at her strangely. "You will be a liability. You should stay here."

"No!" Aria's answer was sharper than she intended, and she tried to smile in apology.

Niamh's eyes were hard and unyielding.

Aria took a deep breath and thought about her words. "I care for him too. I know I'm slow and weak in comparison to you, but I want to help. If I die, then at least I'll know I did something worthwhile with my life."

Everyone stared at her in silence. Cillian's glare was perhaps the most angry, and she tried to think of something that would soften her demand.

"Petro gave *me* the information. Don't you think he might have wanted me to go?"

Cillian blinked as he considered the thought, but Niamh answered. "I imagine he did. But neither altruism nor love convinced him. His interest does not imply compassion."

Ardghal's quiet voice cut through the silence. "And yet, Niamh, she chooses to go. Can we prevent her?"

Aria stared at Ardghal. He was one of the older ones, gaunt and strong and silent. The question was odd.

"What do you mean, *can* you prevent me? I imagine even now any one of you could physically prevent me. You're all much stronger than I am. But that's not the question, is it?"

Niamh nodded for Ardghal to answer. She seemed lost in thought, her gaze distant.

"We have choices, but we cannot interfere with you. Not the way you can with us, I imagine. If you choose to go on the mission, we can tell you the risks, and attempt to change your mind, but we cannot prevent you from going. Not physically. I doubt it would be possible to lie to you directly, and it would be difficult to deliberately deceive you. That is a right that we do not often have, and rarely use." Ardghal glanced at Cillian, who nodded agreement.

Aria felt her understanding slipping, then caught at a thread. The Fae had something in common with Petro then. She pondered the thought, not quite sure she understood, and tucked it away for later. Something to discuss with Owen.

"Right then. You have not changed my mind. I choose to go. I appreciate your desire to protect me," she smiled, trying to seem properly grateful. "But I believe I ought to go."

Cillian and Niamh locked eyes across the circle, and Cillian nodded minutely.

Niamh turned her gaze on Aria. "We have more to discuss among ourselves. You should rest. Eat. We will leave at 8:00."

The dismissal was clear.


ARIA TRUDGED TOWARD the other end of the platform, making her way toward the lanterns scattered about. She was unsure what to do. The books were intriguing, and she was sure there was some message Dandra meant for her. There was also all the material Owen had obtained from the H Street facility. Her eyes burned with exhaustion, and she knew she should rest. Instead, she looked for a face she recognized.

She saw Bartok first, and meandered over to where he was laying on a bedroll, legs stretched out and arms crossed behind his head. A notebook lay open next to him, pages filled with cramped writing.

He blinked up at her. "You're back. Was it as bad as you expected?"

She dropped to sit beside him and leaned forward to put her face in her hands, hair falling forward. Her voice was muffled as she answered. "Nothing bad happened. I think. But it was confusing." She sighed heavily. "Everything is confusing."

Bartok sat up and patted her shoulder once. She could feel his awkward sympathy. They didn't know each other well enough for it not to be awkward, but she obviously needed some comfort.

She sighed again. "Is Gabriel looking at the hard drives yet?"

"I don't think so. He's touchy. You might want to leave him alone right now." Bartok frowned more deeply at her.

"It's not my fault. Is it?" She tried to keep her eyes on his, but felt her gaze slipping back to the floor. *Isn't it? You meant to help, and yet you made it worse. Possibly. Maybe. How can you know? Delusions of heroism. Trying to earn love, as if Owen needed your help, out of everyone here.*

Bartok put one finger under her chin and lifted her face, waiting until she met his eyes again. "No," he said firmly. "It isn't your fault. You meant to help. And you did. It was brave, and I'm sure Owen appreciated it. Jonah certainly does." He withdrew his hand but kept his eyes on hers. His voice softened. "He's married, you know. His wife is out at the safe haven with their two children. They're five and eight. You helped make sure they didn't lose their daddy."

Aria's face crumpled and she buried her face in her hands again. "And sacrificed Owen to do it! How can we know what is right?"

*It's not Bartok's fault. Don't take it out on him.*

"Do you know where Forestgate Imperial Security Facility is?" she sniffled as she looked up again.

"No. Gabriel would. Why?"

"That's where Owen is. Probably."

Bartok's mouth twisted in a frown. "I'll go with you if you want to see Gabriel. If you think it's important."

"I'll tell him what we're doing. But I don't think any humans should go. Except me." She hunched her shoulders. The thought terrified her, but she didn't want to admit it.

"What *are* you doing?" Bartok asked.

"We're going to try to rescue Owen. It could be a total disaster. But we're going to try anyway." She scowled furiously at her clasped hands. "I don't want to, exactly, but I need to. To be able to live with myself." She felt tears welling and brushed at them furiously. "I'm not brave like this, Bartok!"

He put both hands on her shoulders and leaned down to meet her eyes. "None of us are. We do what we need to do. That's all."

She sighed. "They told me to rest. I probably should." She forced a smile. "I bet you were a good pediatrician."

Pleasure flashed across his face. "I enjoyed it. I hope I can do it again someday."

"I'd better go see Gabriel." She didn't want to face him.

247

Bartok pushed himself to his feet and helped her up. "You got it." He led her away from the group toward an alcove near the entrance to one of the tunnels. An electric lantern shed some light, but she didn't see him. "Gabriel?"

"Yes." The answer was a little hoarse. Aria realized he was sitting with his back against the wall closest to them, his boots barely visible.

"Aria wants to talk to you."

"What does she want?"

She heard papers rustling and stepped forward, despite the unfriendly tone of his voice. She gave Bartok a smile she hoped was reassuring.

"Do you want me to stay?" His question was for both of them.

"If you want." Gabriel's frown could be heard, even though she couldn't see it yet. Aria shrugged, and Bartok followed her closer.

She dropped to sit across from Gabriel, not looking at his face yet. Bartok knelt beside her.

"I wanted to tell you that we're going to try to rescue Owen. Cillian and Niall and I went to see Petro. He gave us some information that might help."

"Who's Petro?" Gabriel set the papers aside.

Aria took a deep breath. "I'm not really sure. Someone, some*thing*, they're very frightened of." She didn't know how much she should say. It seemed that the more she knew, the more complicated and tangled things became, and she wasn't sure if it was a good idea to draw Gabriel in to the confusion too. "Something old and powerful."

Gabriel leaned forward and rubbed his hands hard over his face. His shoulders were tense, and she felt a sudden rush of sympathy for him. He

248

was tired, under the pressure of leadership, and grieving, and she knew she was part of the cause.

"I think it will work out. I think we'll get him." She tried to sound more confident than she felt.

Gabriel looked up. "Do you know Colonel Grenidor?"

"I met him. He's the one who arrested me after Owen took my tracker out. Niall said he leads the experimental program." She closed her eyes and took a deep breath. *It will be fine. If it goes well, he'll have Owen for less than 24 hours. Owen will be hurt, but he will be fine.*

Gabriel's eyes shifted away. "Yes."

"Do you know him?"

"Yes." Gabriel did not meet her eyes. He hunched forward a little, frowning, then said, "I'll ask for volunteers if you have a plan to retrieve him."

Aria swallowed. "I don't think anyone should go except Cillian and me. I think it's going to be dangerous. I wouldn't ask it of anyone."

Gabriel met her eyes for a long moment. "I would."

*Am I wrong? Would more people be better? But there is more to risk that way. With only Cillian and me, I think it could work. If not, then only we two die with Owen. I think that is best.*

She reached out to put one hand on his arm and he twitched in surprise. "I think it is best if it is only Cillian and me." She chewed her lip and continued quietly, "The other Fae will provide cover. That way if we fail, which seems likely, you won't have sacrificed any of your fighters. You need to keep going. It's important."

Gabriel held her eyes for a moment longer,

then nodded once. "Understood. Where is he?"

"Forestgate Imperial Security Facility."

Gabriel blinked. "I think we have the plans for that one. Would you check?" he asked Bartok.

Bartok nodded and stood.

"You have the plans?" Aria asked incredulously.

Gabriel frowned, doubt in his eyes. "Jonah worked at the Department of General Services before he was identified as noncompliant. He copied or stole many of the plans for various facilities before he went underground. It was amazing work. Gutsy. Also very useful. We stole most of our equipment and weapons in early missions that relied on those plans. I think Forestgate might be among the facilities we have plans for, but I'm not positive."

They sat in silence for so long that Gabriel pulled the papers toward him again. "This is some of the material Owen retrieved from the H Street facility. I imagine the hard drives have more, but Jonah is still getting a computer set up. It's complicated. They're trying to find power to tap into that won't be obvious. Converters. We have a couple old laptops but nothing that's designed to work with the milspec removable hard drives."

"You can do it though, right?"

"Jonah can do pretty much anything with a computer. It's just taking a while to get everything set up. Then longer to read it, if everything is encrypted." Gabriel peeled off the top few pages and handed them to her. "This is on the brainwashing and such. If you want to read it."

Bartok came jogging back. "No. We don't have that one."

Aria let out a breath she hadn't realized she'd been holding. "Now what? How do we plan, then?"

Bartok handed her a book. "I thought you should see this, though."

"What?" The book was *Memories Kept*, the book that had started her wondering about the past.

Bartok reached over to open it. "Jenison was going through the books you brought from Dandra's, trying to find a common theme, and he found your bookmark. Did you draw this?"

She stared down at the slip of paper. It was torn from one of her pages of thesis notes, an uneven triangle with the penciled ends of words. A black symbol had been drawn on it, the tip just barely protruding from the pages when the book was closed. "What is it?"

He stared at her. "It's a cross. The Christian symbol. You don't remember?"

She blinked. It sounded familiar, but she couldn't think of any details. "Not really. I mean, I remember the word Christian, but I never knew much about them. What does it mean?"

"You didn't draw it?" Bartok and Gabriel were both staring at her.

"No." She shook her head.

"There's more." Bartok turned the paper over to the back, and Aria recognized the shape of the crumpled paper that had been in Dandra's hand the evening Aria met Owen.

The note read, "You must execute your escape plan. You have one day before the soldiers come for you. Petro." The writing was in crisp black ink, a precise all caps print except for the name Petro, which was written with a subdued flourish.

*He wrote it on my bookmark, and I put the book-
mark in the book when I reshelved it. Dandra didn't
have the book out when we left that night. How did it
get in her hand when we were outside?*

Silence.

"Huh," Gabriel said finally.

Aria rubbed her eyes. "This is interesting, but
we're planning a rescue. I don't have any idea how
to do that, so any advice would be welcome."

Gabriel sighed. "Who's going?"

"Cillian and me. And I guess some of them to
provide cover from the walls. We'll need guns."

"Let's talk with them, then." He scooped up
the papers.

Aria led the way back across the platform.
"Resistance fighters don't have coffee, do they? I'm
really, really tired."

Gabriel chuckled softly. "Sorry, but we don't
have any."

Aria sighed. "I thought not." Just one more
trivial comfort that didn't apply to her life anymore.

The Fae looked up coolly as they approached
and said nothing as Aria, Gabriel, and Bartok sat
down near them.

Gabriel took a deep breath and Aria realized
with some surprise that he was nervous. Nervous
about the Fae? About the rescue? About everything, she concluded. He didn't know them well
and probably found them unpredictable. *I should
feel the same way. Maybe I'm just too tired to be nervous.*

"Aria tells me you're planning to try to rescue
Owen. Based on the statements of Petro?"

"Yes," Cillian answered.

"Can you trust him?" Gabriel frowned.

"We believe he did not lie. It is highly likely there is relevant information he is withholding for his own purposes."

Gabriel sat back. "So, the explanation I got from Aria is that Petro is old, and scary, and dangerous. And yet you believe he's telling you the truth. Why on earth would you believe that?"

Cillian and Niamh glanced at each other. Niamh answered, her voice quiet. "I am not sure we understand your question. Why would one not trust Petro's words?"

Bartok and Gabriel stared at them. Finally Gabriel said, "Huh." The single syllable betrayed confusion, and Cillian frowned at him.

"Petro's statement was clear. What is there to doubt?"

Gabriel tilted his head slightly as he stared at them. "You don't think he might lie to you?"

"No." Cillian looked confused by the suggestion.

Gabriel rubbed both hands over his face and sat back. "Fine. When?"

"Tonight at 9:00 at Forestgate Imperial Security Facility. Second basement floor," Aria said.

"Why then? I thought you would want to heal first." Gabriel addressed the question to Cillian.

Cillian nodded. "That is the time Petro specified. It is possible that Owen will not survive past that time, or that he would be moved somewhere else or otherwise be inaccessible if we wait."

"But you don't *know* that. And not to put it too bluntly, but none of you are up to much of a fight right now."

Cillian blinked slowly. "That is immaterial. We

cannot wait longer."

Gabriel said after a long moment, "I will ask for volunteers to provide cover, if you wish."

Niamh frowned slightly, then nodded. "Yes. That would be acceptable. Appreciated."

Cillian stared at Aria, but spoke to Gabriel. "You should convince Aria that it is unwise for her to go. Perhaps you can be more persuasive than we were."

Gabriel turned to study Aria for a moment. "Why do you think she should not go?"

"She will be a liability. We cannot protect her, not as weak as we are, and I will need all my strength for Owen."

Gabriel glanced between Aria and Cillian.

"Also we owe her a blood debt and are obligated to keep her safe until we know it is paid. But we have not the right to prevent her from going, if she chooses. Perhaps you can assist." Cillian's clipped voice betrayed his irritation.

*So much like Owen! When he spoke that way to me, he had reason to, even though I didn't understand at the time. Maybe I should listen to Cillian now.*

Gabriel studied Aria. "And you? What do you say?"

Aria raised her chin. "I think Petro wanted me to go. The information was given to me. Either the rescue will succeed, or it won't. But it might have better chances if I'm there."

Gabriel continued looking at her, then smiled faintly. "I think she has the right to decide. If she believes she should go, maybe she should."

Niamh and Cillian glared at him.

"Do you feel no obligation toward her? She is a human, as you are, and you are the leader of the human resistance. Does that mean nothing to you?" said Cillian.

Gabriel stiffened. "She is an adult, and neither a coward nor a fool. She makes her own decision."

Ardghal, who had said nothing thus far, reached forward to put a calming hand on Cillian's tense arm. He murmured, "Humans are baffling."

Cillian's nostrils flared but he nodded once, sharply. "It is as you say."

Niamh stared at Aria, her glare turning more thoughtful. "Perhaps, if she survives, we will gain useful information from her. Obviously humans see things differently than we do. Perhaps we may discover something enlightening."

Gabriel waited, tension thick in the air, until he said finally, "Will ten be enough to provide cover on the walls?"

"Yes," said Cillian.

"Then I'll leave you." Gabriel rose, and Bartok followed him without a word.

Aria didn't know what to do, but felt the cool irritation in Cillian's gaze and decided that she would go sleep after all. *You'd think I'd rather stay awake for my last hours, but I'm tired. Maybe the rest will help.*

# CHAPTER 11

GABRIEL SHOOK her awake. "I found them. They were in the papers Owen brought out."

"What?" she blinked at him blearily.

"Schematics! Come." He helped her to her feet and pulled her across the platform again toward the Fae.

"What time is it?"

"7:15. There's not much time."

He thrust the papers in front of Cillian. "We found these. Look."

They spread the papers out and studied them in silence for a moment. "Hm," Cillian said finally.

"What?" Aria asked.

He glanced up at her. "I do not think you should go."

"We've discussed this already! I'm going."

Aria glared at him.

His mouth tightened, and he said finally, "Then it will be only us. Niamh, Siofra, Conri, and the humans should stay on the walls and cover us. This is likely suicide. Owen would not wish us to sacrifice more on his behalf." He frowned at the schematics again. "We will enter through the front. Petro said Owen was on the second basement floor. We will use this access stairwell and search the floor from this side."

"I don't think it's *impossible*." Aria frowned. "Maybe improbable. But he gave us the information for a reason."

Niamh said, "But we do not know his reason."

Aria shrugged. "I don't care."

Cillian sighed, as if he had already accepted that the mission was doomed. "If we make it out, I assume my strength will be gone, either through injury or healing Owen as much as I can. Ardghal will meet us here, at the top of the tunnel entrance, and carry Owen the rest of the way. Niall can stand watch and open the sewer as we get close."

Aria studied the floor plan. At first it looked only like a crazed mass of overlapping lines, but after a moment she figured out the symbols for stairwells and doors between rooms. There were four stairwells between each floor; Cillian had indicated they would use the one closest to the eastern side of the building. Perhaps the closed stairwell would limit the number of soldiers who could fire on them at one time. Or perhaps it was merely that it was closest to the outside door. It opened onto a long hallway with many intersections. Plenty of opportunities to be caught or killed. Virtually no cover.

*Way to be optimistic, Aria.*

She frowned at her own thoughts. "Okay. We'll do it."

"There are sensors all along the wall and at the gate to sense our blood." Cillian raised his eyes to meet Niamh's gaze. "Be careful."

Niamh nodded.

"Those on the walls should return here a different way. Perhaps, if we are pursued, they can cause a distraction." Cillian continued frowning at the schematics.

Gabriel put one hand on her shoulder, as if he wanted to be reassuring, and she wondered whether he agreed that the mission was doomed.

"Who else is going?" she asked him.

"Evrial and Jonah's squads." Gabriel waited a moment longer, in case Cillian had anything else to say. "Come. We'll get you a headset and vest."

Aria followed Gabriel back toward the clusters of lanterns at the other end of the platform. He outfitted her, loaded and checked her pistol for her, and finally looked her over with a frown.

"I'd rather you not go, too," he said finally. "But it's your decision."

She didn't answer.

Bartok appeared by Gabriel's shoulder, already wearing his gear. "We found some interesting things in the books you retrieved, in addition to that bookmark. Clint thinks it might be worth going back tomorrow to see if there are any other clues. He used to be a detective."

"Interesting like what?" Aria looked at him curiously.

"We're not sure yet. Deliberate clues, but we don't know what they're pointing to."

258

She frowned at him. "Huh." She would have asked for more detail, but Cillian had joined them.

"We must leave. Petro specified 9:00. We cannot be late."

"Are you going?" Aria asked Gabriel.

He frowned. "No. I've been asked to remain here. But you have good men going. Plus Evrial."

Bartok raised an eyebrow. "I don't think she'd be offended to be grouped in with the men. Not on a mission, anyway."

"Come," Cillian said.

He led the way into a train tunnel. They would split up later, once they were closer to the facility, but for now they travelled in a tense, quiet line, flashlights bobbing in the darkness. It was a long walk, and Aria was already tired. *But it doesn't really matter, does it? Somehow I doubt that my fitness level is the determining factor in whether we succeed or not.* She wasn't confident in the logic of that thought. *If it is, we're doomed whether I'm tired or not. At least no one else is coming in with us.*

She found herself walking next to Bartok, his strides long and confident next to her shorter ones. She pushed down her nerves and tried to smile.

"Are you nervous?" He glanced sideways at her.

"Do I look nervous?"

"A little." He gave her a quick smile. "I'll go in with you, if you want."

The offer gave her pause, and she glanced at him again. "I don't think that's a good idea." *He must know we're probably going to die. Why would he offer something like that?*

He nodded. "I thought you'd say that. But the offer is real."

"Thanks."

They walked in silence for several steps, and Bartok opened his mouth once, then closed it again. Finally he said, "Be careful."

"I will." *For what it's worth.*

Evrial and Jonah led their squads into an access tunnel that would lead them close to Forestgate Imperial Security Facility. Bartok gave Aria a quick pat on the shoulder as he followed them. Evrial patted her shoulder too, a sympathetic touch that left her looking after them into the dark. *Am I stupid to do this? I have to try.* Niamh and several other Fae followed them, all outfitted with pistols and headsets.

She followed Cillian, Niall, and Ardghall a little farther to a different access tunnel and some distance down the dark passage, where they reached the bottom of a long ladder.

Cillian paused to tousle Niall's hair and give him a quick, hard embrace. Niall leaned into him for a moment, thin arms circling his uncle's waist. Cillian hugged Ardghal too, and a murmur passed between them. Then Cillian started up the ladder, his bare feet silent on the rungs.

Ardghal patted Aria on the shoulder. "It is brave, what you are doing. We thank you." His voice was soft, sorrowful.

Niall hesitated, his pale face barely visible in the darkness, and then leaned in to give her a quick hug too. She wrapped her arms around his shoulders, feeling the bones beneath his cool skin.

"I'll do my best."

*They think we're going to die.*

She climbed up the ladder after Cillian, Niall behind her. Cillian waited until she reached him

260

before moving the metal cover aside and slipping out. She climbed out next, and Niall closed the cover behind her, leaving just a crack through which he could watch down the street.

Aria took a deep breath and followed Cillian. They slipped down the street, keeping to the shadows, and circled around to approach the wall from the west side, where they could see the front gate. It was wide enough for two driveways for entering and exiting cars, with a guard post in the middle. The guards were in position, two visible standing outside the gate and at least three inside the gatehouse.

Aria glanced at her watch. Faint ambient light from the spotlights illuminated the face. 8:53 PM.

"What do you think is going to happen?" she murmured to Cillian.

He stared at the guards for a long moment. "Technically, the gate itself is open now. But we should not approach until 9:00."

Aria frowned. She glanced between her watch and the guards.

8:55.

She felt her heart thudding. *What do I expect to happen? This is suicide.*

8:58.

One of the guards turned to speak with another, and then nodded. He disappeared behind the gate. A heartbeat later, the other guard glanced around and walked inside the gate too.

9:00.

"Now." Cillian stepped forward.

Aria followed, hurrying to keep up. He strode toward the gate with apparent confidence. Aria could read his tension only because she'd studied

Owen's face so intently. She kept her pistol hidden under her jacket, hoping that looking innocuous would help somehow. *What about the sensors? He didn't do anything about them. Maybe he can't.*

The guardhouse had bulletproof glass walls on the three sides that faced away from the facility. Aria could see the shapes of the guards inside, bulky forms wearing thick army green jackets with the Imperial insignia. One figure turned briefly toward them, and Aria expected a shout of anger or a cry to halt. But he turned away again, as if Aria and Cillian were either invisible or simply unnoticed. Cillian strode through the wide car entrance and followed the driveway toward the front door of the building.

The driveway curved in front of the main building and continued to a parking area to the left. Floodlights lit the broad paved patio and bathed the driveway and front gate. Aria's heart thudded as she realized how exposed they were.

Cillian hesitated for only a moment before striding up to the large glass doors. He stepped through first, holding one hand out to keep Aria back while he glanced around the empty lobby area before continuing onward. A reception area faced them, with a metal detector for guests and turnstiles operated by badges. Cillian glanced around again before vaulting over a turnstile. She followed, the motion feeling awkward in comparison. She drew her pistol.

Toward the left corner, where a hallway led to the access stairs they had identified on the schematic. Down. And down one more floor.

They saw no one. *Perhaps that isn't so incredible. It is late, after all. But surely a place like this has secu-*

*rity around the clock.* And then, *don't question, Aria.
If we get caught later, so be it.*

Cillian hesitated for a moment at the bottom of
the stairs, his head raised a little.

"What is it?" Aria whispered.

"Blood." Cillian's silent steps quickened as he
followed the long hallway, pausing only briefly at
each intersection before leading her on. He turned
right, then left, and continued straight for another
thirty feet.

He stopped at a metal door. "He is here." He
put his hand on the doorknob, and Aria heard it
unlock with a nearly inaudible click. He pushed it
open.

From the narrow doorway behind Cillian, Aria
saw only that Owen was strapped to a metal table,
head turned slightly away from them to face
Grenidor. The colonel sat in a plastic chair on the
other side of the table, and he looked up, startled,
as the door opened.

Cillian lunged forward and around the table to
wrap his hands around Grenidor's neck. "I should
kill you!"

"Don't." Owen's voice was so faint Aria barely
heard it, but it stopped Cillian.

Grenidor struggled to breathe against Cillian's
harsh grip, his feet dangling six inches in the air. A
clipboard fell from his hands and clattered to the
floor as Cillian bared his teeth and growled.
Grenidor's face darkened with blood as he choked.

"Don't," Owen repeated, only a breath.

Cillian threw Grenidor against the wall ten feet
away. His head cracked against the concrete, and
he slumped to the floor, dazed.

Aria turned her attention to Owen and caught

her breath, tears welling in her eyes.

His left eye was shadowed by a deep bruise, and his right eye was swollen completely shut, the skin taut and dark. The angular line of his cheekbone was completely lost in a mass of bruises and swelling, with a deep cut that seeped blood into his ear. He wore the same clothes, the shirt plastered to him with fresh and caked blood. His chest moved with his breaths in slight, irregular starts.

Cillian moved to him and put a hand on his shoulder.

The bonds were not straps, as Aria had first thought, but metal shackles bolted to the table. She turned to Grenidor. "Where is the key?"

He glared at her, gasping, one hand raised to his throat.

She raised her pistol to aim at his knees, eyes holding his.

He swallowed and finally pointed to the far wall. "Second drawer on the left."

Aria stalked to the desk and opened the drawer, which was empty except for the single key. She hurried back and turned the key in a lock that secured the shackle around Owen's right wrist. She flipped back the metal and glanced at his face.

His eyes were closed, and his free hand lay slack on the table. She looked closer and sucked in her breath. The metal felt cool and smooth against her skin, like any other metal, but it must have been different for Owen. His wrist was raw where the metal had touched it, a livid band of angry red an inch wide.

"What is this?" she turned to Grenidor again.

"Getlaril," he muttered.

Cillian trembled beside her, his anger palpable, but he waited for her to unlock the other shackles, one hand resting on his brother's shoulder. He must have been doing something, because Owen suddenly took a deeper breath, a pained gasp that gurgled in his chest.

Aria was crying, tears streaking down her cheeks unnoticed, and she glared at Grenidor again. "*Why?* Why would you do this?"

Grenidor glared back at her, though he didn't rise. "He's not *human*! This is science. My methods will save lives. *Human* lives! You have no idea what you're dealing with." He cleared his throat with a cough and shot a furious glance at Cillian. "He might look human, but he's an animal. Animals do not have human rights, regardless of how pretty their faces are."

Aria wanted to scream at him, but time pressed upon her. They had to leave, get Owen out before soldiers descended upon them.

"He's better than you are," she muttered, not caring whether he heard or not. Then, "Can we lift him?" On a quick impulse, she unclipped the papers from Grenidor's clipboard and folded them in half to cram into her back pocket. Perhaps they had something that could help his healing.

Cillian frowned down at Owen, lips pressed together, then nodded. He knelt to slip his arm under Owen's shoulders and lift him into a sitting position as Aria shifted Owen's legs toward the floor.

Owen gasped and his left eye fluttered open. "Cillian?"

"Yes. I'm here. We're leaving now." Cillian's voice was low and steady, and he kept his face

265

turned away so Owen wouldn't see his tears. "I'd do more, but I need my strength to carry you."

Owen's head lolled forward, and Aria bent to get his left arm around her shoulders. Cillian was strong, but he was also far from recovered himself, and she imagined the help was welcome.

Aria glanced over her shoulder at Grenidor as they started toward the door. He still crouched against the wall, breath rasping in his throat. But he might not stay that way for long. She considered shooting him, but couldn't bring herself to do it in cold blood. Perhaps, if he'd been chasing them, she would have; but not now, while he only glared.

She wrapped her right arm around Owen's waist and held his left on her shoulder, trying to avoid the burned ring around his wrist. Her right hand was sticky with his blood as she stepped forward, matching Cillian's strides. She glanced back again. Could she block the door somehow? But it opened inward, and there was nothing to use near the door anyway.

Owen's feet barely moved as they dragged him forward, sagging between them.

The alarm finally sounded, a blaring repetitive wail that was deafening in the confined hallway. The lights flickered in time with the sound.

Aria's heart sank into her stomach. There was no way they could escape. Cillian had been right. Niamh and the others would not be able to save them.

She hurried forward anyway.

Grenidor slipped out the door behind them, and she expected a bullet in her back in moments.

Footsteps sounded in a neighboring hallway.

Boots running.

"You keep going. I'll handle it." Aria's breath caught in her throat, but she was proud of how steady her voice was; she sounded confident, competent.

When she started to shift from beneath Owen's arm, he slumped to the side. Cillian struggled to lift him, hitching Owen's right arm further around his shoulder and staggering onward.

Aria glanced behind them again and darted back to the last intersection, where she peeked around the corner. Immediately she pulled back, but not before a shot nearly hit her. The soldier approaching the corner had whipped his gun toward her without aiming in the split second she was visible, but training gave him reflexes much better than hers.

"Stupid, Aria!" she muttered to herself. She flattened herself against the wall and stepped back from the intersection, pistol aimed at the corner. He'd be around it in a moment. She couldn't hear his footsteps; he must be creeping slowly, ready to surprise her. She tried to keep her panicked breathing silent. *Stay calm. Keep it together, girl.*

A metal door slammed across the intersection with a solid thunk. Aria blinked, then backed a step away. The door stayed closed.

*What happened?*

*Don't question, just run.* She sprinted toward Cillian and Owen, who had almost reached the stairwell.

She pulled Owen's arm back over her shoulder and hauled him upward. Cillian was fading, and she imagined he was giving as much to his brother as he could without becoming a burden himself.

Perhaps more than he should have.

"It's not much farther," she muttered, as much for herself as for them.

Owen grunted, not a particularly reassuring sound, but at least it meant he was conscious enough to hear her. She didn't want to think about the long, painfully exposed sprint to the front gate, nor the streets beyond, where the soldiers would easily be able to catch them.

A hailstorm of bullets cracked into the cement beside her, and a metal door clanged shut to her left. Up the stairs. It was a struggle, Owen dead weight between them. Aria's legs burned by the time they reached the top, but she ignored the pain.

Owen muttered something she didn't understand, and Cillian grunted in response. On, through another hallway. She stumbled, nearly dragging Owen down with her before she recovered.

They reached the front door. Aria darted forward again, leaving Owen leaning hard on Cillian as she peered out. "I don't see anyone. Yet. Let's go."

They hurried across the lawn.

*Where are the soldiers? We should be dead by now.*

A shot cracked the glass of the front door behind them, but none tore into her back and she didn't dare slow long enough to look behind her.

*Are the guards asleep? The gate is still open. Go, go, go.*

Teary-eyed and breathless, she stumbled through the gate and down the street.

Another block, and they would make it. *It's impossible. They'll catch us before then.*

She startled when someone matched her steps on the other side. Petro. She stopped, her heart in her throat, then hurried forward again. "What are you doing here?"

His jaw tightened. He seemed reluctant to answer, and then said, "It was required in order to avoid undesirable results."

"Well, I hope you enjoyed the show." Her voice was bitter. *Can you slap a dragon? He deserves it.*

Cillian stared across Owen at Petro, his strides uneven. Petro ignored him, cold green eyes still on Aria as he matched her steps.

Suddenly furious, Aria rounded on him. "I love him! This is painful, and you just watch, like we're some sort of entertainment! It's vulgar!" She brushed angrily at her tears with one hand. "It doesn't matter if he doesn't love me back. That's not the point."

Petro was silent for a long moment, and Aria caught sight of Niall at the sewer opening, the cover open in readiness for them. Finally Petro said, "I've never understood why humans think love is important." He stared at her profile for another few steps.

"Love is everything." Aria didn't know where the words came from, but she meant them with all her heart.

Niall darted forward and pulled Cillian's free hand, helped him down the hole first. Cillian climbed past Ardghal and into the darkness; Ardghal helped Aria maneuver Owen's limp body into the sewer and onto his shoulders. He carried Owen down, breathing heavily with the effort, and Aria and Niall climbed down after him. Petro was gone.

"Where are the others?" Aria whispered as they hurried through the blackness. Ardghal and Cillian supported Owen between them.

"They will meet us," Ardghal answered.

Aria's hand trailing on the wall suddenly felt emptiness, and she followed the corner to the left. Niall's cool hand found hers, and he led her more quickly.

THE TRAIN STATION platform was dimly lit by a few lanterns scattered about. Ardghal was silhouetted briefly as he entered, Owen's unmoving form on his back. Cillian was staggering in exhaustion, his shadow dancing on the walls. Ardghal must have taken Owen's weight from him.

Gabriel cursed and darted forward, but Cillian turned to him with a snarl. "Keep away from him!"

Gabriel stopped, hands raised placatingly. "What do you need?"

Cillian growled something Aria couldn't understand, and Ardghal answered for him. "Keep your distance."

As she hurried in behind them, Aria saw Gabriel frowning. She paused by him for a moment but didn't know what to say.

Finally she choked out, "He's in pretty bad shape."

"I saw." Gabriel's voice was tight. "Is anyone following you?"

Aria took a shaky breath. "I don't think so. I think they would have noticed." She gestured at the Fae.

They stood in silence for a long moment, watching the small group move toward the lanterns at the far end of the platform. Niamh and several of the other Fae who had been on the walls were already there.

"Did everyone else get away?"

Gabriel said, "Yes. We're going over the material from the H Street facility when you want to join us. It's interesting."

Aria nodded, her throat still tight with emotion. "Maybe later."

Gabriel patted her shoulder once before turning away.

She hesitated, but finally made her way toward the Fae encampment. She rubbed at her face, trying to control the tears threatening to overflow.

Aria wasn't sure whether she had the right to be there while they sang for Owen, but she couldn't stay away. Niall saw her face and scooted to the side a little, and she dropped to sit next to him. Owen lay unmoving in the center of the circled Fae, scarcely breathing. The back of his head must have been bleeding too; the hair was thick with caked and crusted blood that had left a smear on the floor.

Niamh spoke, her eyes not leaving Owen's face. "Why did you not kill Grenidor?"

"He forbade it." Cillian's voice was nearly inaudible.

Niamh glanced up at him sharply. "He did *what*?"

"He said, '*Don't.*'" Cillian's nostrils flared but he said nothing else.

Niamh stared at Owen again, and Aria tried to read her expression. Fury. Confusion? Grief.

Doubt, perhaps, though Aria wasn't sure on that one. After a long moment, she closed her eyes and began to sing.

*White stone cliffs fell away into crashing ocean waves. Owen picked his way along the narrow rocky shore, black curls crusted with salt. He knelt to pick up a stone and threw it into the waves. He turned, looked behind him, and smiled, white teeth flashing. He lifted one hand as if in acknowledgement, then looked back toward the water with a pensive expression. A wave surged toward him, and he waited, took a step deeper into the water, the sandy wash tugging at his trousers. He knelt again, pressed both hands to the ground beneath the water. It eddied around him, pulling at the hem of his white shirt, swirling sand and tiny bits of froth in chaotic patterns as it swept away.*

*He looked back over his shoulder again and nodded, but he didn't rise immediately. He stared out at the next wave for a long moment, waiting as it approached, then slowly stood, eyes on the water as it surged around his knees. He opened his hands to let the sand and pebbles fall, disappearing into the water. The wave had begun to recede before he turned and started back toward the narrow beach.*

Aria blinked as she stared at Owen's body. The music faded around her, but she smelled the scent of the ocean, a salty tang in the air.

The difference wasn't obvious at first, but after a moment she realized his breathing was more regular. Niamh leaned forward to touch his forehead with one white hand, and his left eye opened slowly. The right was gruesomely swollen, and Niamh traced the line of his eyebrow with one finger.

"Owen." It was only one word, but there was a

weight of sorrow in her voice that made Aria's heart constrict.

He blinked at her.

Niamh frowned at him. "You should have let Cillian kill him. It is justice."

He said nothing, but his gaze roved slowly around the circle to rest on Aria for a long moment, then back to Niamh. His lips moved, but Aria couldn't tell what he meant to say.

Niamh drew back, her face tight. "Why? You ask *why*?" Her hand clenched.

Owen closed his eye and his lips tightened. Aria wondered whether he was frustrated or simply fighting pain.

"Let him be." Her words came without thought, and she bit her lip as everyone stared at her.

"This is not your concern." Niamh's voice was cool, but her eyes weren't exactly angry as she looked across at Aria. Aria tried to read her face. Was she puzzled?

"Let him be," Aria repeated. "He needs to rest, doesn't he? To heal? Don't bother him with questions, then."

Niamh continued to study her and Aria tried not to squirm.

The next question was addressed to her. "Did Petro help you in there?"

Aria licked her lips and thought. "Possibly. Doors closed, blocking soldiers from shooting us. I didn't do it."

Cillian nodded his head minutely and closed his eyes for a long moment. "There was more. We can discuss it later. Owen saw it too."

Niamh glanced at Owen. He opened his left

eye again, but appeared to gaze thoughtfully into space, not meeting anyone's gaze directly.

"Do you truly love him?"

The question startled Aria, and she blushed. "Yes. But I don't expect anything from him, if that's what you're asking. It's not like I know him that well, really." She chewed her lip and tried to keep her voice from shaking. "I just saw how brave he was, and how he cared for Niall before himself. It's heroic. But it's okay if he doesn't feel the same way. I understand."

She looked up to see his gaze resting on her. His lips twitched, just the merest hint of a smile.

Niamh said finally, "We have done all we can for now." She leaned closer, speaking softly to him. "If you wish, we will leave you." He murmured something, and she leaned in further, her ear close to his mouth. Then she smiled, touched his face again with one hand, and stood. "Come." She led the others a little distance away, where they settled down to rest.

Aria slid forward to sit closer to Owen's face. His eye drifted closed, and then opened again with some effort.

"Can I do anything? Would it help if I did human things? I can wash off the blood and put bandages on. I know it won't heal you." Her voice trailed away and she blinked away tears. She brushed at her eyes in frustration, feeling her face heat as his gaze rested on her.

His voice was nearly inaudible. "If you wish."

"You don't mind? I don't want to hurt you." She swallowed.

"It would be acceptable." He smiled a little, the expression more clear on the left side of his face.

She jogged across the long platform to where the humans were grouped and asked Eli for bandages, tape, scissors, and water. He found a bucket, and she went in search of a faucet to fill it.

Bartok accompanied her. He didn't say anything, but she could feel his quiet sympathy. His company was welcome, because the deep shadows in the upper platform were eerie and echoing. She found a long-abandoned restroom and ran the water for several minutes to let the pipes clear before cramming the bucket underneath the faucet.

"They're less like us than we thought," Bartok said.

Aria frowned more deeply. "I think there's a lot we don't understand. I don't know how important any of it is, though."

Bartok reached out to put a gentle hand on her shoulder for a moment. "Be careful." He didn't say anything else.

He carried the bucket back to Owen for her and then left her with the second lantern, picking his way back across the darkened platform toward the warm circle of light at the far end, where the others were.

Aria settled in front of Owen. He watched her lay out the supplies without a word, and she couldn't read his expression.

"I think I should cut off your shirt. Instead of making you take it off."

He grunted softly, and she decided to take it as assent. She used the scissors to cut the shirt up from the bottom hem. It stuck in many places, and she used one hand to dribble water onto it, loosening the caked blood as she worked the fabric free.

As she pulled the shirt back she caught her

breath, tears in her eyes again. It was even worse than she'd feared. Most of the skin was no longer white; black bruises covered his whole torso, and uneven bumps showed the ends of broken ribs. Dark circles the size of her fingertips filled with crusted blood showed where he'd been shot, eight in his chest and two lower on his right side. She felt his gaze on her face, but she couldn't look up to meet his eye.

"Why did he—" she stopped. Surely she had less right to pester him with questions than his sister did. "Never mind. Just tell me if I make it worse."

Doing something for him, no matter how little it mattered, made her feel better. She folded one of the bandages into a thick square and dipped it into the water, then squeezed it mostly dry. Her hands trembled as she dabbed at the blood smears, circling around each bullet hole.

He kept breathing, but he said nothing and she didn't look at his face for a long time. She focused on the cloth and water, the raw scrapes and bruises. Finally she had cleaned as much as she could and taped small squares of gauze over each visible wound. She didn't imagine it actually mattered, but at least it looked like someone cared.

Finally she looked up to his face. Both eyes were closed, and she hesitated, but finally dipped the cloth into the water again and brought it to his swollen cheek. At the feather light touch, his left eye opened.

"Should I wash your face too?"

"If you wish."

She wished she could read his expression. She wondered what it felt like; if he wasn't warm-blooded, would the cool damp touch feel refreshing on his swollen eye and cheek?

He submitted to her efforts without comment, and she moved on to explore the wound on the back of his head without asking. He turned his head to the right and she moved the lamp closer, but it was still hard to see the extent of the injury through his black curls and the thick, caked blood. With some gentle pouring and working her fingers through his hair, she got the majority of the blood out, and decided that doing anything else would cause more pain than it helped. She folded a dry bandage and slid it beneath his head.

She sat back and looked at him. It would be a stretch to say he looked "better," because some of the wounds had been hidden before. His eye was closed again, and she leaned forward to rest her elbows on her knees, her head hanging down.

The exhaustion of the last three days threatened to overwhelm her. She bit back tears and tried to calm her breathing. *He'll heal. He's strong, and there are others to help him. They love him too, probably better than I do. We're away from the hotel, and Grenidor won't find us here. We have information, if we can decipher it. We're in a better position than we have been since the Revolution. It's just that I didn't know about it before, so I thought everything was fine. But it was never fine. Now we have hope.* The thoughts, logical as they were, didn't keep her from trembling.

She jumped at his touch. Owen had moved his left hand slightly, so the back of his hand rested against her knee.

"Why?" he whispered.

"Why am I crying?" She forced a tired smile.

277

"I'm sorry. For you. I used to think everything was fine. It wasn't. Now I know about it."

He stared at her for a long moment. "Did you go to Petro?"

"Cillian and Niall and I did." She took a deep, shuddering breath and tried to steady her voice. "It was strange. They can tell you about it. Apparently he acted differently around me."

He swallowed. "That was dangerous. They should not have taken you." He closed his eye again and his jaw tightened; it was obvious that speaking was painful.

"They warned me about the danger. But they said they could not prevent me, if I chose to go." She thought back again to their words. *That was odd. As if they spoke of rules understood, rather than a decision agreed upon by the group.*

He continued to watch her face. Finally he asked, "Why did you say 'love is everything' to Petro?"

"He said, 'I've never understood why humans think love is important.' I disagreed." Aria blushed, thinking about what she'd said before that, but it didn't matter. He already knew she loved him, and it probably didn't mean anything to him. That was fine. She'd told everyone already. She didn't expect anything to come of it. *When did I become this brave? I never thought I'd bare my heart like this and care so little if anyone laughed at me.*

Owen blinked and stared at her. "I didn't hear that."

"You were a little out of it."

"I heard what you said before it. I didn't hear Petro's response." He closed his eye and took a slow, painful breath. "Please ask Cillian what he

278

heard."

She blinked at him. "What?"

"I think it might mean something. But I don't know what."

"I will. I think you should rest though." She slipped her hand into his. He didn't react for a moment, but then he squeezed her hand slightly. She smiled, a little sad, a little grateful, and then let him go as she stood.

# CHAPTER 12

ARIA FOUND CILLIAN, but he seemed to be sleeping, lying on his back with one arm thrown over his face. She stood for a moment staring at him, and finally found a bedroll and carried it back to sleep near Owen.

They were all exhausted. Owen's question could wait. He needed to heal, and they needed to rest before they could sing for him again. Perhaps it was improper, but she didn't think he'd mind her staying close. They'd shared a room before, and it felt wrong to leave him lying in the dark alone at the end of the platform.

She turned the lantern down low and curled up under the thin blanket. Cold, hungry, and aching with weariness, she finally drifted off to sleep.

*Shoulders relaxed, Owen stood knee-deep in the*

*sandy ocean water. The cold wind frothed the tips of the waves, but it didn't bother him. As she watched, he stood motionless for long minutes, staring out into the water. The waves moved in and out, tugging at his trousers, the damp fabric dark as it clung to his legs. Birds shrieked, and he looked upward, squinting into the bright sunlight as he watched them pass.*

SHE WOKE to the sound of quiet voices. Cillian and Niamh were closest to her, and they must have heard her wake, for Cillian turned to her immediately.

"We have questions for you." He motioned for her to come closer.

Owen's left eye was open, and the swelling in the right had gone down a little, though it was still probably impossible for him to see with it. He had not moved from his back.

"I thought you'd be able to heal him more by now. There are a lot of you." She meant the words as a question, not an accusation, but Niamh frowned.

"Grenidor did much damage. Most of it is not visible." She ran her hand gently over Owen's forehead. "He is actually better than I'd expected. We wondered if somehow you helped him."

Aria swallowed. "I only cleaned him up a little. I doubt it actually helped any."

They regarded her for a moment. Cillian asked, "What did you hear Petro say as we were leaving?"

"'I've never understood why humans think love is important.' That's what made me so angry. Even if he did help us, he was watching like some creepy voyeur." Even thinking about it made her tense in anger again.

Cillian stared at her and then looked back at Niamh. "You see?"

"See what?" Aria asked.

"I heard him say, 'I am not interested in love.' The difference in meaning may be subtle, but the words were distinctly different. And Owen heard nothing," Cillian said.

Niamh frowned, still looking at Aria. "I am more intrigued by the fact that he helped. Did he explain that to you?"

"He said it was required in order to avoid undesirable results." Aria scowled. "Like us dying, I suppose."

Cillian rubbed his face thoughtfully. "That would not normally be a concern for him," he said.

Owen murmured and they leaned closer to hear him. "We have almost no information about his dealings with humans. Only with us." He stopped to take a slow breath and then continued, "Perhaps the rules are different."

"What rules do you keep talking about?" Aria asked.

Cillian frowned thoughtfully. "Perhaps. You humans have many choices, many options in how you deal with each other. We are more restricted. More bound. We can see many options, as if we were human, but we cannot always choose freely. Sometimes we have a choice, but certain options are much more difficult than others." He must have seen the confusion on her face, because he continued. "Lying. We can lie to each other, but it is very difficult. It is even more difficult to lie to a human. Sometimes impossible. Sometimes merely difficult, with immediate consequences if we dare. It is difficult to withhold information that is directly requested. Especially if the human has a valid reason to request it. Even when it is harmful or dangerous to us, it is virtually impossible to deliberately deceive a human. This is one of many reasons we have kept our distance from humans; for our own safety."

Owen spoke softly. "I lied to Grenidor."

Niamh and Cillian both twitched in surprise. "You did *what*?"

"He wanted information. Your location. And the dark ones. How to contact them." His jaw tensed and he closed his eye for a moment before continuing. "I told him of the hotel after ten hours. I guessed you would have moved by then." Another difficult breath.

Aria chewed her lip as she watched him struggle. She wanted him to rest, but obviously he thought this information was important enough to justify the pain of speaking.

"I lied about the dark ones. I told him it was impossible for humans to interact with them."

Niamh let out a slow sigh and looked back at Cillian. For Aria's benefit, she said, "That should not have been possible. At all. Grenidor, for all his cruelty, genuinely believes in his cause. That gives him the power to compel answers from us. Especially one like Owen, who is so obedient. Perhaps the rules *are* changing."

Cillian leaned closer and touched Owen's shoulder with the tips of his fingers. "And yet I cannot tell." The whisper was soft, confused. "I am glad, my brother, but I don't understand."

Owen twitched his hand; he had something

else to say. "I prayed. For strength. Forgiveness. I didn't think El would answer a prayer for the ability to lie, but He did."

Cillian's nostrils flared, his voice low and angry. "You should give up these beliefs, Owen. They do you no good. If that is why you did not allow me to kill Grenidor, you are *wrong*. He deserved it, more than anyone in both our long lives. You know it would be permitted, and you know it is justice!"

"They have something we don't, Cillian." Owen's voice was fading. "They have choices. I chose. I went against the rules, and it was permitted. But it might be only because I chose mercy."

"But you were wrong!" Niamh cried. Tears spilled down her cheeks, and she reached out to touch Owen's face. "Why? Why would you let him live, after this?"

Owen smiled. "Because I *could*! Don't you see? We have never been permitted such freedom."

Cillian was trembling with anger, but he said nothing for a long moment, his eyes flicking from Niamh to Owen and back. At last he said quietly, "I don't think we understand humans as well as we thought we did. Or Petro. This is important, but perhaps not urgent. We must move soon. Grenidor will be searching for us, and especially you."

Owen's smile faded only slightly as he closed his eye again. "Yes."

Niamh and Cillian frowned at the floor. Aria glanced around. There were several other Fae sitting a little farther back, but no one said anything. Ardghal was staring at her in perplexity, but at last he began to sing. His voice was deeper than those she'd heard before, and in it Aria heard the rush of the ocean waves, the steady strength of ancient oaks.

For the first time, Aria saw other Fae in the singing dream. Perhaps it was a dream. Perhaps it was some truth she did not yet understand. Owen sat on a rocky embankment, bare feet dangling, leaning forward as if listening to someone. Only a few feet below him, the ground spread out in a spacious clearing filled with Fae. They sat on the ground, legs crossed or kneeling, some leaned back on their hands. It was a casual gathering, and there were many smiles among them. Owen nodded and looked toward someone else, a young boy who stood respectfully as he spoke. Niall, his dark hair longer, his shoulders less bony. She couldn't hear his words, perhaps that wasn't permitted in the dream or perhaps she wouldn't have understood them anyway. But it was clear that he *could* speak, and she saw Owen's affection in his face as he listened, a slight smile on his lips. He nodded again, and Niall sat down. Another stood, an older man, and Owen's smile faded into a sorrowful expression.

The song rose around her even as the image shifted into a forest, Owen sitting alone on a high tree branch, leaning back against the trunk as it swayed in the wind. His hair blew into his face and he shook it aside without seeming to notice, one leg hooked around the branch beneath him and the other stretched out in relaxation.

The vision faded, and she saw him again in the center of the circle, bloodied and bruised. Broken. *No. He is* not *broken.*

Niamh leaned forward again to touch his face

285

with the backs of her fingers, barely brushing the skin. Owen did not move, did not react at all, not even a twitch of his closed eyes. "I cannot feel it either, Cillian. No stench of it."

Niall, who had nearly disappeared, scooted forward. He bowed his head to the floor beside Owen and remained there for long minutes, forehead pressed to the concrete.

"Niall," Niamh said at last, in a soft voice.

Niall shook his head, eyes closed, face still toward the floor. His shoulders jerked, and Aria knew he was crying.

She leaned forward to touch his shoulder, conscious of everyone watching her. Niall didn't react at first, but after a long moment he raised his head to study her face. His eyes were red and tears glistened on his thin cheeks, but he kept his eyes on hers. His mouth twitched as if he was going to say something, and he glanced toward his notebook. But he only studied her a moment longer, ducked his head in a slight bow, and nodded toward his mother.

"Is he asleep?" Aria whispered.

"If you can call it that." Cillian's voice had lost the anger.

"Is he in pain? While he's sleeping?"

Cillian's mouth twitched. "It is difficult to tell. He is far from us."

Niamh glanced over Aria's shoulder. "The humans are attempting to gain our attention."

Aria looked back to see Eli silhouetted the lanterns, waving to her. "Please tell me if I can do anything."

They blinked at her, as if surprised by the request, and Cillian nodded solemnly.

ARIA HEADED toward the encampment at the other end of the platform. That area was more brightly lit, with both cool electric lanterns and the warmer tones of oil lanterns spread out across the wide concrete expanse. The supplies had been stacked against the wall at the end, boxes of dried food, ammunition, extra guns, rope, lantern oil, soap, and any number of other things. She didn't really know how they managed to survive, living in tunnels and abandoned buildings, but somehow they did.

Eli waved to her again and she trudged toward him. There was a small circle gathered around an array of papers, glass jars, and the old digital camera.

"We've found some information in the materials Owen brought out from the H Street facility. Come."

She sighed as she sat down next to him. "Like what?"

Bartok, sitting across from her, glanced up. "Are you okay?"

"I'm just hungry. Go on." Her stomach growled to accompany her words, and she winced. "Sorry."

Eli stood. "Carry on." He disappeared, but returned in a moment.

Bartok said, "As part of my residency I did a pharmacology stint. It's been a while, and I focused more on clinical pharmacology and toxicology rather than psycho- and neuropharmacology. However, I can tell a few things about these substances."

He pointed at one jar. "This one contains chlorpromazine, which is generally understood to reduce a subject's aggression and argumentativeness. Valproate, which generally calms the subject without the more obvious signs of sedation. It's sometimes used to treat paranoia and schizophrenia. And methylphenidate, which is used to treat attention disorders and increase focus. I'm not familiar with tricetylethylene and amobarbital. I would guess, based on the chemical names, that they act on inhibitions, somewhat like sodium pentathol, the 'truth drug.' Without knowing what doses were used, I couldn't say for certain what this is used for. But it *could* be used to dramatically alter the subject's state of mind."

Someone put a sandwich in Aria's hand and dropped an apple and a bottle of water in her lap. "Thanks," she said over her shoulder. Whoever it was had already disappeared.

Bartok studied the label on another jar for a long moment. "This one is a little different. Instead of tricetylethylene, it includes chlorpromazine-beta-five. It basically makes the subject very open to suggestion. It looks to me like this is a later variation on that cocktail. This would be used for essentially the same purpose, but would require a lower dose and be more effective. Possibly more dangerous, but highly effective. And this one is propranalol. It's a blood pressure medication but at high doses it can alter and even erase memories."

Gabriel frowned. "So these are the drugs used during the brainwashing?"

Bartok shrugged slightly. "I can't say with certainty. But it's possible. Very likely."

"What can be done to reverse the effects?"

Aria frowned. "What exactly *were* the effects? I

don't remember what they told us in that room. I remember we watched videos, but not what they were about."

Bartok glanced at her. "I'm not a brainwashing expert, nor a psychologist. But I would guess, based on the drugs and your description, that the drugs were used to accustom the subjects to receiving information from a particular source, and to regarding that source as trustworthy. Owen said that some of them also had a magical component. I can't evaluate that, of course, but it seems likely that the magical aspect increased the effective duration. The effects could be compounded, of course. If the source of information was repeatedly shown to be correct, the subjects would eventually cease to question it even after the drug had worn off."

Aria stared at him. "So the drugs might have worn off long ago?"

"I have no way to guess. I could take a blood sample, I suppose, but it would be impossible to evaluate without a lab. Of course, it's also possible for drugs to cause physical changes in the brain, which would persist long after the drug is no longer in the body."

"What about the others?" Gabriel gestured toward the other jars.

Bartok lifted one and read the label. "Hm." He frowned. "This is, or could be, a synthetic form of something that used to be known as scopolamine, or hyoscine. The effects vary. In small doses it was used for reducing labor pains in childbirth, but it had some negative effects so that was discontinued back in the early 1900s. In larger doses, it can be used to essentially eliminate the subject's free will, or critical thinking abilities. They're very suggestible. The natural form has always been difficult to obtain. I wasn't aware that a synthetic form had been created. But this looks very similar in the chemical form; it may not be identical, but it's incredibly close. It may have similar effects."

"So they were experimenting with different drug cocktails? Or they used different ones in succession? Or what?" Aria asked.

Bartok shrugged again. "There's no way for me to know. But it's clear from the selection here that they at least explored medication as one tool in the arsenal." He lifted another jar. "Now these are different. There are several chemical names here I don't recognize at all. Now, I certainly don't know what every drug does, nor can I say with certainty how they were used, but I am reasonably up to date on legitimate medications and their chemical components. These are unusual. First, they aren't strictly chemical names. They're more like descriptions. This one, *lamia sanguis,* translates as 'vampire blood.'" He raised his eyes to catch Aria's eye for a long moment, then looked down again. "This contains several I don't recognize and can't translate. Perhaps something related to breath? The term isn't derived from Latin, like the others. This one, *lupus animum,* translates to 'wolf's mind.' Which doesn't make a lot of sense to me, but that's what it says."

Everyone stared at the jars. Evrial reached forward to pick one up and study it for a moment, then set it back down carefully.

Bartok leaned forward again to put his elbows on his knees. "Owen mentioned that you had something in your brain. Do you know anything about that?"

Aria shook her head. "When he took my tracker out, he put his hand on the back of my head here. I think that's when he sensed it. But he didn't say anything about it until he told you all."

"Maybe we'll find something in the records."

Aria took a deep breath. "Okay. What else is there? Anything in the papers?"

Gabriel pushed them toward her. "Lord Owen saw fit to bring these, out of all the thousands of pages he must have seen. But I'm not sure exactly what he saw in them. Aside from the Forestgate schematic, of course. The hard drives have a lot more. We're still prioritizing."

Aria frowned as she read the top sheet. A bill of lading? A shipment of crates containing un-specified wares, delivered to Eastborn Imperial Security Facility. *It could be food for the mess hall, for all I know. Maybe there is nothing here. Maybe the only thing useful was the schematic.* She paged through slowly, not seeing anything that was immediately valuable or even particularly intriguing. A map of parking areas at Eastborn.

She pulled a few stapled pages out, a list of phone extensions at Eastborn. "Maybe this could be useful."

Gabriel glanced at her. "Maybe."

Bartok didn't seem to have anything else to say, and the others gradually dispersed. He leaned forward elbows on his knees, eyes ranging over the jars again. "You don't remember anything else about the week you spent in that room?" he asked finally.

"No. It's just vague." She frowned. "Even the things before it are still kind of fuzzy. My parents and stuff." She sighed. "I'd like to say it's weird, but I don't remember what it was like to remember it clearly. I have images in my mind, but they're distant."

Bartok's eyes rested on her face, and she felt his sympathy.

"How old were you when the Revolution started?" she asked abruptly. "What do you remember of it?"

"When it really started in the North Quadrant I was in high school. But I lived in the East Quadrant, so I didn't notice anything until I was starting my residency. I was twenty-seven. I was about ten miles south of here in the Rose Hill district, in what used to be called Virginia. The first two years were pretty normal. The third we started getting casualties from the fighting in the North Quadrant, people that didn't want to go to the local hospitals. We heard things, but mostly we focused on treating the injuries."

"I thought you were a pediatrician."

"I was in my emergency and intensive care rotations. I started with a pediatric specialty clinic when I finished. I was thirty. I was only there about a year when everything fell apart." He looked down at his hands and rubbed them on his pants. "The district was suddenly swept up in the fighting. I found myself treating injuries on the street after tanks came through. I hadn't kept up with the politics of it; my residency was pretty intense and I didn't have time to wonder what was going on. So I didn't have a side." He hesitated, then said quietly, "Gabriel's son was fighting with him. He was shot in front of me. He bled out. I'm not sure he would have made it even if we'd been in the ER when it happened. Anyway, he didn't make it. Gabriel was close, and he swept me up with him in their retreat. At first I think he only wanted a doctor. He hated me for a while. But I think he knows now I did everything I could." Bartok hunched forward, not looking at her. "That was a year ago. So here I am." He glanced up at her and then away.

Aria took a shaky breath, caught up in his story. "I'm sorry." She put a hand on his arm.

He sighed.

*But that's recent. I thought all the fighting was over ten years ago! Even in the East Quadrant, I thought it had been over for years.* She swallowed. None of her memories could be completely trusted.

Aria glanced over her shoulder toward the Fae. They hadn't moved, a silent circle around Owen's motionless form.

Bartok glanced at her face and looked like he was considering saying something.

"What?" Aria asked.

He gave a minute shrug. "Never mind." He hesitated, then asked, "Should I go help? I mean, Gabriel told me to stay away. Emphatically. And I know they don't seem to need medical care the way we do, but maybe I can do something."

Aria shook her head. "I cleaned him up a little." Her throat closed with sudden emotion. "They didn't seem to think it would matter. It just made me feel better." She leaned forward to hide her face in her hands.

He rested his hand on her shoulder for just a moment. "It's hard to see someone you care about in pain." His voice was quiet.

She nodded, not looking up.

He sighed and squeezed her shoulder, then withdrew the comforting touch. "It's 4:30 in the morning. You're probably exhausted. Get some sleep."

"It is?" she looked up then.

He gave her a wry smile and rubbed his hands across his face. "Yes. Gabriel wanted to know if any of these things would be useful if you managed to get Owen out. I don't think so. Whatever they're doing, the purpose isn't healing Fae."

Now that she was looking, she could see the shadows under his eyes. He'd been up all night too.

"Thank you." She held his eyes for a moment, to be sure he understood that the thanks was for his kindness, for going on the mission, for his sympathy, not just for the admonition to get some rest.

He nodded slightly. "You're welcome." His smile said he understood.

*Did his smile look sad? Like he'd lost something? Maybe I'm too tired to read expressions well.*

# CHAPTER 13

ARIA DREAMED of strange things. The grey room. Injections. Being stripped naked, paraded in a shivering line with other young women down a hallway. Videos. Even in the dream, she knew she should hold on to the memories, but when she drifted toward wakefulness they faded again. She scowled, still half asleep, and turned over, her back sore and aching.

She lay near Owen, close enough to hear him whisper, if he woke, and far enough to feel that she was not encroaching. Niamh and Cillian slept on his other side, and the others ranged out around them. After she had finished washing his wounds, one of the Fae stayed at his head at all times, silent and watchful. Now it was Niall, his thin shoulders bowed with grief. When she shifted, he looked up at her. The lamp was turned down low, a soft yellow glow that left his expression in shadow.

Aria murmured, "What time is it?"

Niall lifted both hands toward her, fingers splayed, then waggled one hand. *10:00, approximately.*

She assumed he meant AM, not PM. *But what day is it? I've lost track.* She tried to think back. *When did I go to Dandra's? Can I really call it love, if I've known him only for a few weeks? But I'm not asking to marry him! I don't know what I'd say if he asked, and I can't imagine that he would. Call it a crush. Every girl gets those. But it's not without reason. And it doesn't mean the feeling isn't real. I care.*

She slid closer. The bruise around Owen's left eye had deepened as he slept, and the cut on his right cheek had crusted with blood again. His chest moved with faint, uneven breaths, the gauze pads stark white against his black bruises. Niall sat beside him with his legs crossed, the notebook at his knee.

Aria whispered, "Why do you call him Lord Owen?"

Niall glanced at her, and she wondered whether her question was unwelcome. She meant it to be a distraction from his grief. *Because he is Lord Ailill's heir. Lord Ailill is the,* he hesitated, then wrote *High King of our people. There is no word in English that conveys the authority he holds. Lord Ailill has given much of his authority to Lord Owen already. He is old, and he hopes to,* he hesitated again, then made a helpless gesture with one hand.

"Hopes to what?"

*… go away. Ascend? It is not always given to High Kings, but he hopes it will be given to him. It is a great*

*gift. He wants to be ready, and he is wise to rest his authority on Lord Owen before it is necessary. No one would argue with his choice, nor with Lord Owen's authority, but it is wise to support his heir in what may be his last days. His power has weighed on him, but he has always held it lightly. I believe that is counted in his favor.*

"But he's captive, isn't he?"

*Yes, Lord Ailill is captive now. He may be required to die. That is also acceptable to him. We would grieve, but it is not unprecedented. It is only the manner of his death that is objectionable.*

"What authority do you mean?"

*He is given much authority. His decisions are binding in ways that humans cannot understand. We can rebel, but to rebel against him is to rebel against El. That is not something to be chosen lightly. Unless his commands are against El's express order, we obey him as we obey El.*

Aria swallowed. "Yet you argue with Lord Owen."

Niall smiled a little. *Yes, I have pleaded with him. Sometimes my entreaties move him. Sometimes his decision is firm. I obey.*

"When he's unmoved, do you think he's wrong? Like when he didn't let you help open the cells at Eastborn? Do you think he would have gotten away safely if he'd let you help?" Aria wished she'd bitten back the questions as too prying, but her tongue seemed to have a will of its own.

Niall swallowed and remained unmoving, the pen poised over the paper for several minutes. He took a deep breath, put the pen to the page, and then raised it again. He brushed at his eyes angrily with his free hand.

"I'm sorry. I shouldn't have asked that."

*Define "wrong."*

Aria frowned herself, not sure how to answer him.

*For us, "wrong" means disobedient. For humans, I have been told it can mean many things. Incorrect. Defiant. Etc. I do not believe Lord Owen was disobedient in his decision. The outcome was not the outcome I would have chosen. Lord Owen is wiser than I am, and more intimate with El. I do not argue with his decision, though I grieve the cost.* He did not look up at her.

"And when he lied to Grenidor?" she whispered.

He looked up at her then, his clear blue eyes anguished. He shook his head and looked back down at the paper. *It was a sacrifice. He chose the worst possible thing. If he did not have the strength to remain silent,* he paused, the pen trembling over the paper. *I do not blame him for that. But if he did not have the strength, it would have been better to give Grenidor the information. Even if we all died for it. The sacrifice he chose was too great. More than his life for ours. You cannot understand the cost.* He raised the pen again to wipe at his eyes. *All my life, I have looked up to him. He is the example, the most obedient, and the most pure. And now, when he is tested, he chose to lie instead of sacrifice us. I do not understand!* The pen nib tore through the paper and he bent over, burying his face in his hands. His shoulders shook with silent sobs.

Aria reached out to put a sympathetic hand on his shoulder, her head whirling. *What does he mean, the cost is too great? What could be greater than the death of everyone he loves? Who could blame him?*

Owen let out a soft sound that might have

been a moan, if it had been stronger. As it was, it made Aria's heart clench. Niall leaned forward and put his hand on Owen's shoulder, fingers resting lightly on the bruised skin. He frowned, brushed at his eyes again, and turned to Cillian, who sat up and moved to Owen's side.

"How is he?" Aria whispered.

Cillian shook his head. "Perhaps he has strengthened a little. It is difficult to tell. He should not have spoken so much."

Niall glanced at her and then back down at Owen.

"Grenidor will be searching. But I do not want to move him." Cillian frowned more deeply.

A shadow moved, and Niamh slid into the light. She looked up past Aria's shoulder. "What do you want?" The tone was harsh, but she kept her voice quiet.

"I came to see if I could help." Bartok strode closer, his voice quiet and calming. "I know your medical needs are different, but I wanted to offer."

Niamh's nostrils flared angrily, but she said only, "We have no need of your help."

"May I look? I won't touch him."

Cillian answered, his tone only slightly more friendly. "You may look."

Bartok knelt by Aria and set a plastic case down on his other side. He leaned over, eyes taking in everything, face grave. "Do you know if any of the bullets are still in him?"

Cillian said, "Some. Not all. But it doesn't matter. They are lead, not getlaril. They will be eliminated."

Owen's left eye opened. His gaze rested on Bartok first, then moved to the others, one by one, and finally to Aria.

Bartok said, "I could—"

"Leave us. He must rest." Cillian's voice was hard.

Owen murmured so softly that they all leaned forward to hear him. "It is kindness, Cillian."

Cillian frowned and said stiffly, "Thank you for your offer. It is unnecessary. Your human methods cannot help him and will cause pain."

Bartok nodded, his expression gentle. "As you wish. Please let me know if I can help."

Aria put a hand on his arm, suddenly grateful for his understanding. *I bet he's a good doctor. A good man.*

Cillian watched him rise, cold blue eyes following Bartok as he turned and walked back toward the far end of the train platform.

"Should I leave you alone too?" Aria whispered. *Please say no. I couldn't bear to leave him like this. Not for long.*

They seemed to consider the offer, but Niall shook his head just as Owen breathed, "Stay."

Niamh reached out to touch his cheek, her slim fingers smooth and white. She raised her eyes to Cillian and said, "You have not yet told me of Petro's assistance."

Owen closed his eye again.

Cillian shivered but gathered himself and answered. "I believe the human guards will think it easily explained by equipment malfunctions, possibly some slight magic that we did. But there was much more.

"Some alarms that should have alerted the guards malfunctioned. Some functioned as designed but elicited odd responses from the guards;

they noticed but merely logged the alert and switched off the alarms, as if they were conducting equipment drills or tests.

"Moreover, of the few guards who did respond, some their shots were good. Some of the bullets that did not strike us *should* have hit. One passed straight through me without causing injury. Another avoided Aria and hit the wall behind her. The trajectory *curved* around her."

He closed his eyes and shuddered again. "More frightening yet, doors appeared. I saw two, but there may have been others. One closed between Aria and a guard near the beginning of our escape. Another closed later, as we fled down a hallway."

"An equipment malfunction? That Petro initiated?" Aria asked.

Cillian spread the schematics before them. "Look."

"What?" Aria frowned at the papers. Cillian pointed at the two doors in question, neatly labeled as part of the "sector containment" measures that dotted the rest of the diagram.

"Those doors did not exist when we planned the mission. Do you remember?" Cillian stared at her with wide eyes.

She thought and suddenly caught her breath, looking up to see Niamh looking equally stunned. "You're right. They weren't. When we passed by those corridors on the way in, there were no doors. I'm positive."

"Not only did they appear where we needed them, but it appears that they were *always* there. They are on the schematics as original construction." Cillian's voice dropped. "I heard the soldiers through the second door. They were only surprised that the door was triggered, not that it existed."

Aria tried not to shiver. "What are you saying?"

"Petro either added the doors to the facility as they were necessary and altered all references to them, including the schematics and the soldiers' memories, or he actually *altered the past* so that the doors were built, and left us with memories of a past in which the doors did not exist. Either way, this is terrifying." Cillian clasped his hands together. "Either would require power of a higher order than we have ever dreamed existed."

"Why were we exempted from his change?" Aria asked.

Cillian shook his head. "I have no way to guess."

Owen frowned thoughtfully at the ceiling and then shifted his gaze to Aria for a long moment. "I think it has something to do with you."

Aria straightened. "I'm getting credit, or blame, or something, for a lot of things that I don't understand."

"We don't understand them either." Cillian hunched his shoulders, as if he wished to hide.

Owen blinked slowly. "To our knowledge, no one has ever insulted Petro as you did and survived. Many have died for much less."

Aria scowled. "I wasn't brave. I was just angry. I don't think I was wrong to be, either."

Cillian answered her. "I am not sure I disagree. However, Petro is not someone you wish to offend. It has never ended well. Sometimes the offense is never even known."

Owen murmured, "And yet he did not kill her."

The Fae turned their gaze on her again, and Aria shrugged. "I don't know."

There was a long silence while Aria tried not to squirm under their examination.

Finally Owen said, "Petro watched while Grenidor worked. He said nothing, but he was interested."

"In you or in Grenidor?"

"Both. I think." Owen hesitated. "He seemed surprised by my answers, especially the lie. And puzzled as to why I would choose to."

"As are we." Cillian's voice was cool.

Owen smiled faintly. "Are you? You should not be."

Niamh touched his forehead again gently. "Why, Owen? Why would you lie? How could you?"

"How? I do not know. But the why. It was to protect them. And you. Love."

Niamh closed her eyes, as if she could not bear to look at his battered face. Cillian dropped his head too. Only Aria saw Owen smile as his eye closed.

"Was it worth it?" she whispered.

"Yes."


THEY SAT IN SILENCE. Owen might have been asleep or unconscious; it was hard to tell. Cillian glanced at the notebook, then read it silently. Niall turned his face away, sliding back from the light that showed tears streaking down his white cheeks.

Cillian caught his sleeve and shook his head.

He murmured, "We are all surprised. Perhaps disappointment is understandable. But he is still Lord Ailill's heir, and there is no stench of it upon him. Do not be too angry."

Niall looked up, and Aria caught an astonished look on his face. *You are sure of that? He has not begun to,* Niall stopped writing, as if he were reluctant to name his fear.

"He has not."

Niall bent forward, pressing his face into his hands, and Niamh rubbed his back gently.

Aria rubbed her arms; the air was cold and still, and she heard the low susurrus of voices from the other end of the platform. Cillian and Niamh had continued to speak in English. She was grateful for that courtesy, but comprehension hid just out of reach, and she didn't think she had the right to pry too deeply. Not yet. Emotions were too raw.

Owen's song rose like a thread of silver in the dark, a faint sound that brought everything else to stillness. His voice hung in the air, twined around itself, wove into her heart, surged upward and fell. In and around and beneath her, soft gold and clear silver, it rose again. *Owen stood with his back to her on a high precipice, his bare feet on the furthest rocky outcropping, toes curled over the edge. His black hair blew in a gust of wind as he looked out across a green valley. He knelt to put his face to the stone, eyes closed and strong arms stretched out before him. She watched for long minutes, the music rising around her in reverent harmony.*

Owen's voice cracked, and the music shattered and fell away into brilliant shards that left Aria gasping, aching for its lost beauty. She drew a deep breath, fighting tears; the air was fresh, with a faint scent of green growth and morning dew.

Niamh touched his face. "You were not healed." Her voice was heavy with grief.

"I did not ask for healing." His words were barely audible.

"Your pain is greater." Tears spilled down her cheeks.

"I mind it less." He closed his left eye, and Niamh bowed her head over him, her shoulders shaking.

*She's weeping for him. Does he know it? What does it mean, that he didn't ask for healing?*

Cillian raised his head, eyes wide. "Petro is here."

Petro walked toward them from the middle of the platform, steps long and even. *Why did he appear there, instead of here in our midst? To give us time to prepare?*

"I must clarify things with you." He spoke directly to Aria without looking at the others.

"What things?" Aria asked. Her voice didn't shake, and she was proud of that, but her heart still thudded in her chest. *Dragon.* His eyes were the same cold green, his face the same guileless mask it had been before. *He is not human. The face is human, but the eyes are not. No human is both so innocent and so cold.*

As she thought it, his appearance shifted subtly. He grew taller, his face colder, skin shining. She squinted at him. He looked like an incredibly handsome statue, a metallic sheen to his skin. *But what color? Something between silver and copper, changing with the lantern light. What is this appearance supposed to tell me, if anything?* His clothing rippled in a wind she couldn't see, the generic collared shirt and trousers he'd worn before replaced with a robe that hung from one shoulder, belted about his waist. *He's beautiful. Beautiful and hard as a diamond.*

His mouth tightened for a moment before he spoke. "It was made clear to me that the information I provided about Owen's location and the open door could be interpreted as a promise of support in your attempt to rescue him." His words were clipped and painfully precise.

"The attempt would not have succeeded, and it was made clear to me that," he hesitated, then said carefully, "if you died as a result of a choice predicated upon a faulty understanding of my words, which I was aware of and could have prevented, that I would have made a choice I am unwilling to make. My assistance was required in order to avoid this result. Do you understand?" His eyes had not left hers, the green eyes even more striking in his new form.

Aria frowned. "So if I died because you set me up, you'd be held responsible?"

Petro's mouth twitched. "A set up would require the intent for you to die. There was never such an intent. Your death would merely have been a result, neither intended nor unintended."

She frowned even more. "Why are you telling me this? What do you want?"

"My intervention was required in order to avoid making such a choice, with consequences that I do not desire." His eyes flicked away for a moment, and then back to her. "I did not intend to be put in that position when I gave you the information. More importantly, I do not intend to be put in that position again. Any promises to you, implied or otherwise, have been fulfilled. Do you understand and agree?"

*Don't let him off the hook yet. If he's volunteering information, take advantage of it!*

"Why do you think love is so worthless?"

He turned toward Owen and studied him for a long moment before speaking. "I was mistaken when I said I required no further information from Owen. Changes in him are providing valuable data I did not possess before." He circled Owen, eyes roving over his bruised face and body. Owen's left eye followed him, wide and cautious, though he said nothing.

Petro said finally, "You spoke of romantic love, correct?"

"When?"

"When you said, 'I love him! This is painful, and you just watch, like we're some sort of entertainment! It's vulgar! ... It doesn't matter if he doesn't love me back. That's not the point.'"

Aria stared at him, her breath coming fast. Not only were they her words, but it was her *voice* coming from his mouth, her pause while she'd wiped away tears, her breathless anger.

Petro's eyes held hers. "You were referring to romantic love, were you not?"

She closed her eyes for a moment, trying to regain some semblance of equilibrium. "Mostly, yes. But I care for him as a friend too. And as a, well, I'd say human being, but he's not. As a person of some kind, anyway."

Petro's nostrils flared a little. "You complicate things," he said finally.

"Me?" Her voice rose.

"I require more information. That does not imply an intention to intervene in any further matters. I have fulfilled any obligations to you. You agree?"

"What are you studying?" She flung the question at him like a weapon.

He glanced away and then back at her. "I am not required to answer that question."

"No, but you should."

He looked at Owen again for a long moment, as if his answer would be found there. Finally he said, "Choices interest me. Consequences may sometimes be interesting. Your lives are inconsequential. Expect no further assistance from me."

She swallowed. It was more information than she could have hoped for, although she had no idea what it meant. "Agreed."

He was gone.

She barely heard Owen's long exhalation, but she saw the tension in his face. Cillian and Niamh turned away from her, trembling, and she couldn't see their faces.

Aria spoke first. "What did you see that was so terrifying? I mean, he looked *different*, but it wasn't scary, exactly. I already knew he wasn't human."

Niamh shook her head wordlessly, not looking up. Cillian pressed both his hands to his face for a long moment and took a deep, shuddering breath, still not willing to speak. Aria watched them, their reactions frightening her almost more than Petro had.

Owen took a steadying breath and said, "You couldn't see that he was terrified?"

Aria frowned. "He was a little strange, I guess, but I didn't see terrified. I saw precise and excruciatingly clear."

"We saw stark terror. Related to you, but not your person, exactly." He paused, watching Cillian and Niamh for their reactions. "I would guess it would be the 'undesired consequences' of setting you up to die."

Cillian gave one sharp nod, but did not look up.

Niamh whispered, "Which means there are powers much greater than Petro. Powers great enough to terrify him." She was still trembling, shoulders hunched as if she wanted to curl up in a ball.

Cillian ran his hands through his hair and shook out his shoulders, as if consciously deciding not to show his fear any longer. Yet he couldn't hide that his hands were shaking. "If it terrifies Petro, I want no part of it."

Aria thought for a moment. "What did you actually hear him say?"

Cillian and Niamh stared at each other, but Cillian answered. "Almost nothing. I heard your half of the conversation, and nothing while he was speaking. I did not see his lips move, nor feel the vibrations of his speech in the air. I heard 'I must clarify things with you' and 'Expect no further assistance from me.' That's all."

Niamh nodded agreement.

"How did you know he was terrified, then?" Aria asked.

Niamh hid her eyes again, and her voice shook as she answered. "It beat upon us in waves. He could not hide it, though his human form showed little sign of fear. He spoke to you, but he *thought* of fire and pain and a terrible screaming silence."

Aria swallowed. "But he wasn't afraid of *me*."

Owen's voice was faint. "No. Nor I think of El. Not exactly. It was as if he had veered too close to a precipice, and was correcting his course by speaking with you." He hesitated. "I heard more, but perhaps not all he said. Choices, and changes in me."

Cillian looked at his brother more closely. "Hm."

Owen raised one eyebrow.

Finally Cillian murmured, "It's very subtle. I hadn't noticed until you mentioned it. But I do see something different."

"Different in what way?" Aria asked.

"I can't yet tell. If anything, he seems more *human*."

# AFTERWORD

Thank you for purchasing this book. If you enjoyed it, leave a review at your favorite online retailer! This story is continued in *The Dragon's Tongue* (fall/winter 2014).

C. J. Brightley lives in Northern Virginia with her husband and young children. She holds degrees from Clemson University and Texas A&M. You can find more of C. J. Brightley's books at www.CJBrightley.com, including the epic fantasy series Erdemen Honor, which begins with *The King's Sword* and continues in *A Cold Wind* and *Honor's Heir*. You can also find C. J. Brightley on Facebook and Google+.

# THE DRAGON'S TONGUE

## CHAPTER 1

GABRIEL LOOKED at the books spread out before them and the list Jenison, Levi, and Bartok had assembled. "So. Dandra sold history books."

Levi added, "Plus two books on Jewish history and three Bible commentaries."

Aria picked up the book *Memories Kept* and looked at it again. Her bookmark was still between the pages, and she opened the book.

"Did you move the bookmark?" she asked.

"No. That's the page where we found it," Jenison said.

Aria frowned. "That's not where I was reading." A faint green pencil line caught her eye on the right-hand page, underlining the words *beside the wall*.

She flipped through the rest of the book, skimming pages. There were no other markings in the book; no highlights, no notes. Aria never wrote in books, and Dandra was strict about her patrons not defacing the volumes. Few people were inclined to do so, anyway, and fewer still had ever noticed this book. She remembered the conversation about the colored pencil markings used in editing; maybe Dandra had intended this message specifically for her.

"I think Dandra did this. As a message." She turned the book around and showed them.

"We'll go back tonight."


BARTOK, EVRIAL, AND CLINT, a former police detective, went back to Dandra's that evening. Niall accompanied them; he'd volunteered for the duty by showing up at Aria's side as they were leaving. He raised his eyebrows at her.

"You want to go?"

He nodded.

"Okay." Maybe he would see something they couldn't.

It was a long walk, but everyone was silent, subdued. Aria shivered in the cool, still air of the tunnels, and even more once they reached the surface. They emerged from the tunnels through an access hatch hidden beneath a small overpass. Deep in the shadows, they waited for a car to pass on the lower street before darting out and around to the upper road. Another two blocks and Niall stopped at a back door in an alley. White stenciled letters marked it as Dandra's back door.

Clint tried to pull the door open, but it was

locked. Niall touched the door handle and it un-latched with a soft click. He pulled it open and ges-tured for them to enter.

Clint gave him a quick look. "That's a handy trick," he murmured.

Aria smiled a little, but Niall merely nodded.

Inside, they risked a tiny penlight in the stor-age room, though it would be too dangerous in the main shop. With the wide glass windows, any light from the sales floor would be visible to passersby.

"'Beside the wall.' Which wall?" Clint spoke in a whisper.

"I don't know." Aria stared around, biting her lip. "I've never been in the back before."

Niall turned to look away from the light, then motioned that he was going into the front. Clint turned the light off while he slipped through the door, then played it slowly around the walls. He covered the whole room, then began again.

"There." Bartok pointed. "What's that?"

A narrow desk, barely more than a foot deep, stood in one corner against the wall. A green pen-cil lay beneath the desk.

They moved forward and studied it, not touch-ing anything.

"I don't see anything," said Aria. "But that's the green pencil. It must be around here some-where."

"Neither do I." Clint sounded confused. He shifted and considered the pencil and desk from a different angle, playing the light around crack be-tween the desk and the wall.

"There." Aria and Bartok spoke at the same time. Bartok reached down to lay one finger against a green mark on the floorboard near the wall, then pushed it firmly.

The other end of the board some twelve inches away rocked upward, revealing a dark hole. Bartok moved forward to shine his flashlight into it. After a moment, he reached in, the gap barely wide enough for his hand. He had to twist and turn his hand to pull it back out holding a book with some papers folded into the front cover. He shone the penlight around again and then pushed the same button. The trapdoor closed again.

"How did you see that?" Clint asked.

"The pencil tip pointed at the mark." Bartok stared down at the book in his hands.

"What is it?" Aria asked.

Bartok was silent, and Aria moved closer.

Finally Bartok said softly, "It's a Bible."

30260399R00177

Made in the USA
Middletown, DE
18 March 2016